The Holiday Round

by

A. A. Milne

Double 9 BOOKS

The Holiday Round
by A. A. Milne

ISBN: 978-93-62208-54-5

Published by

DOUBLE 9 BOOKS

2/13-B, Ansari Road
Daryaganj, New Delhi – 110002
info@double9books.com
www.double9books.com
Tel. 011-40042856

ABOUT THE AUTHOR

Alan Alexander Milne was an English author best known for his books about the teddy bear Winnie-the-Pooh and for children's poetry. Milne was primarily a dramatist before the enormous popularity of Winnie-the-Pooh eclipsed all of his earlier work. Milne fought in both World Wars, as a lieutenant in the Royal Warwickshire Regiment in WWI and a captain in the Home Guard in WWII. Alan Alexander Milne was born in Kilburn, London, on January 18, 1882, to Jamaican-born John Vine Milne and Sarah Marie Milne. He was raised at Henley House School, 6/7 Mortimer Road (now Crescent), Kilburn, a small independent school owned by his father. H. G. Wells was one of his teachers from 1889 to 1890. Milne attended Westminster School and Trinity College, Cambridge, where he received a mathematics scholarship and graduated with a B.A. in Mathematics in 1903. He edited and wrote for Granta, a student publication. He cooperated with his brother Kenneth on articles that appeared under the letters AKM.

CONTENTS

HOLIDAY TIME

I

THE ORDEAL BY WATER

"We will now bathe," said a voice at the back of my neck.

I gave a grunt and went on with my dream. It was a jolly dream, and nobody got up early in it.

"We will now bathe," repeated Archie.

"Go away," I said distinctly.

Archie sat down on my knees and put his damp towel on my face.

"When my wife and I took this commodious residence for six weeks," he said, "and engaged the sea at great expense to come up to its doors twice a day, it was on the distinct understanding that our guests should plunge into it punctually at seven o'clock every morning."

"Don't be silly, it's about three now. And I wish you'd get off my knees."

"It's a quarter-past seven."

"Then there you are, we've missed it. Well, we must see what we can do for you to-morrow. Good-night."

Archie pulled all the clothes off me and walked with them to the window.

"Jove, what a day!" he said. "And can't you smell the sea?"

"I can. Let that suffice. I say, what's happened to my blanket? I must have swallowed it in my sleep."

"Where's his sponge?" I heard him murmuring to himself as he came away from the window.

"No, no, I'm up," I shouted, and I sprang out of bed and put on a shirt and a pair of trousers with great speed. "Where do I take these off again?" I asked. "I seem to be giving myself a lot of trouble."

"There is a tent."

"Won't the ladies want it? Because, if so, I can easily have my bathe later on."

"The ladies think it's rather too rough to-day."

"Perhaps they're right," I said hopefully. "A woman's instinct—No, I'm NOT a coward."

It wasn't so bad outside—sun and wind and a blue-and-white sky and plenty of movement on the sea.

"Just the day for a swim," said Archie cheerily, as he led the way down to the beach.

"I've nothing against the day; it's the hour I object to. The Lancet says you mustn't bathe within an hour of a heavy meal. Well, I'm going to have a very heavy meal within about twenty minutes. That isn't right, you know."

By the time I was ready the wind had got much colder. I looked out of the tent and shivered.

"Isn't it jolly and fresh?" said Archie, determined to be helpful. "There are points about the early morning, after all."

"There are plenty of points about this morning. Where do they get all the sharp stones from? Look at that one there—he's simply waiting for me."

"You ought to have bought some bathing shoes. I got this pair in the village."

"Why didn't you tell me so last night?"

"It was too late last night."

"Well, it's much too early this morning. If you were a gentleman you'd lend me one of yours, and we'd hop down together."

Archie being no gentleman, he walked and I hobbled to the edge, and there we sat down while he took off his shoes.

"I should like to take this last opportunity," I said, "of telling you that up till now I haven't enjoyed this early morning bathe one little bit. I suppose there will be a notable moment when the ecstasy actually begins, but at present I can't see it coming at all. The only thing I look forward to with any pleasure is the telling Dahlia and Myra at breakfast what I think of their cowardice. That and the breakfast itself. Good-bye."

I got up and waded into the surf.

"One last word," I said as I looked back at him. "In my whole career I shall never know a more absolutely beastly and miserable moment than this." Then a wave knocked me down, and I saw that I had spoken too hastily.

The world may be divided into two classes—those who drink when they swim and those who don't. I am one of the drinkers. For this reason I prefer river bathing to sea bathing.

"It's about time we came out," I shouted to Archie after the third pint. "I'm exceeding my allowance."

"Aren't you glad now you came?" he cried from the top of a wave.

"Very," I said a moment later from inside it.

But I really did feel glad ten minutes afterwards as I sat on the beach in the sun and smoked a cigarette, and threw pebbles lazily into the sea.

"Holbein, how brave of you!" cried a voice behind me.

"Good-morning. I'm not at all sure that I ought to speak to you."

"Have you really been taking the sea so early," said Myra as she sat down between us, "or did you rumple each other's hair so as to deceive me?"

"I have been taking the sea," I confessed. "What you observe out there now is what I left."

"Oh, but that's what *I* do. That's why I didn't come to-day—because I had so much yesterday."

"I'm a three-bottle man. I can go on and on and on. And after all these years I have the most sensitive palate of any man living. For instance, I can distinguish between Scarborough and Llandudno quite easily with my eyes shut. Speaking as an expert, I may say that there is nothing to beat a small Cromer and seltzer; though some prefer a Ventnor and dash. Ilfracombe with a slice of lemon is popular, but hardly appeals to the fastidious."

"Do you know," said Archie, "that you are talking drivel? Nobody ought to drivel before breakfast. It isn't decent. What does Dahlia want to do to-day, Myra?"

"Mr Simpson is coming by the one-thirty."

"Good; then we'll have a slack day. The strain of meeting Simpson will be sufficient for us. I do hope he comes in a yachting cap—we'll send him back if he doesn't."

"I told him to bring one," said Myra. "I put a P.S. in Dahlia's letter—please bring your telescope and yachting cap. She thought we could have a good day's sailing to-morrow, if you'd kindly arrange about the wind."

"I'll talk to the crew about it and see what he can do. If we get becalmed we can always throw somebody overboard, of course. Well, I must go in and finish my toilet."

We got up and climbed slowly back to the house.

"And then," I said, "then for the heavy meal."

II
BECALMED

"Well," said Dahlia, giving up the tiller with a sigh, "if this is all that you and Joe can do in the way of a breeze, you needn't have worried."

"Don't blame the crew," said Archie nobly, "he did his best. He sat up all night whistling."

"ARE we moving?" asked Myra, from a horizontal position on the shady side of the mainsail.

"We are not," I said, from a similar position on the sunny side. "Let's get out."

Simpson took off his yachting cap and fanned himself with a nautical almanac. "How far are we from anywhere?" he asked cheerfully.

"Miles," said Archie. "To be more accurate, we are five miles from a public-house, six from a church, four from a post-office, and three from the spacious walled-in kitchen-garden and tennis-court. On the other hand, we are quite close to the sea."

"You will never see your friends again, Simpson. They will miss you … at first … perhaps; but they will soon forget. The circulation of the papers that you wrote for will go up, the brindled bull-pup will be fed by another and a smaller hand, but otherwise all will be as it was before."

My voice choked, and at the same moment something whizzed past me into the sea.

"Yachting cap overboard! Help!" cried Myra.

"You aren't in The Spectator office now, Simpson," said Archie severely, as he fished with the boat-hook. "There is a time for ballyragging. By the way, I suppose you do want it back again?"

"It's my fault," I confessed remorsefully; "I told him yesterday I didn't like it."

"Myra and I do like it, Mr Simpson. Please save it, Archie."

Archie let it drip from the end of the boat-hook for a minute, and then brought it in.

"Morning, Sir Thomas," I said, saluting it as it came on board. "Lovely day for a sail. We've got the new topmast up, but Her Grace had the last of the potted-meat for lunch yesterday."

Simpson took his cap and stroked it tenderly. "Thirteen and ninepence in the Buckingham Palace Road," he murmured. "Thanks, old chap."

Quiet settled down upon the good ship Armadillo again. There was no cloud in the sky, no ripple on the water, no sound along the deck. The land was hazy in the distance; hazy in the distance was public-house, church, post-office, walled-in kitchen-garden and tennis-court. But in the little cabin Joe was making a pleasant noise with plates....

"Splendid," said Archie, putting down his glass and taking out his pipe. "Now what shall we do? I feel full of energy."

"Then you and Simpson can get the dinghy out and tow," I suggested. "I'll coach from the Armadillo."

"We might go for a long bicycle ride," said Myra; "or call on the Vicarage girls."

"There isn't really very much to do, is there?" said Dahlia, gently. "I'm sorry."

Simpson leapt excitedly into the breach.

"I'll tell you what I'll do—I'll teach you all the different knots and things. I learnt them coming down in the train. Everybody ought to know them. Archie, old man, can you let me have a piece of rope?"

"Certainly. Take any piece you like. Only spare the main-sheet."

Simpson went forward to consult Joe, and came back with enough to hang himself with. He sat down opposite to us, wrapped the rope once round his waist, and then beamed at us over his spectacles.

"Now supposing you had fallen down a well," he began, "and I let this rope down to you, what would you do with YOUR end?"

We thought deeply for a moment.

"I should wait until you were looking over the edge, and then give it a sharp jerk," said Archie.

"One MUST have company in a well," I agreed.

"They're being silly again," apologized Myra. "Tell ME, Mr Simpson! I should love to know—I'm always falling down wells."

"Well, you tie it round you like this. Through there—and over there—and then back under there. You see, it simply CAN'T slip. Then I should pull you up."

"But how nice of you. Let me try. … Oh, yes, that's easy."

"Well, then there's the hangman's knot."

Archie and I looked at each other.

"The predicaments in which Simpson finds himself are extraordinarily varied," I said.

"One of these days he'll be in a well, and we shall let down a rope to him, and he'll hang himself by mistake."

"That would look very determined. On the other hand there must be annoying occasions when he starts out to strangle somebody and finds that he's pulling him out of the cistern."

"Why, how delightful, Mr Simpson," said Myra. "Do show us some more."

"Those are the most important ones. Then there are one or two fancy ones. Do you know the Monkey's Claw?"

"Don't touch it," said Archie solemnly. "It's poison."

"Oh, I must show you that."

Joe showed me the Monkey's Claw afterwards, and it is a beautiful thing, but it was not a bit like Simpson's. Simpson must have started badly, and I think he used too much rope. After about twenty minutes there was hardly any of him visible at all.

"Take your time, Houdini," said Archie, "take your time. Just let us know when you're ready to be put into the safe, that's all."

"You would hardly think, to look at him now," I said a minute later, "that one day he'll be a dear little butterfly."

"Where's the sealing-wax, Maria? You know, I'm certain he'll never go for threepence."

"What I say is, it's simply hypnotic suggestion. There's no rope there at all, really."

An anxious silence followed.

"No," said Simpson suddenly, "I'm doing it wrong."

"From to-night," said Archie, after tea, "you will be put on rations. One cobnut and a thimbleful of sherry wine per diem. I hope somebody's brought a thimble."

"There really isn't so very much left," said Dahlia.

"Then we shall have to draw lots who is to be eaten."

"Don't we eat our boots and things first?" asked Myra.

"The doctor says I mustn't have anything more solid than a lightly-boiled shoe-lace the last thing at night."

"After all, there's always the dinghy," said Archie. "If we put in a tin of corned beef and a compass and a keg of gunpowder, somebody might easily row in and post the letters. Personally, as captain, I must stick to my ship."

"There's another way I've just thought of," I said. "Let's sail in."

I pointed out to sea, and there, unmistakably, was the least little breeze coming over the waters. A minute later and our pennant napped once Simpson moistened a finger and held it up.

The sprint for home had begun.

III
A DAY ASHORE

"Well, which is it to be?" asked Archie.

"Just whichever you like," said Dahlia, "only make up your minds."

"Well, I can do you a very good line in either. I've got a lot of sea in the front of the house, and there's the Armadillo straining at the leash; and I've had some land put down at the back of the house, and there's the Silent-Knight eating her carburettor off in the kennels."

"Oh, what can ail thee, Silent-Knight, alone and palely loitering?" asked Simpson. "Keats," he added kindly.

"Ass (Shakespeare)," I said.

"Of course, if we sailed," Simpson went on eagerly, "and we got becalmed again, I could teach you chaps signalling."

Archie looked from one to the other of us.

"I think that settles it," he said, and went off to see about the motor.

"Little Chagford," said Archie, as he slowed down. "Where are we going to, by the way?"

"I thought we'd just go on until we found a nice place for lunch."

"And then on again till we found a nice place for tea," added Myra.

"And so home to dinner," I concluded.

"Speaking for myself —" began Simpson.

"Oh, why not?"

"I should like to see a church where Katharine of Aragon or somebody was buried."

"Samuel's morbid craving for sensation —"

> "Wait till we get back to London, and I'll take you to Madame Tussaud's, Mr Simpson."

"Well, I think he's quite right," said Dahlia. "There is an old Norman church, I believe, and we ought to go and see it. The Philistines needn't come in if they don't want to."

"Philistines!" I said indignantly. "Well, I'm—"

"Agagged," suggested Archie. "Oh no, he was an Amalekite."

"You've lived in the same country as this famous old Norman church for years and years and years, and you care so little about it that you've never been to see it and aren't sure whether it was Katharine of Aragon or Alice-for-short who was buried here, and now that you HAVE come across it by accident you want to drive up to it in a brand-new 1910 motor-car, with Simpson in his 1910 gent.'s fancy vest knocking out the ashes of his pipe against the lych-gate as he goes in. ... And that's what it is to be one of the elect!"

"Little Chagford's noted back-chat comedians," commented Archie. "Your turn, Dahlia."

"There was once a prince who was walking in a forest near his castle one day—that's how all the nice stories begin—and he suddenly came across a beautiful maiden, and he said to himself, 'I've lived here for years and years and years, and I've never seen her before, and I'm not sure whether her name is Katharine or Alice, or where her uncle was buried, and I've got a new surcoat on which doesn't match her wimple at all, so let's leave her and go home to lunch....' And THAT'S what it is to be one of the elect!"

"Don't go on too long," said Archie. "There are the performing seals to come after you."

I jumped out of the car and joined her in the road.

"Dahlia, I apologize," I said. "You are quite right. We will visit this little church together, and see who was buried there."

Myra looked up from the book she had been studying, Jovial Jaunts Round Jibmouth.

"There isn't a church at Little Chagford," she said. "At least there wasn't two years ago, when this book was published. So that looks as though it can't be VERY early Norman."

"Then let's go on," said Archie, after a deep silence.

We found a most delightful little spot (which wasn't famous for anything) for lunch, and had the baskets out of the car in no time.

"Now, are you going to help get things ready," asked Myra, "or are you going to take advantage of your sex and watch Dahlia and me do all the work?"

> "I thought women always liked to keep the food jobs for themselves," I said. "I know I'm never allowed in the kitchen at home. Besides, I've got more important work to do—I'm going to make the fire."

"What fire?"

"You can't really lead the simple life and feel at home with Nature until you have laid a fire of twigs and branches, rubbed two sticks together to procure a flame, and placed in the ashes the pemmican or whatever it is that falls to your rifle."

"Well, I did go out to look for pemmican this morning, but there were none rising."

"Then I shall have my ham sandwich hot."

"Bread, butter, cheese, eggs, sandwiches, fruit," catalogued Dahlia, as she took them out; "what else do you want?"

"I'm waiting here for cake," I said.

"Bother, I forgot the cake."

"Look here, this picnic isn't going with the swing that one had looked for. No pemmican, no cake, no early Norman church. We might almost as well be back in the Cromwell Road."

"Does your whole happiness depend on cake?" asked Myra scornfully.

"To a large extent it does. Archie," I called out, "there's no cake."

Archie stopped patting the car and came over to us. "Good. Let's begin," he said; "I'm hungry."

"You didn't hear. I said there WASN'T any cake—on the contrary, there is an entire absence of it, a shortage, a vacuum, not to say a lacuna. In the place where it should be there is an aching void or mere hard-boiled eggs or something of that sort. I say, doesn't ANYBODY mind, except me?"

Apparently nobody did, so that it was useless to think of sending Archie back for it. Instead, I did a little wrist-work with the corkscrew....

"Now," said Archie, after lunch, "before you all go off with your butterfly nets, I'd better say that we shall be moving on at about half-past three. That is, unless one of you has discovered the slot of a Large Cabbage White just then, and is following up the trail very keenly."

"I know what I'm going to do," I said, "if the flies will let me alone."

"Tell me quickly before I guess," begged Myra.

"I'm going to lie on my back and think about—who do you think do the hardest work in the world?"

"Stevedores."

"Then I shall think about stevedores."

"Are you sure," asked Simpson, "that you wouldn't like me to show you that signalling now?"

I closed my eyes. You know, I wonder sometimes what it is that makes a picnic so pleasant. Because all the important things, the eating and the sleeping, one can do anywhere.

IV
IN THE WET

Myra gazed out of the window upon the driving rain and shook her head at the weather.

"Ugh!" she said. "Ugly!"

"Beast," I added, in order that there should be no doubt about what we thought. "Utter and deliberate beast."

We had arranged for a particularly pleasant day. We were to have sailed across to the mouth of the—I always forget its name, and then up the river to the famous old castle of-of-no, it's gone again; but anyhow, there was to have been a bathe in the river, and lunch, and a little exploration in the dinghy, and a lesson in the Morse code from Simpson, and tea in the woods with a real fire, and in the cool of the evening a ripping run home before the wind. But now the only thing that seemed certain was the cool of the evening.

"We'll light a fire and do something indoors," said Dahlia.

"This is an extraordinary house," said Archie. "There isn't a single book in it, except a lot of Strand Magazines for 1907. That must have been a very wet year."

"We can play games, dear."

"True, darling. Let's do a charade."

"The last time I played charades," I said, "I was Horatius, thefront part of Elizabeth's favourite palfrey, the arrow which shot Rufus, Jonah, the two little Princes in the Tower, and Mrs Pankhurst."

"Which was your favourite part?" asked Myra.

"The front part of the palfrey. But I was very good as the two little Princes."

"It's no good doing charades, if there's nobody to do them to."

"Thomas is coming to-morrow," said Myra. "We could tell him all about it."

"Clumps is a jolly good game," suggested Simpson.

"The last time I was a clump," I said, "I was the first coin paid on account of the last pair of boots, sandals, or whatnot of the man who laid the first stone of the house where lived the prettiest aunt of the man who reared the goose which laid the egg from which came the goose which provided the last quill pen used by the third man Shakespeare met on the second Wednesday in June, 1595."

"He mightn't have had an aunt," said Myra, after a minute's profound thought.

"He hadn't."

"Well, anyhow, one way and another you've had a very adventurous career, my lad," said Archie. "What happened the last time you played ludo?"

"When I played clumps," put in Simpson, "I was the favourite spoke of Hall Caine's first bicycle. They guessed Hall Caine and the bicycle and the spoke very quickly, but nobody thought of suggesting the favourite spoke."

Myra went to the window again, and came back with the news that it would probably be a fine evening.

"Thank you," we all said.

"But I wasn't just making conversation. I have an idea."

"Silence for Myra's idea."

"Well, it's this. If we can't do anything without an audience, and if the audience won't come to us, let's go to them."

"Be a little more lucid, there's a dear. It isn't that we aren't trying."

"Well then, let's serenade the other houses about here to-night."

There was a powerful silence while everybody considered this.

"Good," said Archie at last. "We will."

The rest of the morning and all the afternoon were spent in preparations. Archie and Myra were all right; one plays the banjo and the other the guitar. (It is a musical family, the Mannerings.) Simpson keeps a cornet which he generally puts in his bag, but I cannot remember anyone asking him to play it. If the question has ever arisen, he has probably been asked not to play it. However, he would bring it out to-night. In any case he has a tolerable voice; while Dahlia has always sung like an angel. In short, I was the chief difficulty.

"I suppose there wouldn't be time to learn the violin?" I asked.

"Why didn't they teach you something when you were a boy?" wondered Myra.

"They did. But my man forgot to put it in my bag when he packed. He put in two tooth-brushes and left out the triangle. Do you think there's a triangle shop in the village? I generally play on an isosceles one, any two sides of which are together greater than the third. Likewise the angles which are opposite to the adjacent sides, each to each."

"Well, you must take the cap round for the money."

"I will. I forgot to say that my own triangle at home, the Strad, is in the chromatic scale of A, and has a splice. It generally gets the chromatics very badly in the winter."

While the others practised their songs, I practised taking the cap round, and by tea-time we all knew our parts perfectly. I had received permission to join in the choruses, and I was also to be allowed to do a little dance with Myra. When you think that I had charge of the financial arrangements as well, you can understand that I felt justified in considering myself the leader of the troupe.

"In fact," I said, "you ought to black your faces so as to distinguish yourselves from me."

"We won't black our faces," said Dahlia, "but we'll wear masks; and we might each carry a little board explaining why we're doing this."

"Right," said Archie; and he sat down and wrote a notice for himself—

"I AM AN ORPHAN. SO ARE THE OTHERS, BUT THEY ARE NOT SO ORPHAN AS I AM. I AM EXTREMELY FREQUENT."

Dahlia said—

"WE ARE DOING THIS FOR AN ADVERTISEMENT. IF YOU LIKE US, SEND A SHILLING FOR A FREE SAMPLE CONCERT, MENTIONING THIS PAPER. YOUR MONEY BACK IF WE ARE NOT SATISFIED WITH IT."

Simpson announced—

"WORLD'S LONG DISTANCE CORNETIST. HOLDER OF THE OBOE RECORD ON GRASS. RUNNER-UP IN THE OCARINA WELTER WEIGHTS (STRANGLE HOLD BARRED). MIXED ZITHER CHAMPION (1907, COVERED COURTS)."

Myra said—

"KIND FRIENDS, HELP US. WE WERE WRECKED THIS AFTERNOON. THE CORNET WAS SINKING FOR THE THIRD TIME WHEN IT WAS RESCUED, AND HAD TO BE BROUGHT ROUND BY ARTIFICIAL RESPIRATION. CAN YOU SPARE US A DRINK OF WATER?"

As for myself I had to hand the Simpson yachting cap round, and my notice said—

"WE WANT YOUR MONEY. IF YOU CANNOT GIVE US ANY, FOR HEAVEN'S SAKE KEEP THE CAP."

We had an early dinner, so as to be in time to serenade our victims when they were finishing their own meal and feeling friendly to the world. Then we went upstairs and dressed. Dahlia and Myra had kimonos, Simpson put on his dressing-gown, in which he fancies himself a good deal, and Archie and I wore brilliantly-coloured pyjamas over our other clothes.

"Let's see," said Simpson, "I start off with 'The Minstrel Boy,' don't I? And then what do we do?"

"Then we help you to escape," said Archie. "After that, Dahlia sings 'Santa Lucia,' and Myra and I give them a duet, and if you're back by then with your false nose properly fixed it might be safe for you to join in the chorus of a coon song. Now then, are we all ready?"

"What's that?" said Myra.

We all listened ... and then we opened the door.

It was pouring.

V
MAROONED

"Stroke, you're late," said Thomas, butting me violently in the back with his oar.

"My dear Thomas, when you have been in the Admiralty a little longer you will know that 'bow' is not the gentleman who sets the time. What do you suppose would happen at Queen's Hall if the second bird-call said to the conductor, 'Henry, you're late'?"

"The whole gallery would go out and get its hair cut," said Archie.

"I'm not used to the Morse system of rowing, that's the trouble," explained Thomas. "Long-short, short-short-long, short-long. You're spelling out the most awful things, if you only knew."

"Be careful how you insult me, Thomas. A little more and I shall tell them what happened to you on the ornamental waters in Regent's Park that rough day."

"Really?" asked Simpson with interest.

"Yes; I fancy he had been rather overdoing it at Swedish drill that morning."

We gave her ten in silence, and then by mutual consent rested on our oars.

"There's a long way yet," said Myra. "Dahlia and I will row if you're tired."

"This is an insult, Thomas. Shall we sit down under it?"

"Yes," said Thomas, getting up; "only in another part of the boat."

We gave up our seats to the ladies (even in a boat one should be polite) and from a position in the stern waited with turned-up coat-collars for the water to come on board.

"We might have sailed up a little higher," remarked Simpson. "It's all right, I'm not a bit wet, thanks."

"It's too shallow, except at high tide," said Myra. "The Armadillo would have gone aground and lost all her—her shell. Do armadilloes have shells, or what?"

"Feathers."

"Well, we're a pretty good bank-holiday crowd for the dinghy," said Archie. "Simpson, if we upset, save the milk and the sandwiches; my wife can swim."

The woods were now beginning to come down to the river on both sides, but on the right a grassy slope broke them at the water's edge for some fifty yards. Thither we rowed, and after a little complicated manoeuvring landed suddenly, Simpson, who was standing in the bows with the boat-hook, being easily the first to reach the shore. He got up quickly, however, apologized, and helped the ladies and the hampers out. Thereafter he was busy for some time, making the dinghy fast with a knot peculiarly his own.

"The first thing to do is to build a palisade to keep the savages off," said Archie, and he stuck the boat-hook into the ground. "After which you are requested to light fires to frighten the wild beasts. The woodbines are very wild at this time of the year."

"We shall have to light a fire anyhow for the tea, so that will be very useful," said the thoughtful Dahlia.

"I myself," I said, "will swim out to the wreck for the musket and the bag of nails."

"As you're going," said Myra, unpacking, "you might get the sugar as well. We've forgotten it."

"Now you've spoilt my whole holiday. It was bad enough with the cake last week, but this is far, far worse. I shall go into the wood and eat berries."

"It's all right, here it is. Now you're happy again. I wish, if you aren't too busy, you'd go into the wood and collect sticks for the fire."

"I am unusually busy," I said, "and there is a long queue of clients waiting for me in the ante-room. An extremely long queue—almost a half-butt in fact."

I wandered into the wood alone. Archie and Dahlia had gone arm-in-arm up the hill to look at a view, Simpson was helping Myra with the hampers, and Thomas, the latest arrival from town, was lying on his back, telling them what he alleged to be a good story now going round London. Myra told it to me afterwards, and we agreed that as a boy it had gone round the world several times first. Yet I heard her laugh unaffectedly—what angels women are!

Ten minutes later I returned with my spoil, and laid it before them.

"A piece of brown bread from the bread-fruit tree, a piece of indiarubber from the mango tree, a chutney from the banana grove, and an omelet from the turtle run, I missed the chutney with my first barrel, and brought it down rather luckily with the ricochet."

"But how funny; they all look just like sticks of wood."

"That is Nature's plan of protective colouring. In the same way apricots have often escaped with their lives by sitting in the cream and pretending to be poached eggs."

"The same instinct of self-preservation," added Archie, "has led many a pill called Beauchamp to pronounce its name Cholmondeley."

Simpson begged to be allowed to show us how to light a fire, and we hadn't the heart to refuse him. It was, he said, the way they lit fires on the veldt (and other places where they wanted fires), and it went out the first time because the wind must have changed round after he had begun to lay the wood. He got the draught in the right place the next time, and for a moment we thought we should have to take to the boats; but the captain averted a panic, and the fire was got under. Then the kettle was put on, and of all the boiled water I have ever tasted this was the best.

"You know," said Archie, "in Simpson the nation has lost a wonderful scoutmaster."

"Oh, Samuel," cried Myra, "tell us how you tracked the mules that afternoon, and knew they were wounded because of the blood."

"Tell us about that time when you bribed the regimental anchovy of Troop B to betray the secret password to you."

"I ignore you because you're jealous. May I have some more tea, Miss Mannering?"

"Call me Myra, Scoutmaster Simpson of The Spectator troop, and you shall."

"I blush for my unblushing sex," said Dahlia.

"I blush for my family," said Archie. "That a young girl of gentle birth, nurtured in a peaceful English home, brought up in an atmosphere of old-world courtesy, should so far forget herself as to attempt to wheedle a promising young scoutmaster, who can light a fire, practically speaking, backwards—this, I repeat, is too much."

It was Thomas who changed the subject so abruptly.

"I suppose the tide comes as far as this?" he said.

"It does, captain."

"Then that would account for the boat having gone."

"That and Simpson's special knot," I said, keeping calm for the sake of the women and children.

Archie jumped up with a shout. The boat was about twenty yards from the shore, going very slowly upstream.

"It's very bad to bathe just after a heavy meal," I reminded him.

"I'm not sure that I'm going to, but I'm quite sure that one of us will have to."

"Walk up the river with it," said Myra, "while Dahlia and I pack, and the one who's first digested goes in."

We walked up. I felt that in my own case the process of assimilation would be a lengthy one.

VI
A LITTLE CRICKET FOR AN ENDING

We came back from a "Men Only" sail to find Myra bubbling over with excitement.

"I've got some news for you," she said, "but I'm not going to tell you till dinner. Be quick and change."

"Bother, she's going to get married," I murmured.

Myra gurgled and drove us off.

"Put on all your medals and orders, Thomas," she called up the stairs; "and, Archie, it's a champagne night."

"I believe, old fellow," said Simpson, "she's married already."

Half an hour later we were all ready for the news.

"Just a moment, Myra," said Archie. "I'd better warn you that we're expecting a good deal, and that if you don't live up to the excitement you've created, you'll be stood in the corner for the rest of dinner."

"She's quite safe," said Dahlia.

"Of course I am. Well, now I'm going to begin. This morning, about eleven, I went and had a bathe, and I met another girl in the sea."

"Horribly crowded the sea is getting nowadays," commented Archie.

"And she began to talk about what a jolly day it was and so on, and I gave her my card—I mean I said, 'I'm Myra Mannering.' And she said, 'I'm sure you're keen on cricket.'"

"I like the way girls talk in the sea," said Archie. "So direct."

"What is there about our Myra," I asked, "that stamps her as a cricketer, even when she's only got her head above water?"

"She'd seen me on land, silly. Well, we went on talking, and at last she said, 'Will you play us at mixed cricket on Saturday?' And a big wave came along and went inside me just as I was saying yes."

"Hooray! Myra, your health."

"We're only six, though," added Archie. "Didn't you swim up against anybody else who looked like a cricketer and might play for us?"

"But we can easily pick up five people by Saturday," said Myra confidently. "And oh, I do hope we're in form; we haven't played for years."

We lost the toss, and Myra led her team out on to the field. The last five places in the eleven had been filled with care: a preparatory school-boy and his little sister (found by Dahlia on the beach), Miss Debenham (found by Simpson on the road with a punctured bicycle), Mrs Oakley (found by Archie at the station and re-discovered by Myra in the Channel), and Sarah, a jolly girl of sixteen (found by me and Thomas in the tobacconist's, where she was buying The Sportsman).

"Where would you all like to field?" asked the captain.

"Let's stand round in groups, just at the start, and then see where we're wanted. Who's going to bowl?"

"Me and Samuel. I wonder if I dare bowl over-hand."

"I'm going to," said Simpson.

"You can't, not with your left hand."

"Why not? Hirst does."

"Then I shan't field point," said Thomas with decision.

However, as it happened, it was short leg who received the first two balls, beautiful swerving wides, while the next two were well caught and returned by third man. Simpson's range being thus established, he made a determined attack on the over proper with lobs, and managed to wipe off half of it. Encouraged by this, he returned with such success to overhand that the very next ball got into the analysis, the batsman reaching out and hitting it over the hedge for six. Two more range-finders followed before Simpson scored another dot with a sneak; and then, at what should have been the last ball, a tragedy occurred.

"Wide," said the umpire.

"But—but I was b-bowling UNDERHAND," stammered Simpson.

"Now you've nothing to fall back on," I pointed out.

Simpson considered the new situation. "Then you fellows can't mind if I go on with overhand," he said joyfully, and he played his twelfth.

It was the batsman's own fault. Like a true gentleman he went after the ball, caught it up near point, and hit it hard in the direction of cover. Sarah shot up a hand unconcernedly.

"One for six," said Simpson, and went over to Miss Debenham to explain how he did it.

"He must come off," said Archie. "We have a reputation to keep up. It's his left hand, of course, but we can't go round to all the spectators and explain that he can really bowl quite decent long hops with his right."

In the next over nothing much happened, except that Miss Debenham missed a sitter. Subsequently Simpson caught her eye from another part of the field, and explained telegraphically to her how she should have drawn her hands in to receive the ball. The third over was entrusted to Sarah.

"So far," said Dahlia, half an hour later, "the Rabbits have not shone. Sarah is doing it all."

"Hang it, Dahlia, Thomas and I discovered the child. Give the credit where it is due."

"Well, why don't you put my Bobby on, then? Boys are allowed to play right-handed, you know."

So Bobby went on, and with Sarah's help finished off the innings.

"Jolly good rot," he said to Simpson, "you're having to bowl left-handed."

"My dear Robert," I said, "Mr Simpson is a natural base-ball pitcher, he has an acquired swerve at bandy, and he is a lepidopterist of considerable charm. But he can't bowl with either hand."

"Coo!" said Bobby.

The allies came out even more strongly when we went in to bat. I was the only Rabbit who made ten, and my whole innings was played in an atmosphere of suspicion very trying to a sensitive man. Mrs Oakley was in when I took guard, and I played out the over with great care, being morally bowled by every ball. At the end of it a horrible thought occurred to me: I had been batting right-handed! Naturally I changed round for my next ball. (Movements of surprise.)

"Hallo," said the wicket-keeper, "I thought you were left-handed; why aren't you playing right?"

"No, I'm really right-handed," I said. "I played that way by mistake just now. Sorry."

He grunted sceptically, and the bowler came up to have things explained to her. The next ball I hit left-handed for six. (LOUD MUTTERS.)

"Is he really right-handed?" the bowler asked Mrs Oakley.

"I don't know," she said, "I've never seen him before." (SENSATION.)

"I think, if you don't mind, we'd rather you played right-handed."

"Certainly." The next ball was a full pitch, and I took a right-handed six. There was an awful hush. I looked round at the field and prepared to run for it. I felt that they suspected me of all the undiscovered crimes of the year.

"Look here," I said, nearly crying, "I'll play any way you like—sideways, or upside down, or hanging on to the branch of a tree, or—"

The atmosphere was too much for me. I trod on my wickets, burst into tears, and bolted to the tent.

"Well," said Dahlia, "we won."

"Yes," we all agreed, "we won."

"Even if we didn't do much of it ourselves," Simpson pointed out, "we had jolly good fun."

"We always have THAT," said Myra.

THE HOUSE-WARMING

I
WORK FOR ALL

"Well," said Dahlia, "what do you think of it?"

I knocked the ashes out of my after-breakfast pipe, arranged the cushions of my deck-chair, and let my eyes wander lazily over the house and its surroundings. After a year of hotels and other people's houses, Dahlia and Archie had come into their own.

"I've no complaints," I said happily.

A vision of white and gold appeared in the doorway and glided over the lawn toward us—Myra with a jug.

"None at all," said Simpson, sitting up eagerly.

"But Thomas isn't quite satisfied with one of the bathrooms, I'm afraid. I heard him saying something in the passage about it this morning when I was inside."

"I asked if you'd gone to sleep in the bath," explained Thomas.

"I hadn't. It is practically impossible, Thomas, to go to sleep in a cold bath."

"Except, perhaps, for a Civil Servant," said Blair.

"Exactly. Of the practice in the Admiralty Thomas can tell us later on. For myself I was at the window looking at the beautiful view."

"Why can't you look at it from your own window instead of keeping people out of the bathroom?" grunted Thomas.

"Because the view from my room is an entirely different one."

"There is no stint in this house," Dahlia pointed out.

"No," said Simpson, jumping up excitedly.

Myra put the jug of cider down in front of us.

"There!" she said. "Please count it, and see that I haven't drunk any on the way."

"This is awfully nice of you, Myra. And a complete surprise to all of us except Simpson. We shall probably be here again to-morrow about the same time."

There was a long silence, broken only by the extremely jolly sound of liquid falling from a height.

Just as it was coming to an end Archie appeared suddenly among us and dropped on the grass by the side of Dahlia. Simpson looked guiltily at the empty jug, and then leant down to his host.

"TO-MORROW!" he said in a stage whisper. "ABOUT THE SAME TIME."

"I doubt it," said Archie.

"I know it for a fact," protested Simpson.

"I'm afraid Myra and Samuel made an assignation for this morning," said Dahlia.

"There's nothing in it, really," said Myra. "He's only trifling with me. He doesn't mean anything."

Simpson buried his confused head in his glass, and proceeded to change the subject.

"We all like your house, Archie," he said.

"We do," I agreed, "and we think it's very nice of you to ask us down to open it."

"It is rather," said Archie.

"We are determined, therefore, to do all we can to give the house a homey appearance. I did what I could for the bathroom this morning. I flatter myself that the taint of newness has now been dispelled."

"I was sure it was you," said Myra. "How do you get the water right up the walls?"

"Easily. Further, Archie, if you want any suggestions as to how to improve the place, our ideas are at your disposal."

"For instance," said Thomas, "where do we play cricket?"

"By the way, you fellows," announced Simpson, "I've given up playing cricket."

We all looked at him in consternation.

"Do you mean you've given up BOWLING?" said Dahlia, with wide-open eyes.

"Aren't you ever going to walk to the wickets again?" asked Blair.

"Aren'tyouevergoingtowalkbacktothepavilionagain?"asked Archie.

"What will Montgomeryshire say?" wondered Myra in tones of awe.

"May I have your belt and your sand-shoes?" I begged.

"It's the cider," said Thomas. "I knew he was overdoing it."

Simpson fixed his glasses firmly on his nose and looked round at us benignly.

"I've given it up for golf," he observed.

"Traitor," said everyone.

"And the Triangular Tournament arranged for, and everything," added Myra.

"You could make a jolly little course round here," went on the infatuated victim. "If you like, Archie, I'll—"

Archie stood up and made a speech.

"Ladies and gentlemen," he said, "at 11.30 to-morrow precisely I invite you to the paddock beyond the kitchen-garden."

"Myra and I have an appointment," put in Simpson hastily.

"A net will be erected," Archie went on, ignoring him, "and Mr Simpson will take his stand therein, while we all bowl at him—or, if any prefer it, at the wicket—for five minutes. He will then bowl at us for an hour, after which he will have another hour's smart fielding practice. If he is still alive and still talks about golf, why then, I won't say but what he mightn't be allowed to plan out a little course—or, at any rate, to do a little preliminary weeding."

"Good man," said Simpson.

"And if anybody else thinks he has given up cricket for ludo or croquet or oranges and lemons, then he can devote himself to planning out a little course for that too—or anyhow to removing a few plantains in preparation for it. In fact, ladies and gentlemen, all I want is for you to make yourselves as happy and as useful as you can."

"It's what you're here for," said Dahlia.

II
A GALA PERFORMANCE

THE sun came into my room early next morning and woke me up. It was followed immediately by a large blue-bottle which settled down to play with me. We adopted the usual formation, the blue-bottle keeping mostly to the back of the court whilst I waited at the net for a kill. After two sets I decided to change my tactics. I looked up at the ceiling and pretended I wasn't playing. The blue-bottle settled on my nose and walked up my forehead. "Heavens!" I cried, clasping my hand suddenly to my brow, "I've forgotten my toothbrush!" This took it completely by surprise, and I removed its corpse into the candlestick.

Then Simpson came in with a golf club in his hand.

"Great Scott," he shouted, "you're not still in bed?"

"I am not. This is telepathic suggestion. You think I'm in bed; I appear to be in bed; in reality there is no bed here. Do go away—I haven't had a wink of sleep yet."

"But, man, look at the lovely morning!"

"Simpson," I said sternly, rolling up the sleeves of my pyjamas with great deliberation, "I have had one visitor already to-day. His corpse is now in the candlestick. It is an omen, Simpson."

"I thought you'd like to come outside with me, and I'd show you my swing."

"Yes, yes, I shall like to see that, but AFTER breakfast, Simpson. I suppose one of the gardeners put it up for you? You must show me your box of soldiers and your tricycle horse, too. But run away now, there's a good boy."

"My golf-swing, idiot."

I sat up in bed and stared at him in sheer amazement. For a long time words wouldn't come to me. Simpson backed nervously to the door.

"I saw the Coronation," I said at last, and I dropped back on my pillow and went to sleep.

"I feel very important," said Archie, coming on to the lawn where Myra and I were playing a quiet game of bowls with the croquet balls. "I've been paying the wages."

"Archie and I do hate it so," said Dahlia. "I'm luckier, because I only pay mine once a month."

"It would be much nicer if they did it for love," said Archie, "and just accepted a tie-pin occasionally. I never know what to say when I hand a man eighteen-and-six."

"Here's eighteen-and-six," I suggested, "and don't bite the half-sovereign, because it may be bad."

"You should shake his hand," said Myra, "and say, 'Thank you very much for the azaleas.'"

"Or you might wrap the money up in paper and leave it for him in one of the beds."

"And then you'd know whether he had made it properly."

"Well, you're all very helpful," said Archie. "Thank you extremely. Where are the others? It's a pity that they should be left out of this."

"Simpson disappeared after breakfast with his golf-clubs. He is in high dudgeon—which is the surname of a small fish—because no one wanted to see his swing."

"Oh, but I do," said Dahlia eagerly. "Where is he?"

"We will track him down," announced Archie. "I will go to the stables, unchain the truffle-hounds, and show them one of his reversible cuffs."

We found Simpson in the pig-sty. The third hole, as he was planning it out for Archie, necessitated the carrying of the farm buildings, which he described as a natural hazard. Unfortunately, his ball had fallen into a casual pig-sty. It had not yet been decided whether the ball could be picked out without penalty—the more immediate need being to find the blessed thing. So Simpson was in the pig-sty, searching.

"If you're looking for the old sow," I said, "there she is, just behind you."

"What's the local rule about loose pigs blown on to the course?" asked Archie.

"Oh, you fellows, there you are," said Simpson rapidly. "I'm getting on first-rate. This is the third hole, Archie. It will be rather good, I think; the green is just the other side of the pond. I can make a very sporting little course."

"We've come to see your swing, Samuel," said Myra. "Can you do it in there, or is it too crowded?"

"I'll come out. This ball's lost, I'm afraid."

"One of the little pigs will eat it," complained Archie, "and we shall have indiarubber crackling."

Simpson came out and proceeded to give his display. Fortunately the weather kept fine, the conditions indeed being all that could be desired. The sun shone brightly, and there was a slight breeze from the south which tempered the heat and in no way militated against the general enjoyment. The performance was divided into two parts. The first part consisted of Mr Simpson's swing WITHOUT the ball, the second part being devoted to Mr Simpson's swing WITH the ball.

"This is my swing," said Simpson.

He settled himself ostentatiously into his stance and placed his club-head stiffly on the ground three feet away from him.

"Middle," said Archie.

Simpson frowned and began to waggle his club. He waggled it carefully a dozen times.

"It's a very nice swing," said Myra at the end of the ninth movement, "but isn't it rather short?"

Simpson said nothing, but drew his club slowly and jerkily back, twisting his body and keeping his eye fixed on an imaginary ball until the back of his neck hid it from sight.

"You can see it better round this side now," suggested Archie.

"He'll split if he goes on," said Thomas anxiously.

"Watch this," I warned Myra. "He's going to pick a pin out of the back of his calf with his teeth."

Then Simpson let himself go, finishing up in a very creditable knot indeed.

"That's quite good," said Dahlia. "Does it do as well when there's a ball?"

"Well, I miss it sometimes, of course."

"We all do that," said Thomas.

Thus encouraged, Simpson put down a ball and began to address it. It was apparent at once that the last address had been only his telegraphic one; this was the genuine affair. After what seemed to be four or five minutes there was a general feeling that some apology was necessary. Simpson recognized this himself.

"I'm a little nervous," he said.

"Not so nervous as the pigs are," said Archie.

Simpson finished his address and got on to his swing. He swung. He hit the ball. The ball, which seemed to have too much left-hand side on it, whizzed off and disappeared into the pond. It sank....

Luckily the weather had held up till the last.

"Well, well," said Archie, "it's time for lunch. We have had a riotous morning. Let's all take it easy this afternoon."

III
UNEXPECTED GUESTS

Sometimes I do a little work in the morning. Doctors are agreed now that an occasional spell of work in the morning doesn't do me any harm. My announcement at breakfast that this was one of the mornings was greeted with a surprised enthusiasm which was most flattering. Archie offered me his own room where he does his thinking; Simpson offered me a nib; and Dahlia promised me a quiet time till lunch. I thanked them all and settled down to work.

But Dahlia didn't keep her promise. My first hour was peaceful, but after that I had inquiries by every post. Blair looked in to know where Myra was; Archie asked if I'd seen Dahlia anywhere; and when finally Thomas's head appeared in the doorway I decided that I had had enough of it.

"Oh, I say," began Thomas, "will you come and—but I suppose you're busy."

"Not too busy," I said, "to spare a word or two for an old friend," and I picked up the dictionary to throw at him. But he was gone before I could take aim.

"This is the end," I said to myself, and after five minutes more decided to give up work and seek refreshment and congenial conversation. To my surprise I found neither. Every room seemed to be empty, the tennis lawn was deserted, and Archie's cricket-bag and Simpson's golf-clubs rested peacefully in the hall. Something was going on. I went back to my work and decided to have the secret out at lunch.

"Now then," I said, when that blessed hour arrived, "tell me about it. You've deserted me all morning, but I'm not going to be left out."

"It's your fault for shutting yourself up."

"Duty," I said, slapping my chest—"duty," and I knocked my glass over with an elbow. "Oh, Dahlia, I'm horribly sorry. May I go and stand in the corner?"

"Let's talk very fast and pretend we didn't notice it," said Myra, helping me to mop. "Go on, Archie."

"Well, it's like this," said Archie. "A little while ago the Vicar called here."

"I don't see that that's any reason for keeping me in the background. I have met clergymen before and I know what to say to them."

"When I say a little while ago I mean about three weeks. We'd have asked you down for the night if we'd known you were so keen on clergymen. Well, as the result of that unfortunate visit, the school treat takes place here this afternoon, and lorblessme if I hadn't forgotten all about it till this morning."

"You'll have to help, please," said Dahlia.

"Only don't spill anything," said Thomas.

They have a poor sense of humour in the Admiralty.

I took a baby in each hand and wandered off to look for bees. Their idea, not mine.

"The best bees are round here," I said, and I led them along to the front of the house. On the lawn was Myra, surrounded by about eight babies.

"Two more for your collection," I announced. "Very fine specimens. The word with them is bees."

"Aren't they darlings? Sit down, babies, and the pretty gentleman will tell us all a story."

"Meaning me?" I asked in surprise. Myra looked beseechingly at me as she arranged the children all round her. I sat down near them and tried to think.

"Once upon a time," I said, "there was a—a—there was a—was a—a bee."

Myra nodded approvingly. She seemed to like the story so far. I didn't. The great dearth of adventures that could happen to a bee was revealed to me in a flash. I saw that I had been hasty.

"At least," I went on, "he thought he was a bee, but as he grew up his friends felt that he was not really a bee at all, but a dear little rabbit. His fur was too long for a bee."

Myra shook her head at me and frowned. My story was getting over-subtle for the infant mind. I determined to straighten it out finally.

"However," I added, "the old name stuck to him, and they all called him a bee. Now then I can get on. Where was I?"

But at this moment my story was interrupted.

"Come here," shouted Archie from the distance. "You're wanted."

"I'm sorry," I said, getting up quickly. "Will you finish the story for me? You'd better leave out the part where he stings the Shah of Persia. That's too exciting. Good-bye." And I hurried after Archie.

"Help Simpson with some of these races," said Archie. "He's getting himself into the dickens of a mess."

Simpson had started two races simultaneously; hence the trouble. In one of them the bigger boys had to race to a sack containing their boots, rescue their own pair, put them on, and race back to the starting-point. Good! In the other the smaller boys, each armed with a paper containing a problem in arithmetic, had to run to their sisters, wait for the problem to be solved, and then run back with the answer. Excellent! Simpson at his most inventive. Unfortunately, when the bootless boys arrived at the turning post, they found nothing but a small problem in arithmetic awaiting them, while on the adjoining stretch of grass young mathematicians were trying, with the help of their sisters, to get into two pairs of boots at once.

"Hallo, there you are," said Simpson. "Do help me; I shall be mobbed in a moment. It's the mothers. They think the whole thing is a scheme for stealing their children's boots. Can't you start a race for them?"

"You never ought to go about without somebody. Where's Thomas?"

"He's playing rounders. He scored a rounder by himself just now from an overthrow, but we shall hear about it at dinner. Look here, there's a game called 'Twos and Threes.' Couldn't you start the mothers at that? You stand in twos, and whenever anyone stands in front of the two then the person behind the two runs away."

"Are you sure?"

"What do you mean?" said Simpson.

"It sounds too exciting to be true. I can't believe it."

"Go on, there's a good chap. They'll know how to play all right."

"Oh, very well. Do they take their boots off first or not?"

Twos and Threes was a great success.

I found that I had quite a FLAIR for the game. I seemed to take to it naturally.

By the time our match was finished Simpson's little footwear trouble was over and he was organizing a grand three-legged race.

"I think they are all enjoying it," said Dahlia.

"They love it," I said; "Thomas is perfectly happy making rounders."

"But I meant the children. Don't you think they love it too? The babies seem so happy with Myra. I suppose she's telling them stories."

"I think so. She's got rather a good one about a bee. Oh, yes, they're happy enough with her."

"I hope they all had enough to eat at tea."

"Allowing for a little natural shyness I think they did well. And I didn't spill anything. Altogether it has been rather a success."

Dahlia stood looking down at the children, young and old, playing in the field beneath her, and gave a sigh of happiness.

"Now," she said, "I feel the house is REALLY warm."

IV
A WORD IN SEASON

"Archie," said Blair, "what's that big empty room above the billiard-room for?"

"That," said Archie, "is where we hide the corpses of our guests. I sleep with the key under my pillow."

"This is rather sudden," I said. "I'm not at all sure that I should have come if I had known that."

"Don't frighten them, dear; tell them the truth."

"Well, the truth is," said Archie, "that there was some idea of a little play-acting there occasionally. Hence the curtain-rod, the emergency exit and other devices."

"Then why haven't we done any? We came down here to open your house for you, and then you go and lock up the most important room of all, and sleep with the key under your pillow."

"It's too hot. But we'll do a little charade to-night if you like—just to air the place."

"Hooray," said Myra, "I know a lovely word."

Myra's little word was in two syllables and required three performers. Archie and I were kindly included in her company. Simpson threatened to follow with something immense and archaic, and Thomas also had something rather good up his sleeve, but I am not going to bother you with these. One word will be enough for you.

FIRST SCENE

"Oh, good-morning," said Myra. She had added a hat and a sunshade to her evening-frock, and was supported by me in a gentleman's lounge-coat and boater for Henley wear.

"Good-morning, mum," said Archie, hitching up his apron and spreading his hands on the table in front of him.

"I just want this ribbon matched, please."

"Certainly, mum. Won't your little boy—I beg pardon, the old gentleman, take a seat too? What colour did you want the ribbon, mum?"

"The same colour as this," I said. "Idiot."

"Your grandfather is in a bit of a draught, I'm afraid, mum. It always stimulates the flow of language. My grandfather was just the same. I'm afraid, mum, we haven't any ribbon as you might say the SAME colour as this."

"If it's very near it will do."

"Now what colour would you call that?" wondered Archie, with his head on one side. "Kind of puce-like, I should put it at. Puce-magenta, as we say in the trade. No; we're right out of puce- magenta."

"Show the lady what you have got," I said sternly.

"Well, mum, I'm right out of ribbon, altogether. The fact is I'm more of an ironmonger really. The draper's is just the other side of the road. You wouldn't like a garden-roller now? I can do you a nice garden-roller for two pound five, and that's simply giving it away."

"Oh, shall we have a nice roller?" said Myra eagerly.

"I'm not going to carry it home," I said.

"That's all right, sir. My little lad will take it up on his bicycle. Two pounds five, mum, and sixpence for the mouse-trap the gentleman's been sitting on. Say three pounds."

Myra took out her purse.

SECOND SCENE

We were back in our ordinary clothes.

"I wonder if they guessed that," said Archie.

"It was very easy," said Myra. "I should have thought they'd have seen it at once."

"But of course they're not a very clever lot," I explained. "That fellow with the spectacles—"

"Simpson his name is," said Archie. "I know him well. He's a professional golfer."

"Well, he LOOKS learned enough. I expect he knows all right. But the others—"

"Do you think they knew that we were supposed to be in a shop?"

"Surely! Why, I should think even—What's that man's name over there? No; that one next to the pretty lady—ah, yes, Thomas. Is that Thomas, the wonderful cueist, by the way? Really! Well, I should think even Thomas guessed that much."

"Why not do it over again to make sure?"

"Oh no, it was perfectly obvious. Let's get on to the final scene."

"I'm afraid that will give it away rather," said Myra.

"I'm afraid so," agreed Archie.

THIRD SCENE

We sat on camp-stools and looked up at the ceiling with our mouths open.

"'E's late," said Archie.

"I don't believe 'e's coming, and I don't mind 'oo 'ears me sye so," said Myra. "So there!"

"'Ot work," I said, wiping my brow.

"Nar, not up there. Not 'ot. Nice and breezy like."

"But 'e's nearer the sun than wot we are, ain't 'e?"

"Ah, but 'e's not 'ot. Not up there."

"'Ere, there 'e is," cried Myra, jumping up excitedly. "Over there. 'Ow naow, it's a bird. I declare I quite thought it was 'im. Silly of me."

There was silence for a little, and then Archie took a sandwich out of his pocket.

"Wunner wot they'll invent next," he said, and munched stolidly.

"Well done," said Dahlia.

"Thomas and I have been trying to guess," said Simpson, "but the strain is terrific. My first idea was 'codfish,' but I suppose that's wrong. It's either 'silkworm' or 'wardrobe.' Thomas suggests 'mangel-wurzel.' He says he never saw anybody who had so much the whole air of a wurzel as Archie. The indefinable elan of the wurzel was there."

"Can't you really guess?" said Myra eagerly.

"I don't know whether I want you to or not. Oh no, I don't want you to."

"Then I withdraw 'mangel-wurzel,'" said Simpson gallantly.

"I think I can guess," said Blair. "It's—"

"Whisper it," said Simpson. "I'm never going to know."

Blair whispered it.

"Yes," said Myra disappointedly, "that's it."

V
UNINVITED GUESTS

"Nine," said Archie, separating his latest victim from the marmalade spoon and dropping it into the hot water. "This is going to be a sanguinary day. With a pretty late cut into the peach jelly Mr A. Mannering reached double figures. Ten. Battles are being won while Thomas still sleeps. Any advance on ten?"

"Does that include MY wasp?" asked Myra.

"There are only ten here," said Archie, looking into the basin, "and they're all mine. I remember them perfectly. What was yours like?"

"Well, I didn't exactly kill him. I smacked him with a teaspoon and asked him to go away. And he went on to your marmalade, so I expect you thought he was yours. But it was really mine, and I don't think it's very sporting of you to kill another person's wasp."

"Have one of mine," I said, pushing my plate across. "Have Bernard—he's sitting on the green-gage."

"I don't really want to kill anything. I killed a rabbit once and I wished I hadn't."

"I nearly killed a rabbit once, and I wished I had."

"Great sportsmen at a glance," said Archie. "Tell us about it before it goes into your reminiscences."

"It was a fierce affair while it lasted. The rabbit was sitting down and I was standing up, so that I rather had the advantage of him at the start. I waited till he seemed to be asleep and then fired."

"And missed him?"

"Y-yes. He heard the report, though. I mean, you mustn't think he ignored me altogether. I moved him. He got up and went away all right."

"A very lucky escape for you," said Archie. "I once knew a man who was gored to death by an angry rabbit." He slashed in the air with his napkin. "Fifteen. Dahlia, let's have breakfast indoors to-morrow. This is very jolly but it's just as hot, and it doesn't get Thomas up any earlier, as we hoped."

All that day we grilled in the heat. Myra and I started a game of croquet in the morning, but after one shot each we agreed to abandon it as a draw — slightly in my favour, because I had given her the chipped mallet. And in the afternoon, Thomas and Simpson made a great effort to get up enthusiasm for lawn-tennis. Each of them returned the other's service into the net until the score stood at eight all, at which point they suddenly realized that nothing but the violent death of one of the competitors would ever end the match. They went on to ten all to make sure, and then retired to the lemonade and wasp jug, Simpson missing a couple of dead bodies by inches only. And after dinner it was hotter than ever.

"The heat in my room," announced Archie, "breaks all records. The thermometer says a hundred and fifty, the barometer says very dry, we've had twenty-five hours' sunshine, and there's not a drop of rain recorded in the soap-dish. Are we going to take this lying down?"

"No," said Thomas, "let's sleep out to-night."

"What do you say, Dahlia?"

"It's a good idea. You can all sleep on the croquet lawn, and Myra and I will take the tennis lawn."

"Hadn't you better have the croquet lawn? Thomas walks in his sleep, and we don't want to have him going through hoops all night."

"You'll have to bring down your own mattresses," went on Dahlia, "and you've not got to walk about the garden in the early morning, at least not until Myra and I are up, and if you're going to fall over croquet hoops you mustn't make a noise. That's all the rules, I think."

"I'm glad we've got the tennis lawn," said Myra; "it's much smoother. Do you prefer the right-hand court, dear, or the left-hand?"

"We shall be very close to Nature to-night," said Archie. "Now we shall know whether it really is the nightjar, or Simpson gargling."

We were very close to Nature that night, but in the early morning still closer. I was awakened by the noise of Simpson talking, as I hoped, in his sleep. However, it appeared that he was awake and quite conscious of the things he was saying.

"I can't help it," he explained to Archie, who had given expression to the general opinion about it; "these bally wasps are all over me."

"It's your own fault," said Archie. "Why do you egg them on? I don't have wasps all over ME."

"Conf—There! I've been stung."

"You've been what?"

"Stung."

"Stung. Where?"

"In the neck."

"In the neck?" Archie turned over to me. "Simpson," he said, "has been stung in the neck. Tell Thomas."

I woke up Thomas. "Simpson," I said, "has been stung in the neck."

"Good," said Thomas, and went to sleep again.

"We've told Thomas," said Archie. "Now, are you satisfied?"

"Get away, you brute," shouted Simpson, suddenly, and dived under the sheet.

Archie and I lay back and shouted with laughter.

"It's really very silly of him," said Archie, "because—go away—because everybody knows that—get away, you ass—that wasps aren't dangerous unless—confound you—unless—I say, isn't it time we got up?"

I came up from under my sheet and looked at my watch.

"Four-thirty," I said, dodged a wasp, and went back again.

"We must wait till five-thirty," said Archie. "Simpson was quite right; he WAS stung, after all. I'll tell him so."

He leant out of bed to tell him so, and then thought better of it and retired beneath the sheets.

At five-thirty a gallant little party made its way to the house, its mattresses over its shoulders.

"Gently," said Archie, as we came in sight of the tennis lawn.

We went very gently. There were only wasps on the tennis lawn, but one does not want to disturb the little fellows.

VI
A FINAL ARRANGEMENT

"Seeing that this is our last day together," began Archie—

"Oh, DON'T," said Myra. "I can't bear it."

"Seeing that this is our first day together, we might have a little tournament of some kind, followed by a small distribution of prizes. What do you think, Dahlia?"

"Well, I daresay I can find something."

"Any old thing that we don't want will do; nothing showy or expensive. Victory is its own reward."

"Yes, but if there IS a pot of home-made marmalade going with it," I said, "so much the better."

"Dahlia, earmark the marmalade for this gentleman. Now, what's it going to be? Golf, Simpson?"

"Why, of course," said Myra. "Hasn't he been getting it ready for days?"

"That will give him an unfair advantage," I pointed out. "He knows every single brick on the greens."

"Oh, I say, there aren't any greens yet," protested Simpson. "That'll take a year or two. But I've marked out white circles and you have to get inside them."

"I saw him doing that," said Archie. "I was afraid he expected us to play prisoners' base with him."

The game fixed upon, we proceeded to draw for partners.

"You'll have to play with me, Archie," said Dahlia, "because I'm no good at all."

"I shall have to play with Myra," I said, "because I'm no good at all."

"Oh, I'm very good," said Myra.

"That looks as though I should have to play with—"
"Simpson," "Thomas," said Thomas and Simpson together.

"You're all giving me a lot of trouble," said Archie, putting his pencil back in his pocket. "I've just written your names out neatly on little bits of paper, and now they're all wasted. You'll have to stick them on yourselves so that the spectators will know who you are as you whizz past." He handed his bits of paper round and went in for his clubs.

It was a stroke competition, and each couple went round by itself.

Myra and I started last.

"Now we've got to win this," she said, "because we shan't play together again for a long time."

"That's a nice cheery thing to say to a person just when he's driving. Now I shall have to address the ball all over again."

"Oh, NO!"

I addressed and despatched the ball. It struck a wall about eighty yards away and dropped. When we got there we found to our disgust that it was nestling at the very foot. Myra looked at it doubtfully.

"Can't you make it climb the wall?" I asked.

"We shall have to go back, I'm afraid. We can pretend we left our pocket-handkerchiefs behind."

She chipped it back about twenty yards, and I sent it on again about a hundred. Unfortunately it landed in a rut. However Myra got it out with great resource, and I was lucky enough with my next to place it inside the magic circle.

"Five," I said. "You know, I don't think you're helping me much. All you did that hole was to go twenty-one yards in the wrong direction."

Myra smiled cheerfully at me and did the next hole in one. "Well played, partner," she said, as he put her club back in its bag.

"Oh, at the short holes I don't deny that you're useful. Where do we go now?"

"Over the barn. This is the long hole."

I got in an excellent drive, but unfortunately it didn't aviate quick enough. While the intrepid spectators were still holding their breath, there was an ominous crash.

"Did you say IN the barn or OVER the barn?" I asked, as we hurried on to find the damage.

"We do play an exciting game, don't we?" said Myra.

We got into the barn and found the ball and a little glass on the floor.

"What a very small hole it made," said Myra, pointing to the broken pane. "What shall I do?"

"You'll have to go back through the hole. It's an awkward little shot."

"I don't think I could."

"No, it IS rather a difficult stroke. You want to stand well behind the ball, and—however, there may be a local rule about it."

"I don't think there is or I should have heard it. Samuel's been telling me EVERYTHING lately."

"Then there's only one thing for it." I pointed to the window at the other end of the barn. "Go straight on."

Myra gave a little gurgle of delight.

"But we shall have to save up our pocket-money," she said.

Her ball hit the wood in between two panes and bounded back. My next shot was just above the glass. Myra took a niblick and got the ball back into the middle of the floor.

"It's simply sickening that we can't break a window when we're really trying to. I should have thought that anyone could have broken a window. Now then."

"Oh, good SHOT!" cried Myra above the crash. We hurried out and did the hole in nine.

At lunch, having completed eighteen holes out of the thirty-six, we were seven strokes behind the leaders, Simpson and Thomas. Simpson, according to Thomas, had been playing like a book. Golf Faults Analysed—that book, I should think.

"But I expect he'll go to pieces in the afternoon," said Thomas. He turned to a servant and added, "Mr Simpson won't have anything more."

We started our second round brilliantly; continued (after an unusual incident on the fifth tee) brilliantly; and ended up brilliantly. At the last tee we had played a hundred and thirty-seven. Myra got in a beautiful drive to within fifty yards of the circle.

"How many?" said the others, coming up excitedly.

"This is terrible," said Myra, putting her hand to her heart. "A hundred and—shall I tell them?—a—a—Oh, dear—a—hundredandthirtyeight."

"Golly," said Thomas, "you've got one for it. We did a hundred and forty."

"We did a hundred and forty-two," said Archie. "Close play at the Oval."

"Oh," said Myra to me, "DO be careful. Oh, but no," she went on quickly, "I don't mind a bit really if we lose. It's only a game. Besides, we—"

"You forget the little pot of home-made marmalade," I said reproachfully. "Dahlia, what ARE the prizes? Because it's just possible that Myra might like the second one better than the first. In that case I should miss this."

"Go on," whispered Myra.

I went on. There was a moment's silence—and then a deep sigh from Myra.

"How about it?" I said calmly.

Loud applause.

"Well," said Dahlia, "you and Myra make a very good couple. I suppose I must find a prize for you."

"It doesn't really matter," said Myra breathlessly, "because on the fifth tee we—we arranged about the prizes."

"We arranged to give each other one," I said, smiling at Dahlia.

Dahlia looked very hard at us.

"You DON'T mean—?"

Myra laughed happily.

"Oh," she said, "but that's just what we do."

AT PLAY

TEN AND EIGHT

The only event of importance last week was my victory over Henry by ten and eight. If you don't want to hear about that, then I shall have to pass on to you a few facts about his motor bicycle. You'd rather have the other? I thought so.

The difference between Henry and me is that he is what I should call a good golfer, and I am what everybody else calls a bad golfer. In consequence of this he insults me with offers of bisques.

"I'll have ten this time," I said, as we walked to the tee.

"Better have twelve. I beat you with eleven yesterday."

"Thank you," I said haughtily, "I will have ten." It is true that he beat me last time, but then owing to bad management on my part I had nine bisques left at the moment of defeat simply eating their heads off.

Henry teed up and drove a "Pink Spot" out of sight. Henry swears by the "Pink Spot" if there is anything of a wind. I use either a "Quo Vadis," which is splendid for going out of bounds, or an "Ostrich," which has a wonderful way of burying itself in the sand. I followed him to the green at my leisure.

"Five," said Henry.

"Seven," said I; "and if I take three bisques it's my hole."

"You must only take one at a time," protested Henry.

"Why? There's nothing in Wisden or Baedeker about it. Besides, I will only take one at a time if it makes it easier for you. I take one and that brings me down to six, and then another one and that brings me down to five, and then another one and that brings me down to four. There! And as you did the hole in five, I win."

"Well, of course, if you like to waste them all at the start—"

"I'm not wasting them, I'm creating a moral effect. Behold, I have won the first hole; let us be photographed together."

Henry went to the next tee slightly ruffled and topped his ball into the road. I had kept mine well this side of it and won in four to five.

"I shan't take any bisques here," I said. "Two up."

At the third tee my "Quo Vadis" darted off suddenly to the left and tried to climb the hill. I headed it off and gave it a nasty dent from behind when it wasn't looking, and with my next shot started it rolling down the mountains with ever-increasing velocity. Not until it was within a foot of the pin did it condescend to stop. Henry, who had reached the green with his drive and had taken one putt too many, halved the hole in four. I took a bisque and was three up.

The fourth hole was prettily played by both of us, and with two bisques I had it absolutely stiff. Unnerved by this Henry went all out at the fifth and tried to carry the stream in two. Unfortunately (I mean unfortunately for him) the stream was six inches too broad in the particular place at which he tried to carry it. My own view is that he should either have chosen another place or else have got a narrower stream from somewhere. As it was I won in an uneventful six, and took with a bisque the short hole which followed.

"Six up," I pointed out to Henry, "and three bisques left. They're jolly little things, bisques, but you want to use them quickly. Bisque dat qui cito dat. Doesn't the sea look ripping to-day?"

"Go on," growled Henry.

"I once did a two at this hole," I said as I teed my ball. "If I did a two now and took a bisque, you'd have to do it in nothing in order to win. A solemn thought."

At this hole you have to drive over a chasm in the cliffs. My ball made a bee line for the beach, bounced on a rock, and disappeared into a cave. Henry's "Pink Spot," which really seemed to have a chance of winning a hole at last, found the wind too much for it and followed me below.

"I'm in this cave," I said when we had found Henry's ball; and with a lighted match in one hand and a niblick in the other I went in and tried to persuade the "Ostrich" to come out. My eighth argument was too much for it, and we re-appeared in the daylight together.

"How many?" I asked Henry.

"Six," he said, as he hit the top of the cliff once more, and shot back on to the beach.

I left him and chivied my ball round to where the cliffs are lowest; then I got it gradually on to a little mound of sand (very delicate work this), took a terrific swing and fairly heaved it on to the grass. Two more strokes put me on to the green in twenty. I lit a pipe and waited for Henry to finish his game of rackets.

"I've played twenty-five," he shouted.

"Then you'll want some of my bisques," I said. "I can lend you three till Monday."

Henry had one more rally and then picked his ball up. I had won seven holes and I had three bisques with which to win the match. I was a little doubtful if I could do this, but Henry settled the question by misjudging yet again the breadth of the stream. What is experience if it teaches us nothing? Henry must really try to enlarge his mind about rivers.

"Dormy nine," I said at the tenth tee, "and no bisques left."

"Thank Heaven for that," sighed Henry.

"But I have only to halve one hole out of nine," I pointed out. "Technically I am on what is known as velvet."

"Oh, shut up and drive."

I am a bad golfer, but even bad golfers do holes in bogey now and then. In the ordinary way I was pretty certain to halve one of the nine holes with Henry, and so win the match. Both the eleventh and the seventeenth, for instance, are favourites of mine. Had I halved one of those, he would have admitted cheerfully that I had played good golf and beaten him fairly. But as things happened—

What happened, put quite briefly, was this. Bogey for the tenth is four. I hooked my drive off the tee and down a little gully to the left, put a good iron shot into a bunker on the right, and than ran down a hundred-yard putt with a niblick for a three. One of those difficult down-hill putts.

"Luck!" said Henry, as soon as he could speak.

"I've been missing those lately," I said.

"Your match," said Henry; "I can't play against luck like that."

It was true that he had given me ten bisques, but, on the other hand, I could have given him a dozen at the seventh and still have beaten him.

However, I was too magnanimous to point that out. All I said was, "Ten and eight."

And then I added thoughtfully, "I don't think I've ever won by more than that."

PAT BALL

"You'll play tennis?" said my hostess absently. "That's right. Let me introduce you to Miss—er—urn."

"Oh, we've met before," smiled Miss—I've forgotten the name again now.

"Thank you," I said gratefully. I thought it was extremely nice of her to remember me. Probably I had spilt lemonade over her at a dance, and in some way the incident had fixed itself in her mind. We do these little things, you know, and think nothing of them at the moment, but all the time—

"Smooth," said a voice.

I looked up and found that a pair of opponents had mysteriously appeared, and that my partner was leading the way on to the court.

"I'll take the right-hand side, if you don't mind," she announced. "Oh, and what about apologizing?" she went on. "Shall we do it after every stroke, or at the end of each game, or when we say good-bye, or never? I get so tired of saying 'sorry.'"

"Oh, but we shan't want to apologize; I'm sure we're going to get on beautifully together."

"I suppose you've played a lot this summer?"

"No, not at all yet, but I'm feeling rather strong, and I've got a new racket. One way and another, I expect to play a very powerful game."

Our male opponent served. He had what I should call a nasty swift service. The first ball rose very suddenly and took my partner on the side of the head. ("Sorry," she apologized. "It's all right," I said magnanimously.) I returned the next into the net; the third clean bowled my partner; and off the last I was caught in the slips. (ONE, LOVE.)

"Will you serve?" said Miss—I wish I could remember her surname. Her Christian name was Hope or Charity or something like that; I know, when I heard it, I thought it was just as well. If I might call her Miss Hope for this once? Thank you.

"Will you serve?" said Miss Hope.

In the right-hand court I use the American service, which means that I never know till the last moment which side of the racket is going to hit the ball. On this occasion it was a dead heat—that is to say, I got it in between with the wood; and the ball sailed away over beds and beds of the most beautiful flowers.

"Oh, is THAT the American service?" said Miss Hope, much interested.

"South American," I explained. "Down in Peru they never use anything else."

In the left-hand court I employ the ordinary Hampstead Smash into the bottom of the net. After four Hampstead Smashes and four Peruvian Teasers (LOVE, TWO) I felt that another explanation was called for.

"I've got a new racket I've never used before," I said. "My old one is being pressed; it went to the shop yesterday to have the creases taken out. Don't you find that with a new racket you—er—exactly."

In the third game we not only got the ball over but kept it between the white lines on several occasions—though not so often as our opponents (THREE, LOVE); and in the fourth game Miss Hope served gentle lobs, while I, at her request, stood close up to the net and defended myself with my racket. I warded off the first two shots amidst applause (THIRTY, LOVE), and dodged the next three (THIRTY, FORTY), but the last one was too quick for me and won the coco-nut with some ease. (GAME. LOVE, FOUR.)

"It's all right, thanks," I said to my partner; "it really doesn't hurt a bit. Now then, let's buck up and play a simply dashing game."

Miss Hope excelled herself in that fifth game, but I was still unable to find a length. To be more accurate, I was unable to find a shortness—my long game was admirably strong and lofty.

"Are you musical?" said my partner at the end of it. (FIVE, LOVE.) She had been very talkative all through.

"Come, come," I said impatiently, "you don't want a song at this very moment. Surely you can wait till the end of the set?"

"Oh, I was only just wondering."

"I quite see your point. You feel that Nature always compensates us in some way, and that as—"

"Oh, no!" said Miss Hope in great confusion. "I didn't mean that at all."

She must have meant it. You don't talk to people about singing in the middle of a game of tennis; certainly not to comparative strangers who have only spilt lemonade over your frock once before. No, no. It was an insult, and it nerved me to a great effort. I discarded—for it was my serve—the Hampstead Smash; I discarded the Peruvian Teaser. Instead, I served two Piccadilly Benders from the right-hand court and two Westminster Welts from the left-hand. The Piccadilly Bender is my own invention. It can only be served from the one court, and it must have a wind against it. You deliver it with your back to the net, which makes the striker think that you have either forgotten all about the game, or else are apologizing to the spectators for your previous exhibition. Then with a violent contortion you slue your body round and serve, whereupon your opponent perceives that you ARE playing, and that it is just one more ordinary fault into the wrong court. So she calls "Fault!" in a contemptuous tone and drops her racket… and then adds hurriedly, "Oh, no, sorry, it wasn't a fault, after all." That being where the wind comes in.

The Westminster Welt is in theory the same as the Hampstead Smash, but goes over the net. One must be in very good form (or have been recently insulted) to bring this off.

Well, we won that game, a breeze having just sprung up; and, carried away by enthusiasm and mutual admiration, we collected another. (FIVE, TWO.) Then it was Miss Hope's serve again.

"Good-bye," I said; "I suppose you want me in the fore-front again?"

"Please."

"I don't mind HER shots—the bottle of scent is absolutely safe; but I'm afraid he'll win another packet of woodbines."

Miss Hope started off with a double, which was rather a pity, and then gave our masculine adversary what is technically called "one to kill." I saw instinctively that I was the one, and I held my racket ready with both hands. Our opponent, who had been wanting his tea for the last two games, was in no mood of dalliance; he fairly let himself go over this shot. In a moment I was down on my knees behind the net … and the next moment I saw through the meshes a very strange thing. The other man, with his racket on the ground, was holding his eye with both hands!

"Don't you think," said Miss Hope (TWO, FIVE—ABANDONED), "that your overhead volleying is just a little severe?"

THE OPENING SEASON

"My dear," said Jeremy, as he folded back his paper at the sporting page, "I have some news for you. Cricket is upon us once again."

"There's a nasty cold upon Baby once again," said Mrs Jeremy. "I hope it doesn't mean measles."

"No child of mine would ever have measles," said Jeremy confidently. "It's beneath us." He cleared his throat and read, "'The coming season will be rendered ever memorable by the fact that for the first time in the history of the game—' You'll never guess what's coming."

"Mr Jeremy Smith is expected to make double figures."

Jeremy sat up indignantly.

"Well of all the wifely things to say! Who was top of our averages last year?"

"Plummer. Because you presented the bat to him yourself."

"That proves nothing. I gave myself a bat too, as it happens; and a better one than Plummer's. After all, his average was only 25. Mine, if the weather had allowed me to finish my solitary innings, would probably have been 26."

"As it was, the weather only allowed you to give a chance to the wicket-keeper off the one ball you had."

"I was getting the pace of the pitch," said Jeremy. "Besides, it wasn't really a chance, because our umpire would never have given the treasurer out first ball. There are certain little courtesies which are bound to be observed."

"Then," said his wife, "it's a pity you don't play more often."

Jeremy got up and made a few strokes with the poker.

"One of us is rather stiff," he said. "Perhaps it's the poker. If I play regularly this season will you promise to bring Baby to watch me?"

"Of course we shall both come."

"And you won't let Baby jeer at me if I'm bowled by a shooter."

"She won't know what a shooter is."

"Then you can tell her that it's the only ball that ever bowls father," said Jeremy. He put down the poker and took up a ball of wool. "I shall probably field somewhere behind the wicket-keeper, where the hottest drives don't come; but if I should miss a catch you must point out to her that the sun was in father's eyes. I want my child to understand the game as soon as possible."

"I'll tell her all that she ought to know," said his wife. "And when you've finished playing with my wool I've got something to do with it."

Jeremy gave himself another catch, threw the wool to his wife and drifted out. He came back in ten minutes with his bat under his arm.

"Really, it has wintered rather well," he said, "considering that it has been in the boot cupboard all the time. We ought to have put some camphor in with it, or—I know there's SOMETHING you do to bats in the winter. Anyhow, the splice is still there."

"It looks very old," said Mrs Jeremy. "Is that really your new one?"

"Yes, this is the one that played the historic innings. It has only had one ball in its whole life, and that was on the edge. The part of the bat that I propose to use this season will therefore come entirely fresh to the business."

"You ought to have oiled it, Jeremy."

"Oil—that was what I meant. I'll do it now. We'll give it a good rub down. I wonder if there's anything else it would like?"

"I think, most of all, it would like a little practice."

"My dear, that's true. It said in the paper that on the County grounds practice was already in full swing." He made an imaginary drive. "I don't think I shall take a FULL swing. It's so much harder to time the ball. I say, do YOU bowl?"

"Very badly, Jeremy."

"The worse you bowl the more practice the bat will get. Or what about Baby? Could she bowl to me this afternoon, do you think, or is her cold too bad?"

"I think she'd better stay in to-day."

"What a pity. Nurse tells me she's left-handed, and I particularly want a lot of that; because Little Buxted has a very hot left-hand bowler called—"

"You don't want your daughter to be an athletic girl, do you?"

Jeremy looked at her in surprise and then sat down on the arm of her chair.

"Surely, dear," he said gravely, "we decided that our child was going to play for Kent?"

"Not a girl!"

"Why not? There's nothing in the rules about it. Rule 197 (B) says that you needn't play if you don't like the Manager, but there's nothing about sex in it. I'm sure Baby would love the Manager."

Mrs Jeremy smiled and ruffled his hair.

"Well," said Jeremy, "if nobody will bowl to me, I can at least take my bat out and let it see the grass. After six months of boots it will be a change for it."

He went out into the garden, and did not appear again until lunch. During the meal he read extracts to his wife from "The Coming Season's Prospects," and spoke cheerfully of the runs he intended to make for the village. After lunch he took her on to the tennis lawn.

"There!" he said proudly, pointing to a cricket pitch beautifully cut and marked with a crease of dazzling white. "Doesn't that look jolly?"

"Heavenly," she said. "You must ask someone up to-morrow. You can get quite good practice here with these deep banks all round."

"Yes, I shall make a lot of runs this season," said Jeremy airily. "But, apart from practice, don't you FEEL how jolly and summery a cricket pitch makes everything?"

Mrs Jeremy took a deep breath. "Yes, there's nothing like a bucket of whitening to make you think of summer."

"I'm glad you think so too," said Jeremy with an air of relief, "because I upset the bucket on the way back to the stables—just underneath the pergola. It ought to bring the roses on like anything."

AN INLAND VOYAGE

Thomas took a day off last Monday in order to play golf with me. For that day the Admiralty had to get along without Thomas. I tremble to think what would have happened if war had broken out on Monday. Could a Thomasless Admiralty have coped with it? I trow not. Even as it was, battleships grounded, crews mutinied, and several awkward questions in the House of Commons had to be postponed till Tuesday.

Something—some premonition of this, no doubt—seemed to be weighing on him all day.

"Rotten weather," he growled, as he came up the steps of the club.

"I'm very sorry," I said. "I keep on complaining to the secretary about it. He does his best."

"What's that?"

"He taps the barometer every morning, and says it will clear up in the afternoon. Shall we go out now, or shall we give it a chance to stop?"

Thomas looked at the rain and decided to let it stop. I made him as comfortable as I could. I gave him a drink, a cigarette, and Mistakes with the Mashie. On the table at his elbow I had in reserve Faulty Play with the Brassy and a West Middlesex Directory. For myself I wandered about restlessly, pausing now and again to read enviously a notice which said that C. D. Topping's handicap was reduced from 24 to 22. Lucky man!

At about half-past eleven the rain stopped for a moment, and we hurried out.

"The course is a little wet," I said apologetically, as we stood on the first tee, "but with your naval experience you won't mind that. By the way, I ought to warn you that this isn't all casual water. Some of it is river."

"How do you know which is which?"

"You'll soon find out. The river is much deeper. Go on—your drive."

Thomas won the first hole very easily. We both took four to the green, Thomas in addition having five splashes of mud on his face while I only had three. Unfortunately the immediate neighbourhood of the hole was under water. Thomas, the bounder, had a small heavy ball, which he managed to sink in nine. My own, being lighter, refused to go into the tin at all, and floated above the hole in the most exasperating way.

"I expect there's a rule about it," I said, "if we only knew, which gives me the match. However, until we find that out, I suppose you must call yourself one up."

"I shall want some dry socks for lunch," he muttered, as he sploshed off to the tee.

"Anything you want for lunch you can have, my dear Thomas. I promise you that you shall not be stinted. The next green is below sea-level altogether, I'm afraid. The first in the water wins."

Honours, it turned out, were divided. I lost the hole, and Thomas lost his ball. The third tee having disappeared, we moved on to the fourth.

"There's rather a nasty place along here," I said.

"The Secretary was sucked in the other day, and only rescued by the hair."

Thomas drove a good one. I topped mine badly, and it settled down in the mud fifty yards off. "Excuse me," I shouted as I ran quickly after it, and I got my niblick on to it just as it was disappearing. It was a very close thing.

"Well," said Thomas, as he reached his ball, "that's not what I call a brassy lie."

"It's what we call a corkscrew lie down here," I explained. "If you haven't got a corkscrew, you'd better dig round it with something, and then when the position is thoroughly undermined—Oh, good shot!"

Thomas had got out of the fairway in one, but he still seemed unhappy.

"My eye," he said, bending down in agony; "I've got about half Middlesex in it."

He walked round in circles saying strange nautical things, and my suggestions that he should (1) rub the other eye, and (2) blow his nose suddenly, were received ungenerously.

"Anything you'd like me to do with my ears?" he asked bitterly. "If you'd come and take some mud out for me, instead of talking rot—"

I approached with my handkerchief and examined the eye carefully.

"See anything?" asked Thomas.

"My dear Thomas, it's FULL of turf. We mustn't forget to replace this if we can get it out. What the Secretary would say—There! How's that?"

"Worse than ever."

"Try not to think about it. Keep the OTHER eye on the ball as much as possible. This is my hole by the way. Your ball is lost."

"How do you know?"

"I saw it losing itself. It went into the bad place I told you about. It's gone to join the Secretary. Oh, no, we got him out, of course; I keep forgetting. Anyhow, it's my hole."

"I think I shall turn my trousers up again," said Thomas, bending down to do so. "Is there a local rule about it?"

"No; it is left entirely to the discretion and good taste of the members. Naturally a little extra licence is allowed on a very muddy day. Of course, if—Oh, I see. You meant a local rule about losing your ball in the mud? No, I don't know of one—unless it comes under the heading of casual land. Be a sportsman, Thomas, and don't begrudge me the hole."

The game proceeded, and we reached the twelfth tee without any further contretemps; save that I accidentally lost the sixth, ninth and tenth holes, and that Thomas lost his iron at the eighth. He had carelessly laid it down for a moment while he got out of a hole with his niblick, and when he turned round for it the thing was gone.

At the twelfth tee it was raining harder than ever. We pounded along with our coat-collars up and reached the green absolutely wet through.

"How about it?" said Thomas.

"My hole, I think; and that makes us all square."

"I mean how about the rain? And it's just one o'clock."

"Just as you like. Well, I suppose it is rather wet. All right, let's have lunch."

We had lunch. Thomas had it in the only dry things he had brought with him—an ulster and a pair of Vardon cuffs, and sat as near the fire as possible. It was still raining in torrents after lunch, and Thomas, who is not what I call keen about golf, preferred to remain before the fire. Perhaps he was right. I raked up an old copy of Strumers with the Niblick for him, and read bits of the Telephone Directory out aloud.

After tea his proper clothes were dry enough in places to put on, and as it was still raining hard, and he seemed disinclined to come out again, I ordered a cab for us both.

"It's really rotten luck," said Thomas, as we prepared to leave, "that on the one day when I take a holiday, it should be so beastly."

"Beastly, Thomas?" I said in amazement. "The ONE day? I'm afraid you don't play inland golf much?"

"I hardly ever play round London."

"I thought not. Then let me tell you that to-day's was the best day's golf I've had for three weeks."

"Golly!" said Thomas.

AN INFORMAL EVENING

DINNER was a very quiet affair. Not a soul drew my chair away from under me as I sat down, and during the meal nobody threw bread about. We talked gently of art and politics and things; and when the ladies left there was no booby trap waiting for them at the door. In a word, nothing to prepare me for what was to follow.

We strolled leisurely into the drawing-room. A glance told me the worst. The ladies were in a cluster round Miss Power, and Miss Power was on the floor. She got up quickly as we came in.

"We were trying to go underneath the poker," she explained. "Can you do it?"

I waved the poker back.

"Let me see you do it again," I said. "I missed the first part."

"Oh, I can never do it. Bob, you show us."

Bob is an active young fellow. He took the poker, rested the end on the floor, and then twisted himself underneath his right arm. I expected to see him come up inside out, but he looked much the same after it. However, no doubt his organs are all on the wrong side now.

"Yes, that's how I should do it," I said hastily.

But Miss Power was firm. She gave me the poker. I pressed it hard on the floor, said good-bye to them all, and dived. I got half-way round, and was supporting myself upside down by one toe and the slippery end of the poker, when it suddenly occurred to me that the earth was revolving at an incredible speed on its own axis, and that, in addition, we were hurtling at thousands of miles a minute round the sun. It seemed impossible in these circumstances that I should keep my balance any longer; and as soon as I realized this, the poker began to slip. I was in no sort of position to do anything about it, and we came down heavily together.

"Oh, what a pity!" said Miss Power. "I quite thought you'd done it."

"Being actually on the spot," I said, "I knew that I hadn't."

"Do try again."

"Not till the ground's a little softer."

"Let's do the jam-pot trick," said another girl.

"I'm not going under a jam-pot for anybody," I murmured.

However, it turned out that this trick was quite different. You place a book (Macaulay's Essays or what not) on the jam-pot and sit on the book, one heel only touching the ground. In the right hand you have a box of matches, in the left a candle. The jam-pot, of course, is on its side, so that it can roll beneath you. Then you light the candle … and hand it to anybody who wants to go to bed.

I was ready to give way to the ladies here, but even while I was bowing and saying, "Not at all," I found myself on one of the jam-pots with Bob next to me on another. To balance with the arms outstretched was not so difficult; but as the matches were then about six feet from the candle and there seemed no way of getting them nearer together the solution of the problem was as remote as ever. Three times I brought my hands together, and three times the jam-pot left me.

"Well played, Bob," said somebody. The bounder had done it.

I looked at his jam-pot.

"There you are," I said, "'Raspberry—1909.' Mine's 'Gooseberry-1911,' a rotten vintage. And look at my book, Alone on the Prairie; and you've got The Mormon's Wedding. No wonder I couldn't do it."

I refused to try it again as I didn't think I was being treated fairly; and after Bob and Miss Power had had a race at it, which Bob won, we got on to something else.

"Ofcourseyoucanpickapinoutofachairwithyourteeth?" said Miss Power.

"Not properly," I said. "I always swallow the pin."

"I suppose it doesn't count if you swallow the pin," said Miss Power thoughtfully.

"I don't know. I've never really thought about that side of it much. Anyhow, unless you've got a whole lot of pins you don't want, don't ask me to do it to-night."

Accordingly we passed on to the water-trick. I refused at this, but Miss Power went full length on the floor with a glass of water balanced on her fore-head and came up again without spilling a single drop. Personally, I shouldn't have minded spilling a single drop; it was the thought of spilling the whole glass that kept me back. Anyway, it is a useless trick, the need for which never arises in an ordinary career. Picking up The Times with the teeth, while clasping the left ankle with the right hand, is another matter. That might come in useful on occasions; as, for instance, if having lost your left arm on the field and having to staunch with the right hand the flow of blood from a bullet wound in the opposite ankle, you desired to glance through the Financial Supplement while waiting for the ambulance.

"Here's a nice little trick," broke in Bob, as I was preparing myself in this way for the German invasion.

He had put two chairs together, front to front, and was standing over them—a foot on the floor on each side of them, if that conveys it to you. Then he jumped up, turned round in the air, and came down facing the other way.

"Can YOU do it?" I said to Miss Power.

"Come and try," said Bob to me. "It's not really difficult."

I went and stood over the chairs. Then I moved them apart and walked over to my hostess.

"Good-bye," I said; "I'm afraid I must go now."

"Coward!" said somebody, who knew me rather better than the others.

"It's much easier than you think," said Bob.

"I don't think it's easy at all," I protested. "I think it's impossible."

I went back and stood over the chairs again. For some time I waited there in deep thought. Then I bent my knees preparatory to the spring, straightened them up, and said:

"What happens if you just miss it?"

"I suppose you bark your shins a bit."

"Yes, that's what I thought."

I bent my knees again, worked my arms up and down, and then stopped suddenly and said:

"What happens if you miss it pretty easily?"

"Oh, YOU can do it, if Bob can," said Miss Power kindly.

"He's practised. I expect he started with two hassocks and worked up to this. I'm not afraid but I want to know the possibilities. If it's only a broken leg or two, I don't mind. If it's permanent disfigurement I think I ought to consult my family first."

I jumped up and came down again the same way for practice.

"Very well," I said. "Now I'm going to try. I haven't the faintest hope of doing it, but you all seem to want to see an accident, and, anyhow, I'm not going to be called a coward. One, two, three…"

"Well done," cried everybody.

"Did I do it?" I whispered, as I sat on the floor and pressed a cushion against my shins.

"Rather!"

"Then," I said, massaging my ankles, "next time I shall try to miss."

THE CONTINENTAL MANNER

OF course I should recognize Simpson anywhere, even at a masked ball. Besides, who but Simpson would go to a fancy-dress dance as a short-sighted executioner, and wear his spectacles outside his mask? But it was a surprise to me to see him there at all.

"Samuel," I said gravely, tapping him on the shoulder, "I shall have to write home about this."

He turned round with a start.

"Hallo!" he said eagerly. "How splendid! But, my dear old chap, why aren't you in costume?"

"I am," I explained. "I've come as an architect. Luckily the evening clothes of an architect are similar to my own. Excuse me, sir, but do you want a house built?"

"How do you like my dress? I am an executioner. I left my axe in the cloak-room."

"So I observe. You know, in real life, one hardly ever meets an executioner who wears spectacles. And yet, of course, if one CAN'T see the head properly without glasses—"

"By Jove," said Simpson, "there she is again."

Columbine in a mask hurried past us and mixed with the crowd. What one could see of her face looked pretty; it seemed to have upset Simpson altogether.

"Ask her for a dance," I suggested. "Be a gay dog, Simpson. Wake London up. At a masked ball one is allowed a certain amount of licence."

"Exactly," said Simpson in some excitement. "One naturally looks for a little Continental ABANDON at these dances." (PORTRAIT OF SIMPSON SHOWING CONTINENTAL abandon.) "And so I did ask her for a dance just now."

"She was cold, Samuel, I fear?"

"She said, 'Sorry, I'm full up.'"

"A ruse, a mere subterfuge. Now, look here, ask her again, and be more debonair and dashing this time. What you want is to endue her with the spirit of revelry. Perhaps you'd better go to the bar first and have a dry ginger-ale, and then you'll feel more in the Continental mood."

"By Jove, I will," said Simpson, with great decision.

I wandered into the ball-room and looked round. Columbine was standing in a corner alone; some outsider had cut her dance. As I looked at her I thought of Simpson letting himself go, and smiled to myself. She caught the edge of the smile and unconsciously smiled back. Remembering the good advice which I had just given another, I decided to risk it.

"Do you ever dance with architects?" I asked her.

"I do sometimes." she said. "Not in Lent," she added.

"In Lent," I agreed, "one has to give up the more furious pleasures. Shall we just finish off this dance? And don't let's talk shop about architecture."

We finished the dance and retired to the stairs.

"I want you to do something for me," I began cautiously.

"Anything except go into supper again. I've just done that for somebody else."

"No, it's not that. The fact is, I have a great friend called Simpson."

"It sounds a case for help," she murmured.

"He is here to-night disguised as an executioner in glasses. He is, in fact, the only spectacled beheader present. You can't miss him."

"All the same, I managed to just now," she gurgled.

"I know. He asked you for a dance and you rebuffed him. Well, he is now fortifying himself with a small dry ginger, and he will then ask you again. Do be kind this time; he's really a delightful person when you get to know him. For instance, both his whiskers are false."

"No doubt I should grow to love him," she agreed; "but I didn't much like his outward appearance. However, if both whiskers are false, and if he's really a friend of yours—"

"He is naturally as harmless as a lamb," I said; "but at a dance like this he considers it his duty to throw a little Continental ABANDON into his manner."

Columbine looked at me thoughtfully, nodding her head, and slowly began to smile.

"You see," I said, "the possibilities."

"He shall have his dance," she said decidedly.

"Thank you very much. I should like to ask for another dance for myself later on, but I am afraid I should try to get out of you what he said, and that wouldn't be fair."

"Of course I shouldn't tell you."

"Well, anyhow, you'll have had enough of us by then. But softly—he approaches, and I must needs fly, lest he should pierce my disguise. Good-bye, and thank you so much."

So I can't say with authority what happened between Simpson and Columbine when they met. But Simpson and I had a cigarette together afterwards and certain things came out; enough to make it plain that she must have enjoyed herself.

"Oh, I say, old chap," he began jauntily, "do you know—match, thanks—er—whereabouts is Finsbury Circus?"

"You're too old to go to a circus now, Simpson. Come and have a day at the Polytechnic instead."

"Don't be an ass; it's a place like Oxford Circus. I suppose it's in the City somewhere? I wonder," he murmured to himself, "what she would be doing in the City at eleven o'clock in the morning."

"Perhaps her rich uncle is in a bank, and she wants to shoot him. I wish you'd tell me what you're talking about."

Simpson took off his mask and spectacles and wiped his brow.

"Dear old chap," he said in a solemn voice, "in the case of a woman one cannot tell even one's best friend. You know how it is."

"Well, if there's going to be a duel you should have chosen some quieter spot than Finsbury Circus. The motor-buses distract one's aim."

Simpson was silent for a minute or two. Then a foolish smile flitted across his face, to be followed suddenly by a look of alarm.

"Don't do anything that your mother wouldn't like," I said warningly.

He frowned and put on his mask again.

"Are chrysanthemums in season?" he asked casually. "Anyhow, I suppose I could always get a yellow one?"

"You could, Simpson. And you could put it in your button-hole, so that you can be recognized, and go to Finsbury Circus to meet somebody at eleven o'clock to-morrow morning. Samuel, I'm ashamed of you. Er—where do you lunch?"

"At the Carlton. Old chap, I got quite carried away. Things seemed to be arranged before I knew where I was."

"And what's she going to wear so that you can recognize HER?"

"Yes," said Simpson, getting up, "that's the worst of it. I told her it was quite out of date, and that only the suburbs wore fashions a year old, but she insisted on it. I had no idea she was that sort of girl. Well, I'm in for it now." He sighed heavily and went off for another ginger-ale.

I think that I must be at Finsbury Circus to-morrow, for certainly no Columbine in a harem skirt will be there. Simpson in his loneliness will be delighted to see me, and then we can throw away his button-hole and have a nice little lunch together.

TWO STORIES

THE MAKING OF A CHRISTMAS STORY

(AS CARRIED OUT IN THE BEST END OF FLEET STREET)

YULETIDE!

London at Yuletide!

A mantle of white lay upon the Embankment, where our story opens, gleaming and glistening as it caught the rays of the cold December sun; an embroidery of white fringed the trees; and under a canopy of white the proud palaces of Savoy and Cecil reared their silent heads. The mighty river in front was motionless, for the finger of Death had laid its icy hand upon it. Above—the hard blue sky stretching to eternity; below—the white purity of innocence. London in the grip of winter!

[EDITOR. Come, I like this. This is going to be good. A cold day, was it not?

AUTHOR. Very.]

All at once the quiet of the morning was disturbed. In the distance a bell rang out, sending a joyous paean to the heavens. Another took up the word, and then another, and another. Westminster caught the message from Bartholomew the son of Thunder, and flung it to Giles Without, who gave it gently to Andrew by the Wardrobe. Suddenly the air was filled with bells, all chanting together of peace and happiness, mirth and jollity—a frenzy of bells.

The Duke, father of four fine children, waking in his Highland castle, heard and smiled as he thought of his little ones....

The Merchant Prince, turning over in his Streatham residence, heard, and turned again to sleep, with love for all mankind in his heart....

The Pauper in his workhouse, up betimes, heard, and chuckled at the prospect of his Christmas dinner....

And, on the Embankment, Robert Hardrow, with a cynical smile on his lips, listened to the splendid irony of it.

> [EDITOR. We really are getting to the story now, are we not? AUTHOR. That was all local colour. I want to make it quite clear that it was Christmas. EDITOR. Yes, yes, quite so. This is certainly a Christmas story. I think I shall like Robert, do you know?]

It was Christmas day, so much at least was clear to him. With that same cynical smile on his lips, he pulled his shivering rags about him, and half unconsciously felt at the growth of beard about his chin. Nobody would recognize him now. His friends (as he had thought them) would pass by without a glance for the poor outcast near them. The women that he had known would draw their skirts away from him in horror. Even Lady Alice—

Lady Alice! The cause of it all!

His thoughts flew back to that last scene, but twenty-four hours ago, when they had parted for ever. As he had entered the hall he had half wondered to himself if there could be anybody in the world that day happier than himself. Tall, well-connected, a vice-president of the Tariff Reform League, and engaged to the sweetest girl in England, he had been the envy of all. Little did he think that that very night he was to receive his conge! What mattered it now how or why they had quarrelled? A few hasty words, a bitter taunt, tears, and then the end.

A last cry from her—"Go, and let me never see your face again!"

A last sneer from him—"I will go, but first give me back the presents I have promised you!"

Then a slammed door and—silence.

What use, without her guidance, to try to keep straight any more? Bereft of her love, Robert had sunk steadily. Gambling, drink, morphia, billiards and cigars—he had taken to them all; until now in the wretched figure of the outcast on the Embankment you would never have recognized the once spruce figure of Handsome Hardrow.

> [EDITOR. It all seems to have happened rather rapidly, does it not? Twenty-four hours ago he had been— AUTHOR. You forget that this is SHORT story.]

Handsome Hardrow! How absurd it sounded now! He had let his beard grow, his clothes were in rags, a scar over one eye testified—

[EDITOR. Yes, yes. Of course, I quite admit that a man might go to the bad in twenty-four hours, but would his beard grow as—AUTHOR. Look here, you've heard of a man going grey with trouble in a single night, haven't you?

EDITOR. Certainly.

AUTHOR. Well, it's the same idea as that.

EDITOR. Ah, quite so, quite so.

AUTHOR. Where was I?

EDITOR. A scar over one eye was just testifying—I suppose he had two eyes in the ordinary way?]

—-testified to a drunken frolic of an hour or two ago. Never before, thought the policeman, as he passed upon his beat, had such a pitiful figure cowered upon the Embankment, and prayed for the night to cover him.

The—

He was—

Er—the—

[EDITOR. Yes?

AUTHOR. To tell the truth I am rather stuck for the moment.

EDITOR. What is the trouble?

AUTHOR. I don't quite know what to do with Robert for ten hours or so.

EDITOR. Couldn't he go somewhere by a local line?

AUTHOR. This is not a humorous story. The point is that I want him to be outside a certain house some twenty miles from town at eight o'clock that evening.

EDITOR. If I were Robert I should certainly start at once.

AUTHOR. No, I have it.]

As he sat there, his thoughts flew over the bridge of years, and he was wafted on the wings of memory to other and happier Yuletides. That Christmas when he had received his first bicycle....

That Christmas abroad....

The merry house-party at the place of his Cambridge friend....

Yuletide at The Towers, where he had first met Alice!

Ah!

Ten hours passed rapidly thus...

[AUTHOR. I put dots to denote the flight of years. EDITOR. Besides, it will give the reader time for a sandwich.]

Robert got up and shook himself.

[EDITOR. One moment. This is a Christmas story. When are you coming to the robin?

AUTHOR. I really can't be bothered about robins just now. I assure you all the best Christmas stories begin like this nowadays. We may get to a robin later; I cannot say.

EDITOR. We must. My readers expect a robin, and they shall have it. And a wassail-bowl, and a turkey, and a Christmas-tree, and a—

AUTHOR. Yes, yes; but wait. We shall come to little Elsie soon, and then perhaps it will be all right.

EDITOR. Little Elsie. Good!]

Robert got up and shook himself. Then he shivered miserably, as the cold wind cut through him like a knife. For a moment he stood motionless, gazing over the stone parapet into the dark river beyond, and as he gazed a thought came into his mind. Why not end it all—here and now? He had nothing to live for. One swift plunge, and—

[EDITOR. YOu forget. The river was frozen.

AUTHOR. Dash it, I was just going to say that.]

But no! Even in this Fate was against him. THE RIVER WAS FROZEN OVER! He turned away with a curse....

What happened afterwards Robert never quite understood. Almost unconsciously he must have crossed one of the numerous bridges which span the river and join North London to South. Once on the other side, he seems to have set his face steadily before him, and to have dragged his weary limbs on and on, regardless of time and place. He walked like one in a dream, his mind drugged by the dull narcotic of physical pain. Suddenly he realized that he had left London behind him, and was in the more open spaces of the country. The houses were more scattered; the recurring villa of the clerk had given place to the isolated mansion of the stock broker. Each residence stood in its own splendid grounds, surrounded by fine old forest trees and approached by a long carriage sweep. Electric—

[EDITOR Quite so. The whole forming a magnificent estate for a retired gentleman. Never mind that.]

Robert stood at the entrance to one of these houses, and the iron entered into his soul. How different was this man's position from his own! What right had this man—a perfect stranger—to be happy and contented in the heart of his family, while he, Robert, stood, a homeless wanderer, alone in the cold?

Almost unconsciously he wandered down the drive, hardly realizing what he was doing until he was brought up by the gay lights of the windows. Still without thinking, he stooped down and peered into the brilliantly lit room above him. Within all was jollity; beautiful women moved to and fro, and the happy laughter of children came to him. "Elsie," he heard someone call, and a childish treble re sponded.

[EDITOR. Now for the robin.

AUTHOR. I am very sorry. I have just remembered something rather sad. The fact is that, two days before, Elsie had forgotten to feed the robin, and in consequence it had died before this story opens.

EDITOR. That is really very awkward. I have already arranged with an artist to do some pictures, AND *I* REMEMBER *I* PARTICULARLY ORDERED A ROBIN AND A WASSAIL. WHAT ABOUT THE WASSAIL?

AUTHOR. ELSIE ALWAYS HAD HER PORRIDGE upstairs.]

A terrible thought had come into Robert's head. It was nearly twelve o'clock. The house-party was retiring to bed. He heard the "Good-nights" wafted through the open window; the lights went out, to reappear upstairs. Presently they too went out, and Robert was alone with the darkened house.

The temptation was too much for a conscience already sodden with billiards, drink and cigars. He flung a leg over the sill and drew himself gently into the room. At least he would have one good meal, he too would have his Christmas dinner before the end came. He switched the light on and turned eagerly to the table. His eyes ravenously scanned the contents. Turkey, mince-pies, plum-pudding— all was there as in the days of his youth.

[EDITOR. THIS IS BETTER. I ORDERED A TURKEY, I REMEMBER. WHAT ABOUT THE MISTLETOE AND HOLLY? I RATHER THINK I ASKED FOR SOME OF THEM.

AUTHOR. WE MUST LET THE READERS TAKE SOMETHING FOR GRANTED

EDITOR. I AM NOT SO SURE. COULDN'T YOU SAY SOMETHING LIKE THIS: "HOLLY AND MISTLETOE HUNG IN FESTOONS UPON THE WALL?"]

Indeed, even holly and mistletoe hung in festoons upon the wall.

[EDITOR. THANK YOU.]

With a sigh of content Hardrow flung himself into a chair, and seized a knife and fork. Soon a plate liberally heaped with good things was before him. Greedily he set to work, with the appetite of a man who had not tasted food for several hours….

"Dood-evening," said a voice. "Are you Father Kwistmas?"

Robert turned suddenly, and gazed in amazement at the white-robed figure in the doorway.

"Elsie," he murmured huskily.

[EDITOR. HOW DID HE KNOW? AND WHY "HUSKILY"?

AUTHOR. HE DIDN'T KNOW, HE GUESSED. AND HIS MOUTH WAS FULL.]

"Are you Father Kwistmas?" repeated Elsie.

Robert felt at his chin, and thanked Heaven again that he had let his beard grow. Almost mechanically he decided to wear the mask—in short, to dissemble.

"Yes, my dear," he said. "I just looked in to know what you would like me to bring you."

"You're late, aren't oo? Oughtn't oo to have come this morning?"

[EDITOR. THIS IS SPLENDID. THIS QUITE RECONCILES ME TO THE ABSENCE OF THE ROBIN. BUT WHAT WAS ELSIE DOING DOWNSTAIRS?

AUTHOR. I AM MAKING ROBERT ASK HER THAT QUESTION DIRECTLY.

EDITOR. YES, BUT JUST TELL ME NOW—BETWEEN FRIENDS.

AUTHOR. SHE HAD LEFT HER GOLLIWOG IN THE ROOM, AND COULDN'T SLEEP WITHOUT HER.

EDITOR. I KNEW THAT WAS IT.]

"If I'm late, dear," said Robert, with a smile, "why, so are you."

The good food and wine in his veins were doing their work, and a pleasant warmth was stealing over Hardrow. He found to his surprise that airy banter still came easy to him.

"To what," he continued lightly, "do I owe the honour of this meeting?"

"I came downstairs for my dolly," said Elsie. "The one you sent me this morning, do you remember?"

"Of course I do, my dear."

"And what have you bwought me now, Father Kwistmas?"

Robert started. If he was to play the role successfully he must find something to give her now. The remains of the turkey, a pair of finger-bowls, his old hat—all these came hastily into his mind, and were dismissed. He had nothing of value on him. All had been pawned long ago.

Stay! The gold locket studded with diamonds and rubies, which contained Alice's photograph. The one memento of her that he had kept, even when the pangs of starvation were upon him. He brought it from its resting-place next his heart.

"A little something to wear round your neck, child," he said. "See!"

"Thank oo," said Elsie. "Why, it opens!"

"Yes, it opens," said Robert moodily.

"Why, it's Alith! Sister Alith!"

[EDITOR. HA!

AUTHOR. I THOUGHT YOU'D LIKE THAT.]

Robert leapt to his feet as if he had been shot.

"Who?" he cried.

"My sister Alith. Does oo know her too?"

Alice's sister! Heavens! He covered his face with his hands.

The door opened.

[EDITOR. HA AGAIN!]

"What are you doing here, Elsie?" said a voice. "Go to bed, child. Why, who is this?"

"Father Kwithmath, thithter."

[EDITOR. HOW EXACTLY DO YOU WORK THE LISPING?

AUTHOR. WHAT DO YOU MEAN? DON'T CHILDREN OF ELSIE'S TENDER YEARS LISP SOMETIMES?

EDITOR. YES; BUT JUST NOW SHE SAID "KWISTMAS" QUITE CORRECTLY—

AUTHOR. I AM GLAD YOU NOTICED THAT. THAT WAS AN EFFECT WHICH I INTENDED TO PRODUCE. LISPING IS BROUGHT ABOUT BY PLACING THE TONGUE UPON THE HARD SURFACE OF THE PALATE, AND IN CASES WHERE THE SUBJECT IS UNDULY EXCITED OR INFLUENCED BY EMOTION THE LISP BECOMES MORE PRONOUNCED. IN THIS CASE—

EDITOR. YETH, I THEE.]

"Send her away," cried Robert, without raising his head.

The door opened, and closed again.

"Well," said Alice calmly, "and who are you? You may have lied to this poor child, but you cannot deceive me. You are NOT Father Christmas."

The miserable man raised his shamefaced head and looked haggardly at her.

"Alice!" he muttered, "don't you remember me?"

She gazed at him earnestly.

"Robert! But how changed!"

"Since we parted, Alice, much has happened."

"Yet it seems only yesterday that I saw you!"

[EDITOR. IT was ONLY YESTERDAY.

AUTHOR. YES, YES. DON'T INTERRUPT NOW, PLEASE.]

"To me it has seemed years."

"But what are you doing here?" said Alice.

"Rather, what are YOU doing here?" answered Robert.

[EDITOR. I THINK ALICE'S QUESTION WAS THE MORE REASONABLE ONE.]

"My uncle Joseph lives here."

Robert gave a sudden cry.

"Your uncle Joseph! Then I have broken into your uncle Joseph's house! Alice, send me away! Put me in prison! Do what you will to me! I can never hold up my head again."

Lady Alice looked gently at the wretched figure in front of her.

"I am glad to see you again," she said. "Because I wanted to say that it was MY fault!"

"Alice!"

"Can you forgive me?"

"Forgive you? If you knew what my life has been since I left you! If you knew into what paths of wickedness I have sunk! How only this evening, unnerved by excess, I have deliberately broken into this house—your uncle Joseph's house—in order to obtain food. Already I have eaten more than half a turkey and the best part of a plum-pudding. If you knew, I—"

With a gesture of infinite compassion she stopped him.

"Then let us forgive each other," she said with a smile. "A new year is beginning, Robert!"

He took her in his arms.

"Listen," he said.

In the distance the bells began to ring in the New Year. A message of hope to all weary travellers on life's highway. It was New Year's Day!

[EDITOR. I THOUGHT CHRISTMAS DAY HAD STARTED ON THE EMBANKMENT. THIS WOULD BE BOXING DAY. AUTHOR. I'M SORRY, BUT IT MUST END LIKE THAT. I MUST HAVE MY BELLS. YOU CAN EXPLAIN SOMEHOW.

EDITOR. THAT'S ALL VERY WELL. I HAVE A GOOD DEAL TO EXPLAIN AS IT IS. SOME OF YOUR STORY DOESN'T FIT THE PICTURES AT ALL, AND IT IS TOO LATE NOW TO GET NEW ONES DONE.

AUTHOR. I AM AFRAID I CANNOT WORK TO ORDER.

EDITOR. YES, I KNOW. THE ARTIST SAID THE SAME THING. WELL, I MUST MANAGE SOMEHOW, I SUPPOSE. GOOD-BYE. ROTTEN WEATHER FOR AUGUST, ISN'T IT?]

A MATTER-OF-FACT FAIRY TALE

Once upon a time there was a King who had three sons. The two eldest were lazy, good-for-nothing young men, but the third son, whose name was Charming, was a delightful youth, who was loved by everybody (outside his family) who knew him. Whenever he rode through the town the people used to stop whatever work they were engaged upon and wave their caps and cry "Hurrah for Prince Charming!"—and even after he had passed they would continue to stop work, in case he might be coming back the same way, when they would wave their caps and cry "Hurrah for Prince Charming!" again. It was wonderful how fond of him they were.

But alas! his father the King was not so fond. He preferred his eldest son; which was funny of him, because he must have known that only the third and youngest son is ever any good in a family. Indeed, the King himself had been a third son, so he had really no excuse for ignorance on the point. I am afraid the truth was that he was jealous of Charming, because the latter was so popular outside his family.

Now there lived in the Palace an old woman called Countess Caramel, who had been governess to Charming when he was young. When the Queen lay dying the Countess had promised her that she would look after her youngest boy for her, and Charming had often confided in Caramel since. One morning, when his family had been particularly rude to him at breakfast, Charming said to her:

"Countess, I have made up my mind, and I am going into the world to seek my fortune."

"I have been waiting for this," said the Countess. "Here is a magic ring. Wear it always on your little finger, and whenever you want help turn it round once and help will come."

Charming thanked her and put the ring on his finger. Then he turned it round once just to make sure that it worked. Immediately the oddest little dwarf appeared in front of him.

"Speak and I will obey," said the dwarf.

Now Charming didn't want anything at all just then, so after thinking for a moment he said, "Go away!"

The dwarf, a little surprised, disappeared.

"This is splendid," thought Charming, and he started on his travels with a light heart.

The sun was at its highest as he came to a thick wood, and in its shade he lay down to rest. He was awakened by the sound of weeping. Rising hastily to his feet he peered through the trees, and there, fifty yards away from him, by the side of a stream sat the most beautiful damsel he had ever seen, wringing her hands and sobbing bitterly. Prince Charming, grieving at the sight of beauty in such distress, coughed and came nearer,

"Princess," he said tenderly, for he knew she must be a Princess, "you are in trouble. How can I help you?"

"Fair Sir," she answered, "I had thought to be alone. But, since you are here, you can help me if you will. I have a—a brother—"

But Charming did not want to talk about brothers. He sat down on a fallen log beside her, and looked at her entranced.

"I think you are the most lovely lady in all the world," he said.

"Am I?" said the Princess, whose name, by the way, was Beauty.

She looked away from him and there was silence between them. Charming, a little at a loss, fidgeted nervously with his ring, and began to speak again.

"Ever since I have known you—"

"You are in need of help?" said the dwarf, appearing suddenly.

"Certainly not," said Charming angrily. "Not in the least. I can manage this quite well by myself."

"Speak, and I will obey."

"Then go away," said Charming; and the dwarf, who was beginning to lose his grip of things, again disappeared.

The Princess, having politely pretended to be looking for something while this was going on, turned to him again.

"Come with me," she said, "and I will show you how you can help me."

She took him by the hand and led him down a narrow glade to a little clearing in the middle of the wood. Then she made him sit down beside her on the grass, and there she told him her tale.

"There is a giant called Blunderbus," she said, "who lives in a great castle ten miles from here. He is a terrible magician, and years ago because I would not marry him he turned my—my brother into a—I don't know how to tell you—into a—a tortoise." She put her hands to her face and sobbed again.

"Why a tortoise?" said Charming, knowing that sympathy was useless, but feeling that he ought to say SOMETHING.

"I don't know. He just thought of it. It—it isn't a very nice thing to be."

"And why should he turn your BROTHER into it? I mean, if he had turned YOU into a tortoise—Of course," he went on hurriedly, "I'm very glad he didn't."

"Thank you," said Beauty.

"But I don't understand why—"

"He knew he could hurt me more by making my brother a tortoise than by making me one," she explained, and looked at him anxiously.

This was a new idea to Charming, who had two brothers of his own; and he looked at her in some surprise.

"Oh, what does it matter WHY he did it?" she cried as he was about to speak. "Why do giants do things? *I* don't know."

"Princess," said Charming remorsefully, and kissed her hand, "tell me how I can help you."

"My brother," said Beauty, "was to have met me here. He is late again." She sighed and added, "He used to be SO punctual."

"But how can I help him?" asked Charming.

"It is like this. The only way in which the enchantment can be taken off him is for someone to kill the Giant. But if once the enchantment has stayed on for seven years, then it stays on for ever."

Here she looked down and burst into tears.

"The seven years," she sobbed, "are over at sundown this afternoon."

"I see," said Charming thoughtfully.

"Here IS my brother," cried Beauty.

An enormous tortoise came slowly into view. Beauty rushed up to him and, having explained the situation rapidly, made the necessary introduction.

"Charmed," said the Tortoise. "You can't miss the castle; it's the only one near here, and Blunderbus is sure to be at home. I need not tell you how grateful I shall be if you kill him. Though I must say," he added, "it puzzles me to think how you are going to do it."

"I have a friend who will help me," said Charming, fingering his ring.

"Well, I only hope you'll be luckier than the others."

"The others?" cried Charming, in surprise.

"Yes; didn't she tell you about the others who had tried?"

"I forgot to," said Beauty, frowning at him.

"Ah, well, perhaps in that case we'd better not go into it now," said the Tortoise. "But before you start I should like to talk to you privately for a moment." He took Charming on one side and whispered, "I say, do YOU know anything about tortoises?"

"Very little," said Charming. "In fact—"

"Then you don't happen to know what they eat?"

"I'm afraid I don't."

"Dash it, why doesn't ANYBODY know? The others all made the most ridiculous suggestions. Steak and kidney puddings—and shrimp sandwiches—and buttered toast. Dear me! The nights we had after the shrimp sandwiches! And the fool swore he had kept tortoises all his life!"

"If I may say so," said Charming, "I should have thought that YOU would have known best."

"The same silly idea they all have," said the Tortoise testily. "When Blunderbus put this enchantment on me, do you suppose he got a blackboard and a piece of chalk and gave me a lecture on the diet and habits of the common tortoise, before showing me out of the front gate? No, he simply turned me into the form of a tortoise and left my mind and soul as it was before. I've got the anatomy of a tortoise, I've got the very delicate inside of a tortoise, but I don't THINK like one, stupid. Else I shouldn't mind being one."

"I never thought of that."

"No one does, except me. And I can think of nothing else." He paused and added confidentially, "We're trying rum omelettes just now. Somehow I don't think tortoises REALLY like them. However, we shall see. I suppose you've never heard anything definite against them?"

"You needn't bother about that," said Charming briskly. "By to-night you will be a man again." And he patted him encouragingly on the shell and returned to take an affectionate farewell of the Princess.

As soon as he was alone, Charming turned the ring round his finger, and the dwarf appeared before him.

"The same as usual?" said the dwarf, preparing to vanish at the word. He was just beginning to get into the swing of it.

"No, no," said Charming hastily. "I really want you this time." He thought for a moment. "I want," he said at last, "a sword. One that will kill giants."

Instantly a gleaming sword was at his feet. He picked it up and examined it.

"Is this really a magic sword?"

"It has but to inflict one scratch," said the dwarf, "and the result is death."

Charming, who had been feeling the blade, took his thumb away hastily.

"Then I shall want a cloak of darkness," he said.

"Behold, here it is. Beneath this cloak the wearer is invisible to the eyes of his enemies."

"One thing more," said Charming. "A pair of seven-league boots....Thank you. That is all to-day."

Directly the dwarf was gone, Charming kicked off his shoes and stepped into the magic boots; then he seized the sword and the cloak and darted off on his lady's behest. He had barely gone a hundred paces before a sudden idea came to him, and he pulled himself up short.

"Let me see," he reflected; "the castle was ten miles away. These are seven-league boots—so that I have come about two thousand miles. I shall have to go back." He took some hasty steps back, and found himself in the wood from which he had started.

"Well?" said Princess Beauty, "have you killed him?"

"No, n-no," stammered Charming, "not exactly killed him. I was just— just practising something. The fact is," he added confidentially, "I've got a pair of new boots on, and—" He saw the look of cold surprise in her face and went on quickly, "I swear, Princess, that I will not return to you again without his head."

He took a quick step in the direction of the castle and found himself soaring over it; turned eleven miles off and stepped back a pace; overshot it again, and arrived at the very feet of the Princess.

"His head!" said Beauty eagerly.

"I—I must have dropped it," said Charming, hastily pretending to feel for it. "I'll just go and—" He stepped off in confusion.

Eleven miles the wrong side of the castle, Charming sat down to think it out. It was but two hours to sundown. Without his magic boots he would get to the castle too late. Of course, what he really wanted to do was to erect an isosceles triangle on a base of eleven miles, having two sides of twenty-one miles each. But this was before Euclid's time.

However, by taking one step to the north and another to the south-west, he found himself close enough. A short but painful walk, with his boots in his hand, brought him to his destination. He had a moment's natural hesitation about making a first call at the castle in his stockinged feet, but consoled himself with the thought that in life-and-death matters one cannot bother about little points of etiquette, and that, anyhow, the giant would not be able to see him. Then, donning the magic cloak, and with the magic sword in his hand, he entered the castle gates. For an instant his heart seemed to stop beating, but the thought of the Princess gave him new courage....

The Giant was sitting in front of the fire, his great spiked club between his knees. At Charming's entry he turned round, gave a start of surprise, bent forward eagerly a moment, and then leant back chuckling. Like most overgrown men he was naturally kind-hearted and had a simple humour, but he could be stubborn when he liked. The original affair of the tortoise seems to have shown him both at his best and at his worst.

"Why do you walk like that?" he said pleasantly to Charming. "The baby is not asleep."

Charming stopped short.

"You see me?" he cried furiously.

"Of course I do! Really, you mustn't expect to come into a house without anything on your feet and not be a LITTLE noticeable. Even in a crowd I should have picked you out."

"That miserable dwarf," said Charming savagely, "swore solemnly to me that beneath this cloak I was invisible to the eyes of my enemies!"

"But then we AREN'T enemies," smiled the Giant sweetly. "I like you immensely. There's something about you—directly you came in ... I think it must be love at first sight."

"So that's how he tricked me!"

"Oh, no, it wasn't really like that. The fact is you are invisible BENEATH that cloak, only—you'll excuse my pointing it out—there are such funny bits of you that aren't beneath the cloak. You've no idea how odd you look; just a head and two legs, and a couple of arms.... Waists," he murmured to himself, "are not being worn this year."

But Charming had had enough of talk. Gripping his sword firmly, he threw aside his useless cloak, dashed forward, and with a beautiful lunge pricked his enemy in the ankle.

"Victory!" he cried, waving his magic sword above his head. "Thus is Beauty's brother delivered!"

The Giant stared at him for a full minute. Then he put his hands to his sides and fell back shaking in his chair.

"Her brother!" he roared. "Well, of all the—Her BROTHER!" He rolled on the floor in a paroxysm of mirth. "Her brother! Oh, you—You'll kill me! Her b-b-b-b-brother! Her b-b-b-b—her b-b-b —her b-b—"

The world suddenly seemed very cold to Charming. He turned the ring on his finger.

"Well?" said the dwarf.

"I want," said Charming curtly, "to be back at home, riding through the streets on my cream palfrey, amidst the cheers of the populace…. At once."

An hour later Princess Beauty and Prince Udo, who was not her brother, gazed into each other's eyes; and Beauty's last illusion went.

"You've altered," she said slowly.

"Yes, I'm not REALLY much like a tortoise," said Udo humorously.

"I meant since seven years ago. You're much stouter than I thought."

"Time hasn't exactly stood still with you, you know, Beauty."

"Yet you saw me every day, and went on loving me."

"Well-er—" He shuffled his feet and looked away.

"DIDN'T you?"

"Well, you see—of course I wanted to get back, you see—and as long as you—I mean if we—if you thought we were in love with each other, then, of course, you were ready to help me. And so—"

"You're quite old and bald. I can't think why I didn't notice it before."

"Well, you wouldn't when I was a tortoise," said Udo pleasantly. "As tortoises go I was really quite a youngster. Besides, anyhow one never notices baldness in a tortoise."

"I think," said Beauty, weighing her words carefully, "I think you've gone off a good deal in looks in the last day or two."

Charming was home in time for dinner; and next morning he was more popular than ever (outside his family) as he rode through the streets of the city. But Blunderbus lay dead in his castle. You and I know that he was killed by the magic sword; yet somehow a strange legend grew up around his death. And ever afterwards in that country, when one man told his neighbour a more than ordinarily humorous anecdote, the latter would cry, in between the gusts of merriment, "Don't! You'll make me die of laughter!" And then he would pull himself together, and add with a sigh—"Like Blunderbus."

AN ODD LOT

THE COMING OF THE CROCUS

"IT'S a bootiful day again, Sir," said my gardener, James, looking in at the study window.

"Bootiful, James, bootiful," I said, as I went on with my work.

"You might almost say as spring was here at last, like."

"Cross your fingers quickly, James, and touch wood. Look here, I'll be out in a minute and give you some orders, but I'm very busy just now."

"Thought praps you'd like to know there's eleven crocuses in the front garden."

"Then send them away—we've got nothing for them."

"Crocuses," shouted James.

I jumped up eagerly, and climbed through the window.

"My dear man," I said, shaking him warmly by the hand, "this is indeed a day. Crocuses! And in the front gar—on the south lawn! Let us go and gaze at them."

There they were—eleven of them. Six golden ones, four white, and a little mauve chap.

"This is a triumph for you, James. It's wonderful. Has anything like this ever happened to you before?"

"There'll be some more up to-morrow, I won't say as not."

"Those really are growing, are they? You haven't been pushing them in from the top? They were actually born on the estate?"

"There'll be a fine one in the back bed soon," said James proudly.

"In the back—my dear James! In the spare bed on the north-east terrace, I suppose you mean. And what have we in the Dutch Ornamental Garden?"

"If I has to look after ornamental gardens and south aspics and all, I ought to have my salary raised," said James, still harping on his one grievance.

"By all means raise some celery," I said coldly.

"Take a spade and raise some for lunch. I shall be only too delighted."

"This here isn't the season for celery, as you know well. This here's the season for crocuses, as anyone can see if they use their eyes."

"James, you're right. Forgive me. It is no day for quarrelling."

It was no day for working either. The sun shone upon the close-cropped green of the deer park, the sky was blue above the rose garden, in the tapioca grove a thrush was singing. I walked up and down my estate and drank in the good fresh air.

"James!" I called to my head gardener.

"What is it now?" he grumbled.

"Are there no daffodils to take the winds of March with beauty?"

"There's these eleven croc—"

"But there should be daffodils too. Is not this March?"

"It may be March, but 'tisn't the time for daffodils—not on three shillings a week."

"Do you only get three shillings a week? I thought it was three shillings an hour."

"Likely an hour!"

"Ah well, I knew it was three shillings. Do you know, James, in the Scilly Islands there are fields and fields and fields of nodding daffodils out now."

"Lor'!" said James.

"Did you say 'lor'' or 'liar'?" I asked suspiciously.

"To think of that now," said James cautiously.

He wandered off to the tapioca grove, leant against it in thought for a moment, and came back to me.

"What's wrong with this little bit of garden—this here park," he began, "is the soil. It's no soil for daffodils. Now what daffodils like is clay."

"Then for Heaven's sake get them some clay. Spare no expense. Get them anything they fancy."

"It's too alloovial—that's what's the matter. Too alloovial. Now, crocuses like a bit of alloovial. That's where you have it."

The matter with James is that he hasn't enough work to do. The rest of the staff is so busily employed that it is hardly ever visible. William, for instance, is occupied entirely with what I might call the poultry; it is his duty, in fact, to see that there are always enough ants' eggs for the goldfish. All these prize Leghorns you hear about are the merest novices compared with William's protegees. Then John looks after the staggery; Henry works the coloured fountain; and Peter paints the peacocks' tails. This keeps them all busy, but James is for ever hanging about.

"Almost seems as if they were yooman," he said, as we stood and listened to the rooks.

"Oh, are you there, James? It's a beautiful day. Who said that first? I believe you did."

"Them there rooks always make a place seem so home-like. Rooks and crocuses, I say—and you don't want anything more."

"Yes; well, if the rooks want to build in the raspberry canes this year, let them, James. Don't be inhospitable."

"Course, some do like to see primroses, I don't say. But—"

"Primroses—I knew there was something. Where are they?"

"It's too early for them," said James hastily. "You won't get primroses now before April."

"Don't say 'now,' as if it were my fault. Why didn't you plant them earlier? I don't believe you know any of the tricks of your profession, James. You never seem to graft anything or prune anything, and I'm sure you don't know how to cut a slip. James, why don't you prune more? Prune now—I should like to watch you. Where's your pruning-hook? You can't possibly do it with a rake."

James spends most of his day with a rake—sometimes leaning on it, sometimes working with it. The beds are always beautifully kept. Only the most hardy annual would dare to poke its head up and spoil the smooth appearance of the soil. For those who like circles and rectangles of unrelieved brown, James is undoubtedly the man.

As I stood in the sun I had a brilliant idea.

"James," I said, "we'll cut the croquet lawn this afternoon."

"You can't play croquet to-day, it's not warm enough."

"I don't pay you to argue, but to obey. At the same time I should like to point out that I never said I was going to play croquet. I said that we, meaning you, would cut the lawn."

"What's the good of that?"

"Why, to encourage the wonderful day, of course. Where is your gratitude, man? Don't you want to do something to help? How can we let a day like this go past without some word of welcome? Out with the mower, and let us hail the passing of winter."

James looked at me in disgust.

"Gratitude!" he said indignantly to Heaven. "And there's my eleven crocuses in the front all a-singing together like anything on three bob a week!"

THE ORDEAL BY FIRE

Our Flame-flower, the Family Flame-flower, is now plainly established in the north-east corner of the pergola, and flourishes exceedingly. There, or thereabouts, it will remain through the generations to come—a cascade of glory to the eye, a fountain of pride to the soul. "Our fathers' fathers," the unborn will say of us, "performed this thing; they toiled and suffered that we might front the world with confidence—a family secure in the knowledge that it has been tried by fire and not found wanting...."

The Atherley's flame-flower, I am glad to inform you, is dead.

We started the work five years ago. I was young and ignorant then—I did not understand. One day they led me to an old apple tree and showed me, fenced in at its foot, two twigs and a hint of leaf. "The flame-flower!" they said, with awe in their voices. I was very young; I said that I didn't think much of it. It was from that moment that my education began....

Everybody who came to see us had to be shown the flame-flower. Visitors were conducted to the apple tree in solemn procession, and presented. They peered over the fence and said, "A-ah!" just as if they knew all about it. Perhaps some of them did. Perhaps some of them had tried to grow it in their own gardens.

As November came on and the air grew cold, the question whether the flame-flower should winter abroad became insistent. After much thought it was moved to the shrubbery on the southern side of the house, where it leant against a laburnum until April. With the spring it returned home, seemingly stronger for the change; but the thought of winter was too much for it, and in October it was ordered south again.

For the next three years it was constantly trying different climates and testing various diets. Though it was touch and go with it all this time our faith was strong, our courage unshaken. June, 1908, found it in the gravel-pit. It seemed our only hope....

And in the August of that year I went and stayed with the Atherleys.

One morning at breakfast I challenged Miss Atherley to an immediate game of tennis.

"Not directly after," said Mrs Atherley, "it's so bad for you. Besides, we must just plant our flame-flower first."

I dropped my knife and fork and gazed at her open-mouthed.

"Plant your—WHAT?" I managed to say at last.

"Flame-flower. Do you know it? John brought one down last night—it looks so pretty growing up anything."

"It won't take a moment," said Miss Atherley, "and then I'll beat you."

"But—but you mustn't—you—you mustn't talk like THAT about it," I stammered." Th-that's not the way to talk about a flame-flower."

"Why, what's wrong?"

"You're just going to plant it! Before you play tennis! It isn't a—a BUTTERCUP! You can't do it like that."

"Oh, but do give us any hints—we shall be only too grateful."

"Hints! Just going to plant it!" I repeated, getting more and more indignant. "I—I suppose Sir Christopher Wren s-said to his wife at breakfast one morning, 'I've just got to design St Paul's Cathedral, dear, and then I'll come and play tennis with you. If you can give me any hints—'"

"Is it really so difficult?" asked Mrs Atherley. "We've seen lots of it in Scotland."

"In Scotland, yes. Not in the South of England." I paused, and then added, "WE have one."

"What soil is yours? Do you plant it very deep? Do they like a lot of water?" These and other technical points were put to me at once.

"Those are mere details of horticulture," I said. "What I am protesting against is the whole spirit in which you approach the business—the light-hearted way in which you assume that you can support a flame-flower. You have to be a very superior family indeed to have a flame-flower growing in your garden."

They laughed. They thought I was joking.

"Well, we're going to plant it now, anyhow," said Miss Atherley. "Come along and help us."

We went out, six of us, Mrs Atherley carrying the precious thing; and we gathered round an old tree trunk in front of the house.

"It would look rather pretty here," said Mrs Atherley. "Don't you think?"

I gave a great groan.

"You—you—you're all wrong again," I said in despair. "You don't put a flame-flower in a place where you think it will look pretty; you try in all humility to find a favoured spot where it will be pleased to grow. There may be such a spot in your garden or there may not. Until I know you better I cannot say. But it is extremely unlikely to be here, right in front of the window."

They laughed again, and began to dig up the ground. I turned my back in horror; I could not watch. And at the last moment some qualms of doubt seized even them. They spoke to me almost humbly.

"How would YOU plant it?" they asked.

It was my last chance of making them realize their responsibility.

"I cannot say at this moment," I began, "exactly how the ceremony should be performed, but I should endeavour to think of something in keeping with the solemnity of the occasion. It may be that Mrs Atherley and I would take the flower and march in procession round the fountain, singing a suitable chant, while Bob and Archie with shaven heads prostrated themselves before the sundial. Miss Atherley might possibly dance the Fire-dance upon the east lawn, while Mr Atherley stood upon one foot in the middle of the herbaceous border and played upon her with the garden hose. These or other symbolic rites we should perform, before we planted it in a place chosen by Chance. Then leaving a saucer of new milk for it lest it should thirst in the night we would go away, and spend the rest of the week in meditation."

I paused for breath.

"That might do it," I added, "or it might not. But at least that is the sort of spirit that you want to show."

Once more they laughed ... and then they planted it.

These have been two difficult years for me. There have been times when I have almost lost faith, and not even the glories of our own flame-flower could cheer me. But at last the news came. I was at home for the week-end and, after rather a tiring day showing visitors the north-east end of the pergola, I went indoors for a rest. On the table there was a letter for me. It was from Mrs Atherley.

"BY THE WAY," she wrote, "THE FLAME-FLOWER IS DEAD."

"By the way"!

But even if they had taken the business seriously, even if they had understood fully what a great thing it was they were attempting—even then I think they would have failed.

For, though I like the Atherleys very much, though I think them all extremely jolly … yet—I doubt, you know, if they are QUITE the family to have a flame-flower growing in their garden.

THE LUCKY MONTH

"KNOW thyself," said the old Greek motto. (In Greek—but this is an English book.) So I bought a little red volume called, tersely enough, WERE YOU BORN IN JANUARY? I was; and, reassured on this point, the author told me all about myself.

For the most part he told me nothing new. "You are," he said in effect, "good-tempered, courageous, ambitious, loyal, quick to resent wrong, an excellent raconteur, and a leader of men." True. "Generous to a fault"— (Yes, I was overdoing that rather)—"you have a ready sympathy with the distressed. People born in this month will always keep their promises." And so on. There was no doubt that the author had the idea all right. Even when he went on to warn me of my weaknesses he maintained the correct note. "People born in January," he said, "must be on their guard against working too strenuously. Their extraordinarily active brains—" Well, you see what he means. It IS a fault perhaps, and I shall be more careful in future. Mind, I do not take offence with him for calling my attention to it. In fact, my only objection to the book is its surface application to ALL the people who were born in January. There should have been more distinction made between me and the rabble.

I have said that he told me little that was new. In one matter, however, he did open my eyes. He introduced me to an aspect of myself entirely unsuspected.

"They," he said-meaning me, "have unusual business capacity, and are destined to be leaders in great commerical enterprises."

One gets at times these flashes of self-revelation. In an instant I realized how wasted my life had been; in an instant I resolved that here and now I would put my great gifts to their proper uses. I would be a leader in an immense commercial enterprise.

One cannot start commercial enterprises without capital. The first thing was to determine the exact nature of my balance at the bank. This was a matter for the bank to arrange, and I drove there rapidly.

"Good-morning," I said to the cashier, "I am in rather a hurry. May I have my pass-book?"

He assented and retired. After an interminable wait, during which many psychological moments for commercial enterprise must have lapsed, he returned.

"I think YOU have it," he said shortly.

"Thank you," I replied, and drove rapidly home again.

A lengthy search followed; but after an hour of it one of those white-hot flashes of thought, such as only occur to the natural business genius, seared my mind and sent me post-haste to the bank again.

"After all," I said to the cashier, "I only want to know my balance. What is it?"

He withdrew and gave himself up to calculation. I paced the floor impatiently. Opportunities were slipping by. At last he pushed a slip of paper across at me. My balance!

It was in four figures. Unfortunately two of them were shillings and pence. Still, there was a matter of fifty pounds odd as well, and fortunes have been built up on less.

Out in the street I had a moment's pause. Hitherto I had regarded my commercial enterprise in the bulk, as a finished monument of industry; the little niggling preliminary details had not come up for consideration. Just for a second I wondered how to begin.

Only for a second. An unsuspected talent which has long lain dormant needs, when waked, a second or so to turn round in. At the end of that time I had made up my mind. I knew exactly what I would do. I would ring up my solicitor.

"Hallo, is that you? Yes, this is me. What? Yes, awfully, thanks. How are you? Good. Look here, come and lunch with me. What? No, at once. Good-bye."

Business, particularly that sort of commercial enterprise to which I had now decided to lend my genius, can only be discussed properly over a cigar. During the meal itself my solicitor and I indulged in the ordinary small-talk of the pleasure-loving world.

"You're looking very fit," said my solicitor. "No, not fat, FIT."

"You don't think I'm looking thin?" I asked anxiously. "People are warning me that I may be overdoing it rather. They tell me that I must be seriously on my guard against brain strain."

"I suppose they think you oughtn't to strain it too suddenly," said my solicitor. Though he is now a solicitor he was once just an ordinary boy like the rest of us, and it was in those days that he acquired the habit of being rude to me, a habit he has never quite forgotten.

"What is an onyx?" I said, changing the conversation.

"Why?" asked my solicitor, with his usual business acumen.

"Well, I was practically certain that I had seen one in the Zoo, in the reptile house, but I have just learnt that it is my lucky month stone. Naturally I want to get one."

The coffee came and we settled down to commerce.

"I was just going to ask you," said my solicitor—"have you any money lying idle at the bank? Because if so—"

"Whatever else it is doing, it isn't lying idle," I protested. "I was at the bank to-day, and there were men chivying it about with shovels all the time."

"Well, how much have you got?"

"About fifty pounds."

"It ought to be more than that."

"That's what I say, but you know what banks are. Actual merit counts for nothing with them."

"Well, what did you want to do with it?"

"Exactly. That was why I rang you up. I—er—" This was really my moment, but somehow I was not quite ready to seize it. My vast commercial enterprise still lacked a few trifling details. "Er—I—well, it's like that."

"I might get you a few ground rents."

"Don't. I shouldn't know where to put them."

"But if you really have fifty pounds simply lying idle I wish you'd lend it to me for a bit. I'm confoundedly hard up."

("GENEROUS TO A FAULT, YOU HAVE A READY SYMPATHY WITH THE DISTRESSED." Dash it, what could I do?)

"Is it quite etiquette for clients to lend solicitors money?" I asked. "I thought it was always solicitors who had to lend it to clients. If I must, I'd rather lend it to you—I mean, I'd dislike it less—as to the old friend of my childhood."

"Yes, that's how I wanted to pay it back."

"Bother. Then I'll send you a cheque to-night," I sighed.

And that's where we are at the moment. "PEOPLE BORN IN THIS MONTH ALWAYS KEEP THEIR PROMISES." The money has got to go to-night. If I hadn't been born in January I shouldn't be sending it; I certainly shouldn't have promised it; I shouldn't even have known that I had it. Sometimes I almost wish that I had been born in one of the decent months. March, say.

A SUMMER COLD

WHEN I am not feeling very well I go to Beatrice for sympathy and advice. Anyhow I get the advice.

"I think," I said carelessly, wishing to break it to her as gently as possible, "I think I have hay-fever."

"Nonsense," said Beatrice.

That annoyed me. Why shouldn't I have hay-fever if I wanted to?

"If you're going to begrudge me every little thing," I began.

"You haven't even got a cold."

As luck would have it a sneeze chose that moment for its arrival.

"There!" I said triumphantly.

"Why, my dear boy, if you had hay-fever you'd be sneezing all day."

"That was only a sample. There are lots more where that came from."

"Don't be so silly. Fancy starting hay-fever in September."

"I'm not starting it. I am, I earnestly hope, just finishing it. If you want to know, I've had a cold all the summer."

"Well, I haven't noticed it."

"That's because I'm such a good actor. I've been playing the part of a man who hasn't had a cold all the summer. My performance is considered to be most life-like."

Beatrice disdained to answer, and by and by I sneezed again.

"You certainly have a cold," she said, putting down her work.

"Come, this is something."

"You must be careful. How did you catch it?"

"I didn't catch it. It caught me."

"Last week-end?"

"No, last May."

Beatrice picked up her work again impatiently. I sneezed a third time.

"Is this more the sort of thing you want?" I said.

"What I say is that you couldn't have had hay-fever all the summer without people knowing."

"But, my dear Beatrice, people do know. In this quiet little suburb you are rather out of the way of the busy world. Rumours of war, depressions on the Stock Exchange, my hay-fever—these things pass you by. But the clubs are full of it. I assure you that, all over the country, England's stately homes have been plunged into mourning by the news of my sufferings, historic piles have bowed their heads and wept."

"I suppose you mean that in every house you've been to this summer you've told them that you had it, and they've been foolish enough to believe you."

"That's putting it a little crudely. What happens is—"

"Well, all I can say is, you know a very silly lot of people."

"What happens is that when the mahogany has been cleared of its polished silver and choice napery, and wine of a rare old vintage is circulating from hand to hand—"

"If they wanted to take any notice of you at all, they could have given you a bread poultice and sent you to bed."

"Then, as we impatiently bite the ends off our priceless Havanas—"

"They might know that you couldn't possibly have hay-fever."

I sat up suddenly and spoke to Beatrice.

"Why on earth SHOULDN'T I have hay-fever?" I demanded. "Have you any idea what hay-fever is? I suppose you think I ought to be running about wildly, trying to eat hay—or yapping and showing an unaccountable aversion from dried grass? I take it that there are grades of hay-fever, as there are of everything else. I have it at present in a mild form. Instead of being thankful that it is no worse, you—"

"My dear boy, hay-fever is a thing people have all their lives, and it comes on every summer. You've never even pretended to have it before this year."

"Yes, but you must start SOME time. I'm a little backward, perhaps. Just because there are a few infant prodigies about, don't despise me. In a year or two I shall be as regular as the rest of them." And I sneezed again.

Beatrice got up with an air of decision and left the room. For a moment I thought she was angry and had gone for a policeman, but as the minutes went by and she didn't return I began to fear that she might have left the house for good. I was wondering how I should break the news to her husband when, to my relief, she came in again.

"You may be right," she said, putting down a small package and unpinning her hat. "Try this. The chemist says it's the best hay-fever cure there is."

"It's in a lot of languages," I said as I took the wrapper off. "I suppose German hay is the same as any other sort of hay? Oh, here it is in English. I say, this is a what-d'-you-call-it cure."

"So the man said."

"Homeopathic. It's made from the pollen that causes hay-fever. Yes. Ah, yes." I coughed slightly and looked at Beatrice out of the corner of my eye. "I suppose," I said carelessly, "if anybody took this who HADN'T got hay-fever, the results might be rather—I mean that he might then find that he-in fact, er—HAD got it."

"Sure to," said Beatrice.

"Yes. That makes us a little thoughtful; we don't want to over-do this thing." I went on reading the instructions. "You know, it's rather odd about my hay-fever—it's generally worse in town than in the country."

"But then you started so late, dear. You haven't really got into the swing of it yet."

"Yes, but still—you know, I have my doubts about the gentleman who invented this. We don't see eye to eye in this matter. Beatrice, you may be right—perhaps I haven't got hay-fever."

"Oh, don't give up."

"But all the same I know I've got something. It's a funny thing about my being worse in town than in the country. That looks rather as if—By Jove, I know what it is—I've got just the opposite of hay-fever."

"What is the opposite of hay?"

"Why, bricks and things."

I gave a last sneeze and began to wrap up the cure.

"Take this pollen stuff back," I said to Beatrice, "and ask the man if he's got anything homoeopathic made from paving-stones. Because, you know, that's what I really want."

"You HAVE got a cold," said Beatrice.

A MODERN CINDERELLA

ONCE upon a time there was a beautiful girl who lived in a mansion in Park Lane with her mother and her two sisters and a crowd of servants. Cinderella, for that was her name, would have dearly loved to have employed herself about the house sometimes; but whenever she did anything useful, like arranging the flowers or giving the pug a bath, her mother used to say, "Cinderella! What DO you think I engage servants for? Please don't make yourself so common."

Cinderella's two sisters were much older and plainer than herself, and their mother had almost given up hope about them, but she used to drag Cinderella to balls and dances night after night, taking care that only the right sort of person was introduced to her. There were many nights when Cinderella would have preferred a book at home in front of the fire, for she soon found that her partners' ideas of waltzing were as catholic as their conversation was limited. It was, indeed, this fondness for the inglenook that had earned her the name of Cinderella.

One day, when she was in the middle of a delightful story, her mother came in suddenly and cried:

"Cinderella! Why aren't you resting, as I told you? You know we are going to the Hogbins' to-night."

"Oh, mother," pleaded Cinderella, "NEED I go to the dance?"

"Don't be so absurd! Of course you're going!"

"But I've got nothing to wear."

"I've told Jennings what you're to wear. Now go and lie down. I want you to look your best to-night, because I hear that young Mr Hogbin is back again from Australia." Young Mr Hogbin was not the King's son; he was the son of a wealthy gelatine manufacturer.

"Then may I come away at twelve?" begged Cinderella.

"You'll come away when I tell you."

Cinderella made a face and went upstairs. "Oh, dear," she thought to herself, "I wish I were as old as my two sisters, and could do what I liked. I'm sure if my godmother were here she would get me off going." But, alas! her godmother lived at Leamington, and Cinderella, after a week at Leamington, had left her there only yesterday.

Cinderella indeed looked beautiful as they started for the ball; but her mother, who held a review of her in the drawing-room, was not quite satisfied.

"Cinderella!" she said. "You know I said you were to wear the silver slippers!"

"Oh, mother, they ARE so tight," pleaded Cinderella. "Don't you remember I told you at the time they were much too small for me?"

"Nonsense. Go and put them on at once."

The dance was in full swing when Cinderella arrived. Although her lovely appearance caused several of the guests to look at her, they did not ask each other eagerly who she was, for most of them knew her already as Miss Partington-Smith. A brewer's son led her off to dance.

The night wore on slowly. One young man after another trod on Cinderella's toes, trotted in circles round her, ran her violently backwards into some other man, or swooped with her into the fireplace. Cinderella, whose feet seemed mechanically to adapt themselves to the interpretation of the Boston that was forming in her partner's brain, bore it from each one as long as she could; and then led the way to a quiet corner, where she confessed frankly that she had NOT bought all her Christmas presents yet, and that she WAS going to Switzerland for the winter.

The gelatine manufacturer's son took her in to supper. It was noticed that Cinderella looked much happier as soon as they had sat down, and indeed throughout the meal she was in the highest spirits. For some reason or other she seemed to find even Mr Hogbin endurable. But just as they were about to return to the ball-room an expression of absolute dismay came over her face.

"Anything the matter?" said her partner.

"N—no," said Cinderella; but she made no effort to move.

"Well, shall we come?"

"Y—yes."

She waited a moment longer, dropped her fan under the table, picked it up slowly, and followed him out.

"Let's sit down here," she said in the hall; "not upstairs."

They sat in silence; for he had exhausted his stock of questions at the end of their first dance, and had told her all about Australia during supper; while she apparently had no desire for conversation of any kind, being wrapped up in her thoughts.

"I'll wait here," she said, as a dance began. "If you see mother, I wish you'd send her to me."

Her mother came up eagerly.

"Well, dear?" she said.

"Mother," said Cinderella, "do take me home at once. Something extraordinary has happened."

"It's young Mr Hogbin! I knew it!"

"Who? Oh—er—yes, of course. I'll tell you all about it in the carriage, mother."

"Is my little girl going to be happy?"

"I don't know," said Cinderella anxiously. "There's just a chance."

The chance must have come off, for, once in the carriage, Cinderella gave a deep sigh of happiness.

"Well, dear?" said her mother again.

"You'll NEVER guess, mother," laughed Cinderella. "Try."

"I guess that my little daughter thinks of running away from me," said her mother archly. "Am I right?"

"Oh, how lovely! Why, running away is simply the LAST thing I could do. Look!" She stretched out her foot-clothed only in a pale blue stocking.

"Cinderella!"

"I TOLD you they were too tight," she explained rapidly, "and I was trodden on by every man in the place, and I simply HAD to kick them off at supper, and—and I only got one back. I don't know what happened to the other; I suppose it got pushed along somewhere, but, anyhow, I wasn't going under the table after it." She laughed suddenly and softly to herself. "I wonder what they'll do when they find the slipper?" she said.

Of course the King's son (or anyhow, Mr Hogbin) ought to have sent it round to all the ladies in Mayfair, taking knightly oath to marry her whom it fitted. But what actually happened was that a footman found it, and, being very sentimental and knowing that nobody would ever dare to claim it, carried it about with him ever afterwards—thereby gaining a great reputation with his cronies as a nut.

> Oh, and by the way—I ought to put in a good word for the godmother. She did her best.

"Cinderella!" said her mother at lunch next day, as she looked up from her letters. "Why didn't you tell me your godmother was ill?"

"She wasn't very well when I left her, but I didn't think it was anything much. Is she bad? I AM sorry."

"She writes that she has obtained measles. I suppose that means YOU'RE infectious. Really, it's very inconvenient. Well, I'm glad we didn't know yesterday or you couldn't have gone to the dance."

"Dear fairy godmother!" said Cinderella to herself. "She was a day too late, but how sweet of her to think of it at all!"

A LITERARY LIGHT

ANNESLEY BUPP was born one of the Bupps of Hampshire—the Fighting Bupps, as they were called. A sudden death in the family left him destitute at the early age of thirty, and he decided to take seriously to journalism for a living. That was twelve years ago. He is now a member of the Authors' Club; a popular after-dinner speaker in reply to the toast of Literature; and one of the best-paid writers in Fleet Street. Who's Who tells the world that he has a flat at Knightsbridge and a cottage on the river. If you ask him to what he owes his success he will assure you, with the conscious modesty of all great men, that he has been lucky; pressed further, that Hard Work and Method have been his watchwords. But to the young aspirant he adds that of course if you have it in you it is bound to come out.

I

When Annesley started journalism he realized at once that it was necessary for him to specialize in some subject. Of such subjects two occurred to him—"George Herbert" and "Trams." For a time he hesitated, and it was only the sudden publication of a brief but authoritative life of the poet which led him finally to the study of one of the least explored of our transit systems. Meanwhile he had to support himself. For this purpose he bought a roll-top desk, a typewriter, and an almanac; he placed the almanac on top of the desk, seated himself at the typewriter, and began.

It was the month of February; the almanac told him that it wanted a week to Shrove Tuesday. In four days he had written as many articles, entitled respectively Shrovetide Customs, The Pancake, Lenten Observances, and Tuesdays Known to Fame. The Pancake, giving as it did the context of every reference in literature to pancakes, was the most scholarly of the four; the Tuesday article, which hazarded the opinion that Rome may at least have been begun on a Tuesday, the most daring. But all of them were published.

This early success showed Annesley the possibilities of the topical article; it led him also to construct a revised calendar for his own use. In the "Bupp Almanac" the events of the day were put back a fortnight; so that, if the Feast of St Simon and St Jude fell upon the 17th, Annesley's attention was called to it upon the 3rd, and upon the 3rd he surveyed the Famous Partnerships of the epoch. Similarly, The Origin of Lord Mayor's Day was put in hand on October 26th.

He did not, however, only glorify the past; current events claimed their meed of copy. In the days of his dependence Annesley had travelled, so that he could well provide the local colour for such sketches as Kimberley as I Knew It (1901) and Birmingham by Moonlight (1903). His Recollections of St Peter's at Rome were hazy, yet sufficient to furnish an article with that title at the time of the Coronation. But I must confess that Dashes for the Pole came entirely from his invaluable Encyclopaedia....

II

Annesley Bupp had devoted himself to literature for two years before his first article on trams was written. This was called Voltage, was highly technical, and convinced every editor to whom it was sent (and by whom it was returned) that the author knew his subject thoroughly. So when he followed it up with How to be a Tram Conductor, he had the satisfaction not only of seeing it in print within a week, but of reading an editorial reference to himself as "the noted expert on our overhead system." Two other articles in the same paper—Some Curious Tram Accidents and Tram or Bus: Which?— established his position.

Once recognized as the authority on trams, Bupp was never at a loss for a subject. In the first place there were certain articles, such as Tramways in 1904, Progress of Tramway Construction in the Past Year, Tramway Inventions of the Last Twelvemonth, and The Tram: Its Future in 1905, which flowed annually from his pen. From time to time there would arise the occasion for the topical article on trams—Trams as Army Transports and How our Trams fared during the Recent Snow, to give two obvious examples. And always there was a market for such staple articles as Trams in Fiction....

III

You will understand, then, that by the end of 1906 Annesley Bupp had a reputation; to be exact, he had two reputations. In Fleet Street he was known as a writer upon whom a sub-editor could depend; a furnisher of what got to be called "buppy"—matter which is paid at a slightly higher rate than ordinary copy, because the length and quality of it never vary. Outside Fleet Street he was regarded simply as a literary light; Annesley Bupp, the fellow whose name you saw in every paper; an accepted author.

It was not surprising, therefore, that at the beginning of 1907 public opinion forced Annesley into (sic) n wer fields of literature. It demanded from him, among other things, a weekly review of current fiction entitled Fireside Friends. He wrote this with extraordinary fluency; a few words of introduction, followed by a large fragment of the book before him, pasted beneath the line, "Take this, for instance." An opinion of any kind he rarely ventured; an adverse opinion, like a good friend, never.

About this time he was commissioned to write three paragraphs each day for an evening paper. The first of them always began: "Mr Asquith's admission in the House of Commons yesterday that he had never done so and so is not without parallel. In 1746 the elder Pitt ..." The second always began: "Mention of the elder Pitt recalls the fact that ..." The third always began: "It may not be generally known ..."

Until he began to write these paragraphs Annesley Bupp had no definite political views.

IV

Annesley Bupp is now at the zenith of his fame. The "buppy" of old days he still writes occasionally, but he no longer signs it in full. A modest "A. B." in the corner, supposed by the ignorant to stand for "Arthur Balfour," is the only evidence of the author. (I say "the only evidence," for he has had, like all great men, his countless imitators.) Trams also he deserted with the publication of his great work on the subject—Tramiana. But as a writer on Literature and Old London he has a European reputation, and his recent book, In the Track of Shakespeare: A Record of a Visit to Stratford-on-Avon, created no little stir.

He is in great request at public dinners, where his speech in reply to the toast of Literature is eagerly attended.

He contributes to every symposium in the popular magazines.

It is all the more to be regretted that his autobiography, The Last of the Bupps, is to be published posthumously.

LITTLE PLAYS FOR AMATEURS

"FAIR MISTRESS DOROTHY"

THE SCENE IS AN APARTMENT IN THE MANSION OF Sir Thomas Farthingale. THERE IS NO NEED TO DESCRIBE THE FURNITURE IN IT, AS REHEARSALS WILL GRADUALLY SHOW WHAT IS WANTED. A PICTURE OR TWO OF PREVIOUS Sir

Thomas's MIGHT BE SEEN ON THE WALLS, IF YOU
HAVE AN ARTISTIC FRIEND WHO COULD ARRANGE
THIS; BUT IT IS A MISTAKE TO HANG UP YOUR
OWN ANCESTORS AS SOME OF YOUR GUESTS MAY
RECOGNIZE THEM, AND THUS PIERCE BENEATH THE
VRAISEMBLANCE OF THE SCENE.

THE PERIOD IS THAT OF CROMWELL—SIXTEEN SOMETHING.

THE COSTUMES ARE, IF POSSIBLE, OF THE SAME PERIOD.

Mistress Dorothy Farthingale IS SEATED IN THE
MIDDLE OF THE STAGE, READING A LETTER AND
OCCASIONALLY SIGHING.

ENTER My Lord Carey.

CAREY. Mistress Dorothy alone! Truly Fortune smiles upon me.

DOROTHY (HIDING THE LETTER QUICKLY). An she smiles, my lord, I needs must frown.

CAREY (USED TO THIS SORT OF THING AND NO LONGER PUT OFF BY IT). Nay, give me but one smile, sweet mistress. (SHE SIGHS HEAVILY.) You sigh! Is't for me?

DOROTHY (FEELING THAT THE SOONER HE AND THE
AUDIENCE UNDERSTAND THE
SITUATION THE BETTER). I sigh for another, my lord,
who is absent.

CAREY (ANNOYED). Zounds, and zounds again!

A pest upon the fellow! (He strides up and down the room, keeping out of the way of his sword as much as possible.) Would that I might pink the pesky knave!

DOROTHY (turning upon him a look of hate). Would that you might have the chance, my lord, so it were in fair fighting. Methinks Roger's sword-arm will not have lost its cunning in the wars.

CAREY. A traitor to fight against his King!

DOROTHY. He fights for what he thinks is right. (She takes out his letter and kisses it.)

CAREY (observing the action). You have a letter from him!

DOROTHY (hastily concealing it, and turning pale). How know you that?

CAREY. Give it to me! (She shrieks and rises.) By heavens, madam, I will have it! [He struggles with her and seizes it.

Enter Sir Thomas.

SIR THOMAS. Odds life, my lord, what means this?

CAREY (straightening himself). It means, Sir Thomas, that you harbour a rebel within your walls. Master Roger Dale, traitor, corresponds secretly with your daughter. [Who, I forgot to say, has swooned.

SIR THOMAS (sternly). Give me the letter. Ay, 'tis Roger's hand, I know it well. (He reads the letter, which is full of thoughtful metaphors about love, aloud to the audience. Suddenly his eyebrows go up and down to express surprise. He seizes Lord Carey by the arm.) Ha! Listen! "To-morrow, when the sun is upon the western window of the gallery, I will be with thee." The villain!

CAREY (who does not know the house very well). When is that?

SIR THOMAS. Why, 'tis now, for I have but recently passed through the gallery and did mark the sun.

CAREY (FIERCELY). In the name of the King, Sir Thomas, I call upon you to arrest this traitor.

SIR THOMAS (sighing). I loved the boy well, yet—[He shrugs his shoulders expressively and goes out with Lord Carey to collect sufficient force for the arrest.

Enter Roger by a secret door, R.

ROGER. My love!

DOROTHY (opening her eyes). Roger!

ROGER. At last!

[For the moment they talk in short sentences like this. Then DOROTHY puts her hand to her brow as if she is remembering something horrible.

DOROTHY. Roger! Now I remember! It is not safe for you to stay!

ROGER (very brave). Am I a puling child to be afraid?

DOROTHY. My Lord Carey is here. He has read your letter.

ROGER. The black-livered dog! Would I had him at my sword's point to teach him manners.

[He puts his hand to his heart and staggers into a chair.

DOROTHY. Oh, you are wounded!

ROGER. Faugh,'tis but a scratch. Am I a puling—

[He faints. She binds up his ankle.

Enter Lord Carey with two soldiers.

CAREY. Arrest this traitor! (ROGER is led away by the soldiers.)

Dorothy (stretching out her hands to him). Roger! (She sinks into a chair.)

Carey (choosing quite the wrong moment for a proposal). Dorothy, I love you! Think no more of this traitor, for he will surely hang. 'Tis your father's wish that you and I should wed.

Dorothy (refusing him). Go, lest I call in the grooms to whip you.

Carey. By heaven—(thinking better of it) I go to fetch your father.

[Exit.

Enter Roger by secret door, L.

Dorothy. Roger! You have escaped!

Roger. Knowest not the secret passage from the wine cellar, where we so often played as children? 'Twas in that same cellar the thick-skulled knaves immured me.

Dorothy. Roger, you must fly! Wilt wear a cloak of mine to elude our enemies?

Roger (missing the point rather). Nay, if I die, let me die like a man, not like a puling girl. Yet, sweetheart—

Enter Lord Carey by ordinary door.

Carey (forgetting himself in his confusion). Odds my zounds, dod sink me! What murrain is this?

Roger (seizing Sir Thomas's sword, which had been accidentally left behind on the table, as I ought to have said before, and advancing threateningly). It means, my lord, that a villain's time has come. Wilt say a prayer?

[They fight, and Carey is disarmed before they can hurt each other.

Carey (dying game). Strike, Master Dale!

Roger. Nay, I cannot kill in cold blood.

[He throws down his sword. Lord Carey exhibits considerable emotion at this, and decides to turn over an entirely new leaf.

Enter two soldiers.

Carey. Arrest that man! (Roger is seized again.) Mistress Dorothy, it is for you to say what shall be done with the prisoner.

Dorothy (standing up if she was sitting down, and sitting down if she was standing up). Ah, give him to me, my lord!

Carey (joining the hands of Roger and Dorothy). I trust to you, sweet mistress, to see that the prisoner does not escape again.

[Dorothy and Roger embrace each other, if they can do it without causing a scandal in the neighbourhood, and the curtain goes down.

"A SLIGHT MISUNDERSTANDING"

The scene is a drawing-room (in which the men are allowed to smoke—or a smoking-room in which the women are allowed to draw—it doesn't much matter) in the house of somebody or other in the country. George Turnbull and his old College friend, Henry Peterson, are confiding in each other, as old friends will, over their whiskies and cigars. It is about three o'clock in the afternoon.

George (dreamily helping himself to a stiff soda). Henry, do you remember that evening at Christ Church College, Oxford, five years ago, when we opened our hearts to each other...

Henry (lighting a cigar and hiding it in a fern-pot). That moonlight evening on the Backs, George, when I had failed in my Matriculation examination?

George. Yes; and we promised that when either of us fell in love the other should be the first to hear of it? (Rising solemnly.) Henry, the moment has come. (With shining eyes.) I am in love.

Henry (jumping up and grasping him by both hands). George! My dear old George! (In a voice broken with emotion.) Bless you, George!

[He pats him thoughtfully on the back three times, nods his own head twice, gives him a final grip of the hand, and returns to his chair.

George (more moved by this than he cares to show). Thank you, Henry. (Hoarsely.) You're a good fellow.

Henry (airily, with a typically British desire to conceal his emotion). Who is the lucky little lady?

George (taking out a picture postcard of the British Museum and kissing it passionately). Isobel Barley!

[If Henry is not careful he will probably give a start of surprise here, with the idea of suggesting to the audience that he (1) knows something about the lady's past, or (2) is in love with her himself. He is, however, thinking of a different play. We shall come to that one in a moment.

Henry (in a slightly dashing manner). Little Isobel? Lucky dog!

George. I wish I could think so. (Sighs.) But I have yet to approach her, and she may be another's. (Fiercely.) Heavens, Henry, if she should be another's!

Enter Isobel.

Isobel (brightly). So I've run you to earth at last. Now, what have you got to say for yourselves?

Henry (like a man). By Jove! (looking at his watch)—I had no idea—is it really—poor old Joe—waiting—

[Dashes out tactfully in a state of incoherence.

George (rising and leading Isobel to the front of the stage). Miss Barley, now that we are alone, I have something I want to say to you.

Isobel (looking at her watch). Well, you must be quick. Because I'm engaged—

[George drops her hand and staggers away from her.

Isobel. Why, what's the matter?

George (to the audience, in a voice expressing the very deeps of emotion). Engaged! She is engaged! I am too late!

[He sinks into a chair and covers his face with his hands.

Isobel (surprised). Mr Turnbull! What has happened?

George (waving her away with one hand). Go! Leave me! I can bear this best alone. (Exit Isobel.) Merciful heavens, she is plighted to another!

Enter Henry.

Henry (eagerly). Well, old man?

George (raising a face white with misery—that is to say, if he has remembered to put the French chalk in the palms of his hands). Henry, I am too late! She is another's!

Henry (in surprise). Whose?

George (with dignity). I did not ask her. It is nothing to me. Good-bye, Henry. Be kind to her.

Henry. Why, where are you going?

George (firmly). To the Rocky Mountains. I shall shoot some bears. Grizzly ones. It may be that thus I shall forget my grief.

Henry (after a pause). Perhaps you are right, George. What shall I tell—her?

George. Tell her—nothing. But should anything (feeling casually in his pockets) happen to me—if (going over them again quickly) I do not come back, then (searching them all, including the waistcoat ones, in desperate haste), give her—give her—give her (triumphantly bringing his handkerchief out of the last pocket) this, and say that my last thought was of her. Good-bye, my old friend. Good-bye.

[Exit to Rocky Mountains.

Enter Isobel.

Isabel. Why, where's Mr Turnbull?

Henry (sadly). He's gone.

Isabel. Gone? Where?

Henry. To the Rocky Mountains—to shoot bears. (Feeling that some further explanation is needed.) Grizzly ones.

Isobel. But he was HERE a moment ago.

Henry. Yes, he's only JUST gone.

Isobel. Why didn't he say good-bye? (Eagerly.) But perhaps he left a message for me? (Henry shakes his head.) Nothing? (Henry bows silently and leaves the room.) Oh! (She gives a cry and throws herself on the sofa.) And I loved him! George, George, why didn't you speak?

Enter George hurriedly. He is fully dressed for a shooting expedition in the Rocky Mountains, and carries a rifle under his arm.

George (to the audience). I have just come back for my pocket-handkerchief. I must have dropped it in here somewhere. (He begins to search for it, and in the ordinary course of things comes upon Isobel on the sofa. He puts his rifle down carefully on a table, with the muzzle pointing at the prompter rather than at the audience, and staggers back.) Merciful heavens! Isobel! Dead! (He falls on his knees beside the sofa.) My love, speak to me!

Isobel (softly). George!

George. She is alive! Isobel!

Isobel. Don't go, George!

George. My dear, I love you! But when I heard that you were another's, honour compelled me—

Isobel (sitting up quickly). What do you mean by another's?

George. You said you were engaged!

Isobel (suddenly realizing how the dreadful misunderstanding arose which nearly wrecked two lives). But I only meant I was engaged to play tennis with Lady Carbrook!

George. What a fool I have been! (He hurries on before the audience can assent.) Then, Isobel, you WILL be mine?

Isobel. Yes, George. And you won't go and shoot nasty bears, will you, dear? Not even grizzly ones?

George (taking her in his arms). Never, darling. That was only (turning to the audience with the air of one who is making his best point) A Slight Misunderstanding.

CURTAIN.

"MISS PRENDERGAST"

As the curtain goes up two ladies are discovered in the morning-room of Honeysuckle Lodge engaged in work of a feminine nature. Miss Alice Prendergast is doing something delicate with a crochet-hook, but it is obvious that her thoughts are far away. She sighs at intervals, and occasionally lays down her work and presses both hands to her heart. A sympathetic audience will have no difficulty in guessing that she is in love. On the other hand, her elder sister, Miss Prendergast, is completely wrapped up in a sock for one of the poorer classes, over which she frowns formidably. The sock, however, has no real bearing upon the plot, and she must not make too much of it.

Alice (hiding her emotions). Did you have a pleasant dinner-party last night, Jane?

Jane (to herself). Seventeen, eighteen, nineteen, twenty. (Looking up.) Very pleasant indeed, Alice. The Blizzards were there, and the Podbys, and the Slumphs. (These people are not important and should not be over-emphasized.) Mrs Podby's maid has given notice.

Alice. Who took you in?

Jane (brightening up). Such an interesting man, my dear. He talked most agreeably about Art during dinner, and we renewed the conversation in the drawing-room. We found that we agreed upon all the main principles of Art, considered as such.

Alice (with a look in her eyes which shows that she is recalling a tender memory). When I was in Shropshire last week—What was your man's name?

Jane (with a warning glance at the audience). You know how difficult it is to catch names when one is introduced. I am certain he never heard mine. (As the plot depends partly upon this, she pauses for it to sink in.) But I inquired about him afterwards, and I find that he is a Mr—

Enter Mary, the Parlour-maid.

Mary (handing letter). A letter for you, miss.

Jane (taking it). Thank you, Mary. (Exit Mary to work up her next line.) A letter! I wonder who it is from! (Reading the envelope.) "Miss Prendergast, Honeysuckle Lodge." (She opens it with the air of one who has often received letters before, but feels that this one may play an important part in her life.) "Dear Miss Prendergast, I hope you will pardon the presumption of what I am about to write to you, but whether you pardon me or not, I ask you to listen to me. I know of no woman for whose talents I have a greater admiration, or for whose qualities I have a more sincere affection than yourself. Since I have known you, you have been the lodestar of my existence, the fountain of my inspiration. I feel that, were your life joined to mine, the joint path upon which we trod would be the path to happiness, such as I have as yet hardly dared to dream of. In short, dear Miss Prendergast, I ask you to marry me, and I will come in person for my answer. Yours truly—" (In a voice of intense surprise) "Jas. Bootle!"

[At the word "Bootle," a wave of warm colour rushes over Alice and dyes her from neck to brow. If she is not an actress of sufficient calibre to ensure this, she must do the best she can by starting abruptly and putting her hand to her throat.

Alice (aside, in a choking voice). Mr Bootle! In love with Jane!

Jane. My dear! The man who took me down to dinner! Well!

Alice (picking up her work again and trying to be calm). What will you say?

Jane (rather pleased with herself). Well, really—I—this is—Mr Bootle! Fancy!

Alice (starting up). Was that a ring? (She frowns at the prompter and a bell is heard to ring.) It is Mr Bootle! I know his ring, I mean I know—Dear, I think I will go and lie down. I have a headache.

[She looks miserably at the audience, closes her eyes, and goes off with her handkerchief to her mouth, taking care not to fall over the furniture.

Enter Mary, followed by James Bootle.

Mary. Mr Bootle. (Exit finally.)

Jane. Good-morning, Mr Bootle!

Bootle. I beg—I thought—Why, of course! It's Miss—er-h'm, yes—How do you do? Did you get back safely last night?

Jane. Yes, thank you, (Coyly.) I got your letter.

Bootle. My letter? (Sees his letter on the table. Furiously.) You opened my letter!

Jane (mistaking his fury for passion). Yes—James. And (looking down on the ground) the answer is "Yes."

Bootle (realizing the situation). By George!

(Aside.) I have proposed to the wrong lady! Tchck!

Jane. You may kiss me, James.

Bootle. Have you a sister?

Jane (missing the connection). Yes, I have a younger sister, Alice. (Coldly.) But I hardly see—

Bootle (beginning to understand how he made the mistake). A younger sister! Then you are Miss Prendergast? And my letter—Ah!

Enter Alice.

Alice. You are wanted, Jane, a moment.

Jane. Will you excuse me, Mr Bootle? [Exit.

Bootle (to Alice, as she follows her sister out). Don't go!

Alice (wanly—if she knows how). Am I to stay and congratulate you?

Bootle. Alice! (They approach the footlights, while Jane, having finished her business, comes in unobserved and watches from the back.) It is all a mistake! I didn't know your Christian name—I didn't know you had a sister. The letter I addressed to Miss Prendergast I meant for Miss Alice Prendergast.

Alice. James! My love! But what can we do?

Bootle (gloomily). Nothing. As a man of honour I cannot withdraw. So two lives are ruined!

Alice. You are right, James. Jane must never know. Good-bye!

[They give each other a farewell embrace.

Jane (aside). They love. (Fiercely.) But he is mine; I will hold him to his promise! (Picking up a photograph of Alice as a small child from an occasional table.) Little Alice! And I promised to take care of her—to protect her from the cruel world Baby Alice! (She puts her handkerchief to her eyes.) No! I will not spoil two lives! (Aloud.) Why "Good-bye," Alice?

[Bootle and Alice, who have been embracing all this time—unless they can think of something else to do—break away in surprise.

Alice. Jane—we—I—

Jane (calmly). Dear Alice! I understand perfectly. Mr Bootle said in his letter to you that he was coming for his answer, and I see what answer you have given him. (To Bootle.) You remember I told you it would be "Yes." I know my little sister, you see.

Bootle (tactlessly). But—you told me I could kiss you!

Jane (smiling). And I tell you again now. I believe it is usual for men to kiss their sisters-in-law? (She offers her cheek. Bootle, whose day it is, salutes her respectfully.) And now (gaily) perhaps I had better leave you young people alone!

[Exit, with a backward look at the audience expressive of the fact that she has been wearing the mask.

Bootle. Alice, then you are mine, after all.

Alice. James! (They k—No, perhaps better not. There has been quite enough for one evening.) And to think that she knew all the time! Now I am quite, quite happy. And James—you WILL remember in future that I am Miss ALICE Prendergast?

Bootle (gaily). My dear, I shall only be able to remember that you are The Future Mrs Bootle!

CURTAIN.

"AT DEAD OF NIGHT"

The stage is in semi-darkness as Dick Trayle throws open the window from outside, puts his knee on the sill, and falls carefully into the drawing-room of Beeste Hall. He is dressed in a knickerbocker suit with arrows on it (such as can always be borrowed from a friend), and, to judge from the noises which he emits, is not in the best of training. The lights go on suddenly; and, he should seize this moment to stagger to the door and turn on the switch. This done, he sinks into the nearest chair and closes his eyes.

If he has been dancing very late the night before he may drop into a peaceful sleep; in which case the play ends here. Otherwise, no sooner are his eyes closed than he opens them with a sudden start and looks round in terror.

Dick (striking the keynote at once). No, no! Let me out—I am innocent! (He gives a gasp of relief as he realizes the situation.) Free! It is true, then! I have escaped! I dreamed that I was back in prison again! (He shudders and helps himself to a large whisky-and-soda, which he swallows at a gulp.) That's better! Now I feel a new man—the man I was three years ago. Three years! It has been a lifetime! (Pathetically to the audience.) Where is Millicent now?

[He falls into a reverie, from which he is suddenly wakened by a noise outside. He starts, and then creeps rapidly to the switch, arriving there at the moment when the lights go out. Thence he goes swiftly behind the window curtain. The lights go up again as Jasper Beeste comes in with a revolver in one hand and a bull's-eye lantern of apparently enormous candle-power in the other.

Jasper (in immaculate evening dress). I thought I heard a noise, so I slipped on some old things hurriedly and came down. (Fingering his perfectly-tied tie.) But there seems to be nobody here. (Turns round suddenly to the window.) Ha, who's there? Hands up, blow you—(He ought to swear rather badly here, really)—hands up, or I fire!

[The stage is suddenly plunged into darkness, there is the noise of a struggle, and the lights go on to reveal Jasper by the door covering Dick with his revolver.

Jasper. Let's have a little light on you. (Brutally.) Now then, my man, what have you got to say for yourself? Ha! An escaped convict, eh?

Dick (to himself in amazement). Jasper Beeste!

Jasper. So you know my name?

Dick (in the tones of a man whose whole life has been blighted by the machinations of a false friend). Yes, Jasper Beeste, I know your name. For two years I have said it to myself every night, when I prayed Heaven that I should meet you again.

Jasper. Again? (Uneasily.) We have met before?

Dick (slowly). We have met before, Jasper Beeste. Since then I have lived a lifetime of misery. You may well fail to recognize me.

Enter Millicent Wilsdon—in a dressing-gown, with her hair over her shoulders, if the county will stand it.

Millicent (to Jasper). I couldn't sleep—I heard a noise—I—(suddenly seeing the other) Dick! (She trembles.)

Dick. Millicent! (He trembles too.)

Jasper. Trayle! (So does he.)

Dick (bitterly). You shrink from me, Millicent. (With strong common sense.) What is an escaped convict to the beautiful Miss Wilsdon?

Millicent. Dick—I—you—when you were sentenced—

Dick. When I was sentenced—the evidence was black against me, I admit—I wrote and released you from your engagement. You are married now?

Millicent (throwing herself on the sofa). Oh, Dick!

Jasper (recovering himself). Enough of this. Miss Wilsdon is going to marry me to-morrow.

Dick. To marry YOU! (He strides over to the sofa and pulls Millicent to her feet.) Millicent, look me in the eyes! Do you love him? (She turns away.) Say "Yes," and I will go back quietly to my prison. (She raises her eyes to his.) Ha! I thought so! You don't love him! Now then I can speak.

> Jasper (advancing threateningly). Yes, to your friends the warders. Millicent, ring the bell.

Dick (wresting the revolver from his grasp). Ha, would you? Now stand over there and listen to me. (He arranges his audience, Millicent on a sofa on the right, Jasper, biting his finger-nails, on the left.) Three years ago

Lady Wilsdon's diamond necklace was stolen. My flat was searched and the necklace was found in my hatbox. Although I protested my innocence, I was tried, found guilty, and sentenced to ten years' penal servitude, followed by fifteen years' police supervision.

Millicent (raising herself on the sofa). Dick, you were innocent—I know it. (She falls back again.)

Dick. I was. But how could I prove it? I went to prison. For a year black despair gnawed at my heart. And then something happened. The prisoner in the cell next to mine tried to communicate with me by means of taps. We soon arranged a system and held conversations together. One day he told me of a robbery in which he and another man had been engaged—the robbery of a diamond necklace.

Jasper (jauntily). Well?

Dick (sternly). A diamond necklace, Jasper Beeste, which the other man hid in the hatbox of another man in order that he might woo the other man's fiancee! (Millicent shrieks.)

Jasper (blusteringly). Bah!

Dick (quietly). The man in the cell next to mine wants to meet this gentleman again. It seems that he has some old scores to pay off.

Jasper (sneeringly). And where is he?

Dick. Ah, where is he? (He goes to the window and gives a low whistle. A Stranger in knickerbockers jumps in and advances with a crab-like movement.) Good! here you are. Allow me to present you to Mr Jasper Beeste.

Jasper (in horror). Two-toed Thomas! I am undone!

Two-toed Thomas (after a series of unintelligible snarls). Say the word, guv'nor, and I'll kill him. (He prowls round Jasper thoughtfully.)

Dick (sternly). Stand back! Now, Jasper Beeste, what have you to say?

Jasper (hysterically). I confess. I will sign anything. I will go to prison. Only keep that man off me.

Dick (going up to a bureau and writing aloud at incredible speed). "I, Jasper Beeste, of Beeste Hall, do hereby declare that I stole Lady Wilsdon's diamond necklace and hid it in the hatbox of Richard Trayle; and I further declare that the said Richard Trayle is innocent of any complicity in the affair." (Advancing with the paper and a fountain pen.) Sign, please.

[Jasper signs. At this moment two warders burst into the room.

First Warder. There they are!

[He seizes Dick. Two-toed Thomas leaps from the window, pursued by the second Warder. Millicent picks up the confession and advances dramatically.

Millicent. Do not touch that man! Read this!

[She hands him the confession with an air of superb pride.

First Warder (reading). Jasper Beeste! (Slipping a pair of handcuffs on Jasper.) You come along with me, my man. We've had our suspicions of you for some time. (To Millicent, with a nod at Dick.) You'll look after that gentleman, miss?

Millicent. Of course! Why, he's engaged to me. Aren't you, Dick?

Dick. This time, Millicent, for ever!

CURTAIN.

"THE LOST HEIRESS"

The scene is laid outside a village inn in that county of curious dialects, Loamshire. The inn is easily indicated by a round table bearing two mugs of liquid, while a fallen log emphasizes the rural nature of the scene. Gaffer Jarge and Gaffer Willyum are seated at the table, surrounded by a fringe of whisker, Jarge being slightly more of a gaffer than Willyum.

Jarge (who missed his dinner through nervousness and has been ordered to sustain himself with soup—as he puts down the steaming mug). Eh, bor, but this be rare beer. So it be.

Willyum (who had too much dinner and is now draining his sanatogen). You be right, Gaffer Jarge. Her be main rare beer. (He feels up his sleeve, but thinking better of it wipes his mouth with the back of his hand.) Main rare beer, zo her be. (Gagging.) Zure-lie.

Jarge. Did I ever tell 'ee, bor, about t' new squoire o' these parts—him wot cum hum yesterday from furren lands? Gaffer Henry wor a-telling me.

Willyum (privately bored). Thee didst tell 'un, lad, sartain sure thee didst. And Gaffer Henry, he didst tell 'un too. But tell 'un again. It du me good to hear 'un, zo it du. Zure-lie.

Jarge. A rackun it be a main queer tale, queerer nor any them writing chaps tell about. It wor like this. (Dropping into English, in his hurry to get his long speech over before he forgets it.) The old Squire had a daughter who disappeared when she was three weeks old, eighteen years ago. It was always thought she was stolen by somebody, and the Squire would have it that she was still alive. When he died a year ago he left the estate and all his money to a distant cousin in Australia, with the condition that if he did not discover the missing baby within twelve months everything was to go to the hospitals. (Remembering his smock and whiskers with a start.) And here du be the last day, zo it be, and t' Squoire's daughter, her ain't found.

Willyum (puffing at a new and empty clay pipe). Zure-lie. (Jarge, a trifle jealous of Willyum's gag, pulls out a similar pipe, but smokes it with the bowl upside down to show his independence.) T' Squire's darter (Jarge frowns), her bain't (Jarge wishes he had thought of "bain't")—her bain't found. (There is a dramatic pause, only broken by the prompter.) Her ud be little Rachel's age now, bor?

> Jarge (reflectively). Ay, ay. A main queer lass little Rachel du be. Her bain't like one of us.

Willyum. Her do be that fond of zoap and water. (Laughter.)

Jarge (leaving nothing to chance). Happen she might be a real grand lady by birth, bor.

Enter Rachel, beautifully dressed in the sort of costume in which one would go to a fancy-dress ball as a village maiden.

Rachel (in the most expensive accent). Now Uncle George (shaking a finger at him), didn't you promise me you'd go straight home? It would serve you right if I never tied your tie for you again. (She smiles brightly at him.)

Jarge (slapping his thigh in ecstasy). Eh, lass, yer du keep us old 'uns in order. (He bursts into a falsetto chuckle, loses the note, blushes and buries his head in his mug.)

Willyum (rising). Us best be gettin' down along, Jarge, a rackun.

> Jarge. Ay, bor, time us chaps was moving. Don't 'e be long, lass.
> [Exeunt, limping heavily.

Rachel (sitting down on the log). Dear old men! How I love them all in this village! I have known it all my life. How strange it is that I have never had a father or mother. Sometimes I seem to remember a life different to this—a life in fine houses and spacious parks, among beautifully dressed people (which is surprising, seeing that she was only three weeks old at the time; but the audience must be given a hint of the plot), and then it all fades away again. (She looks fixedly into space.)

Enter Hugh Fitzhugh, Squire.

Fitzhugh (standing behind Rachel, but missing her somehow). Did ever man come into stranger inheritance? A wanderer in Central Australia, I hear unexpectedly of my cousin's death through an advertisement in an old copy of a Sunday newspaper. I hasten home—too late to soothe his dying hours; too late indeed to enjoy my good fortune for more than one short day. To-morrow I must give up all to the hospitals, unless by some stroke of Fate this missing girl turns up. (Impatiently.) Pshaw! She is dead. (Suddenly he notices Rachel.) By heaven, a pretty girl in this out-of-the-way village! (He walks round her.) Gad, she is lovely! Hugh, my boy, you are in luck. (He takes off his hat.) Good-evening, my dear!

Rachel (with a start). Good-evening.

Fitzhugh (aside). She is adorable. She can be no common village wench. (Aloud.) Do you live here, my girl?

Rachel. Yes, I have always lived here. (Aside.) How handsome he is. Down, fluttering heart.

Fitzhugh (sitting on the log beside her). And who is the lucky village lad who is privileged to woo such beauty?

Rachel. I have no lover, sir.

Fitzhugh (taking her hand). Can Hodge be so blind?

Rachel (innocently). Are you making love to me?

Fitzhugh. Upon my word I—(He gets up from the log, which is not really comfortable.) What is your name?

Rachel. Rachel. (She rises.)

Fitzhugh. It is the most beautiful name in the world. Rachel, will you be my wife?

Rachel. But we have known each other such a short time!

Fitzhugh (lying bravely). We have known each other for ever.

Rachel. And you are a rich gentleman, while I—

Fitzhugh. A gentleman, I hope, but rich—no. To-morrow I shall be a beggar. No, not a beggar, if I have your love, Rachel.

Rachel (making a lucky shot at his name). Hugh! (They embrace.)

Fitzhugh. Let us plight our troth here. See, I give you my ring!

Rachel. And I give you mine.

[She takes one from the end of a chain which is round her neck, and puts it on his finger. Fitzhugh looks at it and staggers back.

Fitzhugh. Heavens! They are the same ring! (In great excitement.) Child, child, who are you? How came you by the crest of the Fitzhughs?

Rachel. Ah, who am I? I never had any parents. When they found me they found that ring on me, and I have kept it ever since!

Fitzhugh. Let me look at you! It must be! The Squire's missing daughter!

[Gaffers Jarge and Willyum, having entered unobserved at the back some time ago, have been putting in a lot of heavy byplay until wanted.

Jarge (at last). Lor' bless 'ee, Willyum, if it bain't Squire a-kissin' our Rachel!

Willyum. Zo it du be. Here du be goings-on! What will t' passon say?

Jarge (struck with an idea). Zay, bor, don't 'ee zee a zort o' loikeness atween t' maid and t' Squire?

Willyum. Jarge, if you bain't right, lad. Happen she do have t' same nose!

[Hearing something, Fitzhugh and Rachel turn round.

Fitzhugh. Ah, my men! I'm your new Squire. Do you know who this is?

Willyum. Why, her du be our Rachel.

Fitzhugh. On the contrary, allow me to introduce you to Miss Fitzhugh, daughter of the late Squire!

Jarge. Well, this du be a day! To think of our Rachel now!

Fitzhugh. MY Rachel now.

Rachel (who, it is to be hoped, has been amusing herself somehow since her last speech). Your Rachel always!

CURTAIN.

"WILLIAM SMITH, EDITOR"

The scene is the Editor's room in the office of The Lark. Two walls of the room are completely hidden from floor to ceiling by magnificently-bound books: the third wall at the back is hidden by boxes of immensely expensive cigars. The windows, of course, are in the fourth wall, which, however, need not be described, as it is never quite practicable on the stage. The floor of this apartment is chastely covered with rugs shot by the Editor in his travels, or in the Tottenham Court Road; or, in some cases, presented by admiring readers from abroad. The furniture is both elegant and commodious.

William Smith, Editor, comes in. He is superbly dressed in a fur coat and an expensive cigar. There is a blue pencil behind his ear, and a sheaf of what we call in the profession "typewritten manuscripts" under his arm. He sits down at his desk and pulls the telephone towards him.

Smith (at the telephone). Hallo, is that you, Jones? ... Yes, it's me. Just come up a moment. (Puts down telephone and begins to open his letters.)

Enter Jones, his favourite sub-editor. He is dressed quite commonly, and is covered with ink. He salutes respectfully as he comes into the room.

Jones. Good-afternoon, chief.

Smith. Good-afternoon. Have a cigar?

Jones. Thank you, chief.

Smith. Have you anything to tell me?

Jones. The circulation is still going up, chief. It was three million and eight last week.

Smith (testily). How often have I told you not to call me "chief," except when there are ladies present? Why can't you do what you're told?

Jones. Sorry, sir, but the fact is there ARE ladies present.

Smith (fingering his moustache). Show them up. Who are they?

Jones. There is only one. She says she's the lady who has been writing our anonymous "Secrets of the Boudoir" series which has made such a sensation.

Smith (in amazement). I thought you told me YOU wrote these.

Jones (simply). I did.

Smith. Then why—

Jones. I mean I did tell you. The truth is, they came in anonymously, and I thought they were more likely to be accepted if I said I had written them. (With great emotion.) Forgive me, chief, but it was for the paper's sake. (In matter-of-fact tones.) There were one or two peculiarities of style I had to alter. She had a way of—

Smith (sternly). How many cheques for them have you accepted for the paper's sake?

Jones. Eight. For a thousand pounds each.

Smith (with tears in his eyes). If your mother were to hear of this—

Jones (sadly). Ah, chief, I have never had a mother.

Smith (slightly put out, but recovering himself quickly). What would your father say, if—

Jones. Alas, I have no relations. I was a foundling.

Smith (nettled). In that case, I shall certainly tell the master of your workhouse. To think that there should be a thief in this office!

Jones (with great pathos). Chief, chief, I am not so vile as that. I have carefully kept all the cheques in an old stocking, and—

Smith (in surprise). Do you wear stockings?

Jones. When I bicycle. And as soon as the contributor comes forward—

Smith (stretching out his hand and grasping that of Jones). My dear boy, forgive me. You have been hasty, perhaps, but zealous. In any case, your honesty is above suspicion. Leave me now. I have much to think of. (Rests his head on his hands. Then, dreamily.) YOU have never seen your father; for thirty years *I* have not seen my wife. ... Ah, Arabella!

Jones. Yes, sir. (Rings bell.)

Smith. She WOULD split her infinitives. ... We quarrelled. ... She left me. ... I have never seen her again.

Jones (excitedly). Did you say she split her infinitives?

Smith. Yes. That was what led to our separation. Why?

Jones. Nothing, only—it's very odd. I wonder—

Enter Boy.

Boy. Did you ring, sir?

Smith. No. But you can show the lady up. (Exit Boy.) You'd better clear out, Jones. I'll explain to her about the money.

Jones. Right you are, sir.

[Exit.

[Smith leans back in his chair and stares in front of him.

Smith (to himself). Arabella!

Enter Boy, followed by a stylishly-dressed lady of middle age.

Boy. Mrs Robinson.

[Exit.

[Mrs Robinson stops short in the middle of the room and stares at the Editor; then staggers and drops on to the sofa.

Smith (in wonder). Arabella!

Mrs Robinson. William!

[They fall into each other's arms.

Arabella. I had begun to almost despair. (Smith winces.) "Almost to despair," I mean, darling.

Smith (with a great effort). No, no, dear. You were right.

Arabella. How sweet of you to think so, William.

Smith. Yes, yes, it's the least I can say. ... I have been very lonely without you, dear. ... And now, what shall we do? Shall we get married again quietly?

Arabella. Wouldn't that be bigamy?

Smith. I think not, but I will ask the printer's reader. He knows everything. You see, there will be such a lot to explain otherwise.

Arabella. Dear, can you afford to marry?

Smith. Well, my salary as editor is only twenty thousand a year, but I do a little reviewing for other papers.

Arabella. And I have—nothing. How can I come to you without even a trousseau?

Smith. Yes, that's true. ... (Suddenly.) By Jove, though, you have got something! You have eight thousand pounds! We owe you that for your articles. (With a return to his professional manner.) Did I tell you how greatly we all appreciated them? (Goes to telephone.) Is that you, Jones? Just come here a moment. (To Arabella.) Jones is my sub-editor; he is keeping your money for you.

Enter Jones.

Jones (producing an old stocking). I've just been round to my rooms to get that money—(sees Arabella)—oh, I beg your pardon.

Smith (waving an introduction). Mrs Smith—my wife. This is our sub-editor, dear—Mr Jones. (Arabella puts her hand to her heart and seems about to faint.) Why, what's the matter?

Arabella (hoarsely). Where did you get that stocking?

Smith (pleasantly). It's one he wears when he goes bicycling.

Jones. No; I misled you this afternoon, chief. This stocking was all the luggage I had when I first entered the Leamington workhouse.

Arabella (throwing herself into his arms). My son! This is your father! William—our boy!

Smith (shaking hands with Jones). How are you. I say, Arabella, then that was one of MY stockings?

Arabella (to her boy). When I saw you on the stairs you seemed to dimly remind me—

Jones. To remind you dimly, mother.

Smith. No, my boy. In future, nothing but split infinitives will appear in our paper. Please remember that.

Jones (with emotion). I will endeavour to always remember it, dad.

CURTAIN.

A CHAPTER OF ACCIDENTS

John walked eight miles over the cliffs to the nearest town in order to buy tobacco. He came back to the farmhouse with no tobacco and the news that he had met some friends in the town who had invited us to dinner and Bridge the next evening.

"But that's no reason why you should have forgotten the tobacco," I said.

"One can't remember everything. I accepted for both of us. We needn't dress. Put on that nice blue flannel suit of yours—"

"And that nice pair of climbing boots with the nails—"

"Is that all you've got?"

"All I'm going to walk eight miles in on a muddy path."

"Then we shall have to take a bag with us. And we can put in pyjamas and stay the night at an hotel; it will save us walking back in the dark. We don't want to lose you over the cliff."

I took out a cigar.

"This is the last," I said. "If, instead of wandering about and collecting invitations, you had only remembered—Shall we cut it up or smoke half each?"

"Call," said John, bringing out a penny. "Heads it is. You begin."

I struck a match and began.

Next day, after lunch, John brought out his little brown bag.

"It won't be very heavy," he said, "and we can carry it in turns. An hour each."

"I don't think that's quite fair," I said. "After all, it's YOUR bag. If you take it for an hour and a half, I don't mind taking the other half."

"Your shoes are heavier than mine, anyhow."

"My pyjamas weigh less. Such a light blue as they are."

"Ah, but my tooth-brush has lost seven bristles. That makes a difference."

"What I say is, let every man carry his own bag. This is a rotten business, John. I don't wish to be anything but polite, but for a silly ass commend me to the owner of that brown thing."

John took no notice and went on packing.

"I shall buy a collar in the town," he said.

"Better let me do it for you. You would only go getting an invitation to a garden-party from the haberdasher. And that would mean another eight miles with a portmanteau."

"There we are," said John, as he closed the bag, "quite small and light. Now, who'll take the first hour?"

"We'd better toss, if you're quite sure you won't carry it all the way. Tails. Just my luck."

John looked out of the window and then at his watch.

"They say two to three is the hottest hour of the day," he said. "It will be cooler later on. I shall put you in."

I led the way up the cliffs with that wretched bag. I insisted upon that condition anyhow — that the man with the bag should lead the way. I wasn't going to have John dashing off at six miles an hour, and leaving himself only two miles at the end.

"But you can come and talk to me," I said to him after ten minutes of it. "I only meant that I was going to set the pace."

"No, no, I like watching you. You do it so gracefully. This is my man," he explained to some children who were blackberrying. "He is just carrying my bag over the cliffs for me. No, he is not very strong."

"You wait," I growled.

John laughed. "Fifty minutes more," he said. And then after a little silence, "I think the bag-carrying profession is overrated. What made you take it up, my lad? The drink? Ah, just so. Dear, dear, what a lesson to all of us."

"There's a good time coming," I murmured to myself, and changed hands for the eighth time.

"I don't care what people say," said John, argumentatively; "brown and blue DO go together. If you wouldn't mind —"

For the tenth time I rammed the sharp corner of the bag into the back of my knee.

"There, that's what I mean. You see it perfectly like that—the brown against the blue of the flannel. Thank you very much."

I stumbled up a steep little bit of slippery grass, and told myself that in three-quarters of an hour I would get some of my own back again. He little knew how heavy that bag could become.

"They say," said John to the heavens, "that if you have weights in your hands you can jump these little eminences much more easily. I suppose one hand alone doesn't do. What a pity he didn't tell me before—I would have lent him another bag with pleasure."

"Nobody likes blackberries more than I do," said John. "But even I would hesitate to come out here on a hot afternoon and fill a great brown bag with blackberries, and then carry them eight miles home. Besides, it looks rather greedy…. I beg your pardon, my lad, I didn't understand. You are taking them home to your aged mother? Of course, of course. Very commendable. If I had a penny, I would lend it to you. No, I only have a sixpence on me, and I have to give that to the little fellow who is carrying my bag over the cliffs for me…. Yes, I picked him up about a couple of miles back. He has mud all up his trousers, I know."

"Half an hour more," I told myself, and went on doggedly, my right shoulder on fire.

"Dear, dear," he said solicitously, "how lopsided the youth of to-day is getting. Too much lawn-tennis, I suppose. How much better the simply healthy exercises of our forefathers; the weightlifting after lunch, the—"

He was silent for ten minutes, and then broke out rapturously once more.

"What a heavenly day! I AM glad we didn't bring a bag—it would have spoilt it altogether. We can easily borrow some slippers, and it will be jolly walking back by moonlight. Now, if you had had your way—"

"One minute more," I said joyfully; "and oh, my boy, how glad I am we brought a bag. What a splendid idea of yours! By the way, you haven't said much lately. A little tired by the walk?"

"I make it TWO minutes," said John.

"Half a minute now…. There! And may I never carry the confounded thing another yard."

I threw the bag down and fell upon the grass. The bag rolled a yard or two away. Then it rolled another yard, slipped over the edge, and started bouncing down the cliff. Finally it leapt away from the earth altogether, and dropped two hundred feet into the sea.

"MY bag," said John stupidly.

And that did for me altogether.

"I don't care a hang about your bag," I cried. "And I don't care a hang if I've lost my pyjamas and my best shoes and my only razor. And I've been through an hour's torture for nothing, and I don't mind that. But oh!—to think that you aren't going to have YOUR hour—"

"By Jove, neither I am," said John, and he sat down and roared with laughter.

A CROWN OF SORROWS

There is something on my mind, of which I must relieve myself. If I am ever to face the world again with a smile I must share my trouble with others. I cannot bear my burden alone.

Friends, I have lost my hat. Will the gentleman who took it by mistake, and forgot to leave his own in its place, kindly return my hat to me at once?

I am very miserable without my hat. It was one of those nice soft ones with a dent down the middle to collect the rain; one of those soft hats which wrap themselves so lovingly round the cranium that they ultimately absorb the personality of the wearer underneath, responding to his every emotion. When people said nice things about me my hat would swell in sympathy; when they said nasty things, or when I had had my hair cut, it would adapt itself automatically to my lesser requirements. In a word, it fitted—and that is more than can be said for your hard unyielding bowler.

My hat and I dropped into a hall of music one night last week. I placed it under the seat, put a coat on it to keep it warm, and settled down to enjoy myself. My hat could see nothing, but it knew that it would hear all about the entertainment on the way home. When the last moving picture had moved away, my hat and I prepared to depart together. I drew out the coat and felt around for my—Where on earth …

I was calm at first.

"Excuse me," I said politely to the man next to me, "but have you got two hats?"

"Several," he replied, mistaking my meaning.

I dived under the seat again, and came up with some more dust.

"Someone," I said to a programme girl, "has taken my hat."

"Have you looked under the seat for it?" she asked.

It was such a sound suggestion that I went under the seat for the third time.

"It may have been kicked further along," suggested another attendant. She walked up and down the row looking for it, and, in case somebody had kicked it into the row above, walked up and down that one too; and, in case somebody had found touch with it on the other side of the house, many other girls spread themselves in pursuit; and soon we had the whole pack hunting for it.

Then the fireman came up, suspecting the worst. I told him it was even worse than that—my hat had been stolen.

He had a flash of inspiration.

"Are you sure you brought it with you?" he asked.

The programme girls seemed to think that it would solve the whole mystery if I hadn't brought it with me.

"Are you sure you are the fireman?" I said coldly.

He thought for a moment, and then unburdened himself of another idea.

"Perhaps it's just been kicked under the seat," he said.

I left him under the seat and went downstairs with a heavy heart. At the door I said to the hall porter, "Have you seen anybody going out with two hats by mistake?"

"What's the matter?" he said. "Lost your hat?"

"It has been stolen."

"Have you looked under the seats? It may have been kicked along a bit."

"Perhaps I'd better see the manager," I said. "Is it any good looking under the seats for HIM?"

"I expect it's just been kicked along a bit," the hall porter repeated confidently. "I'll come up with you and look for it."

"If there's any more talk about being kicked along a bit," I said bitterly, "somebody WILL be. I want the manager."

I was led to the manager's room, and there I explained the matter to him. He was very pleasant about it.

"I expect you haven't looked for it properly," he said, with a charming smile. "Just take this gentleman up," he added to the hall porter, "and find his hat for him. It has probably been kicked under one of the other seats."

We were smiled irresistibly out, and I was dragged up to the grand circle again. The seats by this time were laid out in white draperies; the house looked very desolate; I knew that my poor hat was dead. With an air of cheery confidence the hall porter turned into the first row of seats....

"It may have been kicked on to the stage," I said, as he began to slow down. "It may have jumped into one of the boxes. It may have turned into a rabbit. You know, I expect you aren't looking for it properly."

The manager was extremely sympathetic when we came back to him. He said, "Oh, I'm sorry." Just like that—"Oh, I'm sorry."

"My hat," I said firmly, "has been stolen."

"I'm sorry," he repeated with a bored smile, and turned to look at himself in the glass.

Then I became angry with him and his attendants and his whole blessed theatre.

"My hat," I said bitingly, "has been stolen from me—while I slept."

You must have seen me wearing it in the dear old days. Greeny brown it was in colour; but it wasn't the colour that drew your eyes to it—no, nor yet the shape, nor the angle at which it sat. It was just the essential rightness of it. If you have ever seen a hat which you felt instinctively was a clever hat, an alive hat, a profound hat, then that was my hat—and that was myself underneath it.

NAPOLEON AT WORK

When I am in any doubt or difficulty I say to myself, "What would Napoleon have done?" The answer generally comes at once: "He would have borrowed from Henry," or "He would have said his aunt was ill" — the one obviously right and proper thing. Then I weigh in and do it.

"What station is this?" said Beatrice, as the train began to slow up. "Baby and I want to get home."

"Whitecroft, I expect," said John, who was reading the paper. "Only four more."

"It's grown since we were here last," I observed. "Getting quite a big place."

"Good; then we're at Hillstead. Only three more stations."

I looked out of the window, and had a sudden suspicion.

"Where have I heard the name Byres before?" I murmured thoughtfully.

"You haven't," said John. "Nobody has."

"Say 'Byres,' baby," urged Beatrice happily.

"You're quite sure that there isn't anything advertised called 'Byres'? You're sure you can't drink Byres or rub yourself down with Byres?"

"Quite."

"Well, then, we must be AT Byres."

There was a shriek from Beatrice, as she rushed to the window.

"We're in the wrong train — Quick! Get the bags! — Have you got the rug? — Where's the umbrella? — Open the window, stupid!"

I got up and moved her from the door.

"Leave this to me," I said calmly. "Porter! — PORTER!! — PORTER!!! — Oh, guard, what station's this?"

"Byres, sir."

"Byres?"

"Yes, sir." He blew his whistle and the train went on again.

"At any rate we know now that it WAS Byres," I remarked, when the silence began to get oppressive.

"It's all very well for you," Beatrice burst out indignantly, "but you don't think about Baby. We don't know a bit where we are—"

"That's the one thing we do know," I said. "We're at this little Byres place."

"It was the porter's fault at Liverpool Street," said John consolingly. "He told us it was a through carriage."

"I don't care whose fault it was; I'm only thinking of Baby."

"What time do babies go to bed as a rule?" I asked.

"This one goes at six."

"Well, then, she's got another hour. Now, what would Napoleon have done?"

"Napoleon," said John, after careful thought, "would have turned all your clothes out of your bag, would have put the baby in it diagonally, and have bored holes in the top for ventilation. That's as good as going to bed—you avoid the worst of the evening mists. And people would only think you kept caterpillars."

Beatrice looked at him coldly.

"That's a way to talk of your daughter," she said in scorn.

"Don't kill him," I begged, "We may want him. Now I've got another idea. If you look out of the window you observe that we are on a SINGLE line."

"Well, I envy it. And, however single it is, we're going away from home in it."

"True. But the point is that no train can come back on it until we've stopped going forward. So, you see, there's no object in getting out of this train until it has finished for the day. Probably it will go back itself before long, out of sheer boredom. And it's much better waiting here than on a draughty Byres platform."

Beatrice, quite seeing the point, changed the subject.

"There's my trunk will go on to Brookfield, and the wagonette will meet the train, and as we aren't there it will go away without the trunk, and all baby's things are in it."

"She's not complaining," I said. "She's just mentioning it."

"Look here," said John reproachfully, "we're doing all we can. We're both thinking like anything." He picked up his paper again.

I was beginning to get annoyed. It was, of course, no good to get as anxious and excited as Beatrice; that wouldn't help matters at all. On the other hand, the entire indifference of John and the baby was equally out of place. It seemed to me that there was a middle and Napoleonic path in between these two extremes which only I was following. To be convinced that one is the only person doing the right thing is always annoying.

"I've just made another discovery," I said in a hurt voice. "There's a map over John's head, if he'd only had the sense to look there before. There we are," and I pointed with my stick; "there's Byres. The line goes round and round and eventually goes through Dearmer. We get out at Dearmer, and we're only three miles from Brookfield."

"What they call a loop line," assisted John, "because it's in the shape of a loop."

"It's not so bad as it might be," admitted Beatrice grudgingly, after studying the map, "but it's five miles home from Dearmer; and what about my trunk?"

I sighed and pulled out a pencil.

"It's very simple. We write a telegram:—

'Stationmaster, Brookfield. Send wagonette and trunk to wait for us at Dearmer Station.'"

"Love to mother and the children," added John.

Our train stopped again. I summoned a porter and gave him the telegram.

"It's so absurdly simple," I repeated, as the train went on. "Just a little presence of mind; that's all."

We got out at Dearmer and gave up our tickets to the porter-station-master-signalman.

"What's this?" he said. "These are no good to me."

"Well, they're no good to us. We've finished with them."

We sat in the waiting-room with him for half an hour and explained the situation. We said that, highly as we thought of Dearmer, we had not wantonly tried to defraud the Company in order to get a sight of the place;

and that, so far from owing him three shillings apiece, we were prepared to take a sovereign to say nothing more about it.... And still the wagonette didn't come.

"Is there a post-office here?" I asked the man. "Or a horse?"

"There might be a horse at the 'Lion.' There's no post-office."

"Well, I suppose I could wire to Brookfield Station from here?"

"Not to Brookfield."

"But supposing you want to tell the station-master there that the train's off the line, or that you've won the first prize at the Flower Show in the vegetable class, how would you do it?"

"Brookfield's not on this line. That's why you've got to pay three shill—"

"Yes, yes. You said all that. Then I shall go and explore the village."

I explored, as Napoleon would have done, and I came back with a plan.

"There is no horse," I said to my eager audience; "but I have found a bicycle. The landlady of the 'Lion' will be delighted to look after Beatrice and the baby, and will give her tea; John will stay here with the bags in case the wagonette turns up, and I will ride to Brookfield and summon help."

"That's all right," said John, "only I would suggest that *I* go to the 'Lion' and have tea, and Beatrice and the child—"

We left him in disgust at his selfishness. I established the ladies at the inn, mounted the bicycle, and rode off. It was a windy day, and I had a long coat and a bowler hat. After an extremely unpleasant two miles something drove past me. I lifted up my head and looked round. It was the wagonette.

I rode back behind it in triumph. When it turned up the road to the station, I hurried straight on to the "Lion" to prepare Beatrice. I knocked, and peered into rooms, and knocked again, and at last the landlady came.

"Er—is the lady—"

"Oh, she's gone, sir, a long time ago. A gentleman she knew drove past, and she asked him to give her a lift home in his trap. She was going to tell the other gentleman, and he'd wait for you."

"Oh yes. That's all right."

I returned my bicycle to its owner, distributed coppers to his children, and went up to the station. The porter came out to meet me. He seemed surprised.

"The gentleman thought you wouldn't be coming back, sir, as you didn't come with the wagonette."

"I just went up to the 'Lion' — "

"Yessir. Well, he drove off quarter of an hour ago; said it was no good waiting for you, as you'd ride straight 'ome when you found at Brookfield that the wagonette 'ad come."

And now I ask you—What would Napoleon have said?

THE PORTUGUESE CIGAR

EVERYTHING promised well for my week-end with Charles. The weather was warm and sunny, I was bringing my golf clubs down with me, and I had just discovered (and meant to put into practice) an entirely new stance which made it impossible to miss the object ball. It was this that I was explaining to Charles and his wife at dinner on Friday, when the interruption occurred.

"By the way," said Charles, as I took out a cigarette, "I've got a cigar for you. Don't smoke that thing."

"You haven't let him go in for cigars?" I said reproachfully to Mrs Charles. I can be very firm about other people's extravagances.

"This is one I picked up in Portugal," explained Charles. "You can get them absurdly cheap out there. Let's see, dear; where did I put it?"

"I saw it on your dressing-table last week," said his wife, getting up to leave us. He followed her out and went in search of it, while I waited with an interest which I made no effort to conceal. I had never heard before of a man going all the way to Portugal to buy one cigar for a friend.

"Here it is," said Charles, coming in again. He put down in front of me an ash-tray, the matches and a—and a—well, as I say, a cigar. I examined it slowly. Half of it looked very tired.

"Well," said Charles, "what do you think of it?"

"When you say you—er—PICKED IT UP in Portugal," I began carefully, "I suppose you don't mean—" I stopped and tried to bite the end off.

"Have a knife," said Charles.

I had another bite, and then I decided to be frank.

"WHY did you pick it up?" I asked.

"The fact was," said Charles, "I found myself one day in Lisbon without my pipe, and so I bought that thing; I never smoke them in the ordinary way."

"Did you smoke this?" I asked. It was obvious that SOMETHING had happened to it.

"No, you see, I found some cigarettes at the last moment, and so, knowing that you liked cigars, I thought I'd bring it home for you."

"It's very nice of you, Charles. Of course I can see that it has travelled. Well, we must do what we can with it."

I took the knife and started chipping away at the mahogany end. The other end—the brown-paper end, which had come ungummed—I intended to reserve for the match. When everything was ready I applied a light, leant back in my chair, and pulled.

"That's all right, isn't it?" said Charles. "And you'd be surprised if I told you what I paid for it."

"No, no, you mustn't think that," I protested. "Probably things are dearer in Portugal." I put it down by my plate for a moment's rest. "All I've got against it at present is that its pores don't act as freely as they should."

"I've got a cigar-cutter somewhere, if—"

"No, don't bother. I think I can do it with the nut-crackers. There's no doubt it was a good cigar once, but it hasn't wintered well."

I squeezed it as hard as I could, lit it again, pressed my feet against the table and pulled.

"Now it's going," said Charles.

"I'm afraid it keeps very reticent at my end. The follow-through is poor. Is your end alight still?"

"Burning beautifully."

"It's a pity that I should be missing all that. How would it be if we were to make a knitting-needle red-hot, and bore a tunnel from this end? We might establish a draught that way. Only there's always the danger, of course, of coming out at the side."

I took the cigar up and put it to my ear.

"I can't HEAR anything wrong," I said. "I expect what it really wants is massage."

Charles filled his pipe again and got up. "Let's go for a stroll," he said. "It's a beautiful night. Bring your cigar with you."

"It may prefer the open air," I said. "There's always that. You know we mustn't lose sight of the fact that the Portuguese climate is different from ours. The thing's pores may have acted more readily in the South. On the other hand, the unfastened end may have been more adhesive. I gather that though you have never actually met anybody who has smoked a cigar like this, yet you understand that the experiment is a practicable one. As far as you know, this had no brothers. No, no, Charles, I'm going on with it, but I should like to know all that you can tell me of its parentage. It had a Portuguese father and an American mother, I should say, and there has been a good deal of trouble in the family. One moment"—and as we went outside I stopped and cracked it in the door.

It was an inspiration. At the very next application of the match I found that I had established a connection with the lighted end. Not a long and steady connection, but one that came in gusts. After two gusts I decided that it was perhaps safer to blow from my end, and for a little while we had in this way as much smoke around us as the most fastidious cigar-smoker could want. Then I accidentally dropped it; something in the middle of it shifted, I suppose—and for the rest of my stay behind it only one end was at work.

"Well," said Charles, when we were back in the smoking-room, and I was giving the cigar a short breather, "it's not a bad one, is it?"

"I have enjoyed it," I said truthfully, for I like trying to get the mastery over a thing that defies me.

"You'll never guess what it cost," he chuckled.

"Tell me," I said. "I daren't guess."

"Well, in English money it works out at exactly three farthings."

I looked at him for a long time and then shook my head sadly.

"Charles, old friend," I said, "you've been done."

A COLD WORLD

Herbert is a man who knows all about railway tickets, and packing, and being in time for trains, and things like that. But I fancy I have taught him a lesson at last. He won't talk quite so much about tickets in future.

I was just thinking about getting up when he came into my room. He looked at me in horror.

"My dear fellow!" he said. "And you haven't even packed! You'll be late. Here, get up, and I'll pack for you while you dress."

"Do," I said briefly.

"First of all, what clothes are you going to travel in?"

There was no help for it. I sat up in bed and directed operations.

"Right," said Herbert. "Now, what about your return ticket? You mustn't forget that."

"You remind me of a little story," I said. "I'll tell it you while you pack—that will be nice for you. Once upon a time I lost my return ticket, and I had to pay two pounds for another. And a month afterwards I met a man—a man like you who knows all about tickets—and he said, 'You could have got the money back if you had applied at once.' So I said, 'Give me a cigarette now, and I'll transfer all my rights in the business to you.' And he gave me a cigarette; but unfortunately—"

"It was too late?"

"No. Unfortunately it wasn't. He got the two pounds. The most expensive cigarette I've ever smoked."

"Well, that just shows you," said Herbert. "Here's your ticket. Put it in your waistcoat pocket now."

"But I haven't got a waistcoat on, silly."

"Which one are you going to put on?"

"I don't know yet. This is a matter which requires thought. Give me time, give me air."

"Well, I shall put the ticket here on the dressing-table, and then you can't miss it." He looked at his watch. "And the trap starts in half an hour."

"Help!" I cried, and I leapt out of bed.

Half an hour later I was saying good-bye to Herbert.

"I've had an awfully jolly time," I said, "and I'll come again."

"You've got the ticket all right?"

"Rather!" and I drove away amidst cheers. Cheers of sorrow.

It was half an hour's drive to the station. For the first ten minutes I thought how sickening it was to be leaving the country; then I had a slight shock; and for the next twenty minutes I tried to remember how much a third single to the nearest part of London cost. Because I had left my ticket on the dressing-table after all.

I gave my luggage to a porter and went off to the station-master.

"I wonder if you can help me," I said. "I've left my return ticket on the dress—Well, we needn't worry about that, I've left it at home."

He didn't seem intensely excited.

"What did you think of doing?" he asked.

"I had rather hoped that YOU would do something."

"You can buy another ticket, and get the money back afterwards."

"Yes, yes; but can I? I've only got about one pound six."

"The fare to London is one pound five and tenpence ha'penny."

"Ah; well, that leaves a penny ha'penny to be divided between the porter this end, lunch, tea, the porter the other end, and the cab. I don't believe it's enough. Even if I gave it all to the porter here, think how reproachfully he would look at you ever afterwards. It would haunt you."

The station-master was evidently moved. He thought for a moment, and then asked if I knew anybody who would vouch for me. I mentioned Herbert confidently. He had never even heard of Herbert.

"I've got a tie-pin," I said (station-masters have a weakness for tie-pins), "and a watch and a cigarette case. I shall be happy to lend you any of those."

The idea didn't appeal to him.

"The best thing you can do," he said, "is to take a ticket to the next station and talk to them there. This is only a branch line, and I have no power to give you a pass."

So that was what I had to do. I began to see myself taking a ticket at every stop and appealing to the station-master at the next. Well, the money would last longer that way, but unless I could overcome quickly the distrust which I seemed to inspire in station-masters there would not be much left for lunch. I gave the porter all I could afford—a ha'penny, mentioned apologetically that I was coming back, and stepped into the train.

At the junction I jumped out quickly and dived into the sacred office.

"I've left my ticket on the dressing—that is to say I forgot—well, anyhow I haven't got it," I began, and we plunged into explanations once more. This station-master was even more unemotional than the last. He asked me if I knew anybody who could vouch for me—I mentioned Herbert diffidently. He had never even heard of Herbert. I showed him my gold watch, my silver cigarette case, and my emerald and diamond tie-pin—that was the sort of man I was.

"The best thing you can do," he said, walking with me to the door," is to take a ticket to Plymouth and speak to the station-master there—"

"This is a most interesting game," I said bitterly. "What is 'home'? When you speak to the station-master at London, I suppose? I've a good mind to say 'Snap!'"

Extremely annoyed I strode out, and bumped into—you'll never guess—Herbert!

"Ah, here you are," he panted; "I rode after you—the train was just going—jumped into it—been looking all over the station for you."

"It's awfully nice of you, Herbert. Didn't I say good-bye?"

"Your ticket." He produced it. "Left it on the dressing-table." He took a deep breath. "I told you you would."

"Bless you," I said, as I got happily into my train. "You've saved my life. I've had an awful time. I say, do you know, I've met two station-masters already this morning who've never even heard of you. You must inquire into it."

At that moment a porter came up.

"Did you give up your ticket, sir?" he asked Herbert.

"I hadn't time to get one," said Herbert, quite at his ease. "I'll pay now," and he began to feel in his pockets…. The train moved out of the station.

A look of horror came over Herbert's face. I knew what it meant. He hadn't any money on him. "Hi!" he shouted to me, and then we swung round a bend out of sight....

Well, well, he'll have to get home somehow. His watch is only nickel and his cigarette case leather, but luckily that sort of thing doesn't weigh much with station-masters. What they want is a well- known name as a reference. Herbert is better off than I was: he can give them MY name. It will be idle for them to pretend that they have never heard of me.

THE DOCTOR

"May I look at my watch?" I asked my partner, breaking a silence which had lasted from the beginning of the waltz.

"Oh, HAVE you got a watch?" she drawled. "How exciting!"

"I wasn't going to show it to you," I said, "But I always think it looks so bad for a man to remove his arm from a lady's waist in order to look at his watch—I mean without some sort of apology or explanation. As though he were wondering if he could possibly stick another five minutes of it."

"Let me know when the apology is beginning," said Miss White. Perhaps, after all, her name wasn't White, but, anyhow, she was dressed in white, and it's her own fault if wrong impressions arise.

"It begins at once. I've got to catch a train home. There's one at 12.45, I believe. If I started now I could just miss it."

"You don't live in these Northern Heights then?"

"No. Do you?"

"Yes."

I looked at my watch again.

"I should love to discuss with you the relative advantages of London and Greater London," I said; "the flats and cats of one and the big gardens of the other. But just at the moment the only thing I can think of is whether I shall like the walk home. Are there any dangerous passes to cross?"

"It's a nice wet night for a walk," said Miss White reflectively.

"If only I had brought my bicycle."

"A watch AND a bicycle! You ARE lucky!"

"Look here, it may be a joke to you, but I don't fancy myself coming down the mountains at night."

"The last train goes at one o'clock, if that's any good to you."

"All the good in the world," I said joyfully. "Then I needn't walk." I looked at my watch. "That gives us five minutes more. I could almost tell you all about myself in the time."

"It generally takes longer than that," said Miss White. "At least it seems to." She sighed and added, "My partners have been very autobiographical to-night."

I looked at her severely.

"I'm afraid you're a Suffragette," I said.

As soon as the next dance began I hurried off to find my hostess. I had just caught sight of her, when—

"Our dance, isn't it?" said a voice.

I turned and recognized a girl in blue.

"Ah," I said, coldly cheerful, "I was just looking for you. Come along."

We broke into a gay and happy step, suggestive of twin hearts utterly free from care.

"Why do you look so thoughtful?" asked the girl in blue after ten minutes of it.

"I've just heard some good news," I said.

"Oh, do tell me!"

"I don't know if it would really interest you."

"I'm sure it would."

"Well, several miles from here there may be a tram, if one can find it, which goes nobody quite knows where up till one-thirty in the morning probably. It is now," I added, looking at my watch (I was getting quite good at this), "just on one o'clock and raining hard. All is well."

The dance over, I searched in vain for my hostess. Every minute I took out my watch and seemed to feel that another tram was just starting off to some unknown destination. At last I could bear it no longer and, deciding to write a letter of explanation on the morrow, I dashed off.

My instructions from Miss White with regard to the habitat of trams (thrown in by her at the last moment in case the train failed me) were vague. Five minutes' walk convinced me that I had completely lost any good that they might ever have been to me. Instinct and common sense were the only guides left. I must settle down to some heavy detective work.

The steady rain had washed out any footprints that might have been of assistance, and I was unable to follow up the slot of a tram conductor of which I had discovered traces in Two-hundred-and- fifty-first Street. In Three-thousand-eight-hundred- and-ninety-seventh Street I lay with my ear to the ground and listened intently, for I seemed to hear the ting-ting of the electric car, but nothing came of it; and in Four-millionth Street I made a new resolution. I decided to give up looking for trams and to search instead for London—the London that I knew.

I felt pretty certain that I was still in one of the Home Counties, and I did not seem to remember having crossed the Thames, so that if only I could find a star which pointed to the south I was in a fair way to get home. I set out to look for a star; with the natural result that, having abandoned all hope of finding a man, I immediately ran into him.

"Now then," he said good-naturedly.

"Could you tell me the way to—" I tried to think of some place near my London—"to Westminster Abbey?"

He looked at me in astonishment. His feeling seemed to be that I was too late for the Coronation and too early for the morning service.

"Or—or anywhere," I said hurriedly. "Trams, for instance."

He pointed nervously to the right and disappeared.

Imagine my joy; there were tram-lines, and, better still, a tram approaching. I tumbled in, gave the conductor a penny, and got a workman's ticket in exchange. Ten minutes later we reached the terminus.

I had wondered where we should arrive, whether Gray's Inn Road or Southampton Row, but didn't much mind so long as I was again within reach of a cab. However, as soon as I stepped out of the tram, I knew at once where I was.

"Tell me," I said to the conductor; "do you now go back again?"

"In ten minutes. There's a tram from here every half-hour."

"When is the last?"

"There's no last. Backwards and forwards all night."

I should have liked to stop and sympathize, but it was getting late. I walked a hundred yards up the hill and turned to the right....As I entered the gates I could hear the sound of music.

"Isn't this our dance?" I said to Miss White, who was taking a breather at the hall door. "One moment," I added, and I got out of my coat and umbrella.

"Is it? I thought you'd gone."

"Oh no, I decided to stay after all. I found out that the trams go all night."

We walked in together.

"I won't be more autobiographical than I can help," I said, "but I must say it's a hard life, a doctor's. One is called away in the middle of a dance to a difficult case of—of mumps or something, and—well, there you are. A delightful evening spoilt. If one is lucky, one may get back in time for a waltz or two at the end.

"Indeed," I said, as we began to dance; "at one time to-night I quite thought I wasn't going to get back here at all."

THE THINGS THAT MATTER

RONALD, surveying the world from his taxi—that pleasant corner of the world, St James's Park—gave a sigh of happiness. The blue sky, the lawn of daffodils, the mist of green upon the trees were but a promise of the better things which the country held for him. Beautiful as he thought the daffodils, he found for the moment an even greater beauty in the Gladstone bags at his feet. His eyes wandered from one to the other, and his heart sang to him, "I'm going away—I'm going away—I'm going away."

The train was advertised to go at 2.22, and at 2.20 Ronald joined the Easter holiday crowd upon the platform. A porter put down his luggage and was then swallowed up in a sea of perambulators and flustered parents. Ronald never saw him again. At 2.40, amidst some applause, the train came in.

Ronald seized a lost porter.

"Just put these in for me," he said. "A first smoker."

"All this lot yours, sir?"

"The three bags—not the milk-cans," said Ronald.

It had been a beautiful day before, but when a family of sixteen which joined Ronald in his carriage was ruthlessly hauled out by the guard, the sun seemed to shine with a warmth more caressing than ever. Even when the train moved out of the station, and the children who had been mislaid emerged from their hiding-places and were bundled in anywhere by the married porters, Ronald still remained splendidly alone ... and the sky took on yet a deeper shade of blue.

He lay back in his corner, thinking. For a time his mind was occupied with the thoughts common to most of us when we go away—thoughts of all the things we have forgotten to pack. I don't think you could fairly have called Ronald over-anxious about clothes. He recognized that it was the inner virtues which counted; that a well-dressed exterior was nothing without some graces of mind or body. But at the same time he did feel strongly that, if you are going to stay at a house where you have never visited before, and if you are particularly anxious to make a good impression, it IS a pity that an accident of packing should force you to appear at dinner in green knickerbockers and somebody else's velvet smoking-jacket.

Ronald couldn't help feeling that he had forgotten something. It wasn't the spare sponge; it wasn't the extra shaving-brush; it wasn't the second pair of bedroom slippers. Just for a moment the sun went behind a cloud as he wondered if he had included the reserve razor-strop; but no, he distinctly remembered packing that.

The reason for his vague feeling of unrest was this. He had been interrupted while getting ready that afternoon; and as he left whatever he had been doing in order to speak to his housekeeper he had said to himself, "If you're not careful, you'll forget about that when you come back." And now he could not remember what it was he had been doing, nor whether he HAD in the end forgotten to go on with it. Was he selecting his ties, or brushing his hair, or—

The country was appearing field by field; the train rushed through cuttings gay with spring flowers; blue was the sky between the baby clouds … but it all missed Ronald. What COULD he have forgotten?

He went over the days that were coming; he went through all the changes of toilet that the hours might bring. He had packed this and this and this and this—he was all right for the evening. Supposing they played golf? … He was all right for golf. He might want to ride …. He would be able to ride. It was too early for lawn-tennis, but … well, anyhow, he had put in flannels.

As he considered all the possible clothes that he might want, it really seemed that he had provided for everything. If he liked, he could go to church on Friday morning; hunt otters from twelve to one on Saturday; toboggan or dig for badgers on Monday. He had the different suits necessary for those who attend a water-polo meeting, who play chess, or who go out after moths with a pot of treacle. And even, in the last resort, he could go to bed.

Yes, he was all right. He had packed EVERYTHING; moreover, his hair was brushed and he had no smut upon his face. With a sigh of relief he lowered the window and his soul drank in the beautiful afternoon. "We are going away—we are going away—we are going away," sang the train.

At the prettiest of wayside stations the train stopped and Ronald got out. There were horses to meet him. "Better than a car," thought Ronald, "on an afternoon like this." The luggage was collected—"Nothing left out," he chuckled to himself, and was seized with an insane desire to tell the coach-man so; and then they drove off through the fresh green hedgerows, Ronald trying hard not to cheer.

His host was at the door as they arrived. Ronald, as happy as a child, jumped out and shook him warmly by the hand, and told him what a heavenly day it was; receiving with smiles of pleasure the news in return that it was almost like summer.

"You're just in time for tea. Really, we might have it in the garden."

"By Jove, we might," said Ronald, beaming.

However, they had it in the hall, with the doors wide open. Ronald, sitting lazily with his legs stretched out and a cup of tea in his hands, and feeling already on the friendliest terms with everybody, wondered again at the difference which the weather could make to one's happiness.

"You know," he said to the girl on his right, "on a day like this, NOTHING seems to matter."

And then suddenly he knew that he was wrong; for he had discovered what it was which he had told himself not to forget ... what it was which he had indeed forgotten.

And suddenly the birds stopped singing and there was a bitter chill in the air.

And the sun went violently out.

He was wearing only half a pair of spats.

STORIES OF SUCCESSFUL LIVES

THE SOLICITOR

The office was at its busiest, for it was Friday afternoon.
John Blunt leant back in his comfortable chair and
toyed with the key of the safe, while he tried to realize
his new position. He, John Blunt, was junior partner in
the great London firm of Macnaughton, Macnaughton,
Macnaughton, Macnaughton & Macnaughton!

He closed his eyes, and his thoughts wandered back to the day when he had first entered the doors of the firm as one of two hundred and seventy-eight applicants for the post of office-boy. They had been interviewed in batches, and old Mr Sanderson, the senior partner, had taken the first batch.

"I like your face, my boy," he had said heartily to John.

"And I like yours," replied John, not to be outdone in politeness.

"Now I wonder if you can spell 'mortgage'?"

"One 'm'?" said John tentatively.

Mr Sanderson was delighted with the lad's knowledge, and engaged him at once.

For three years John had done his duty faithfully. During this time he had saved the firm more than once by his readiness—particularly on one occasion, when he had called old Mr Sanderson's attention to the fact that he had signed a letter to a firm of stockbrokers, "Your loving husband Macnaughton, Macnaughton, Macnaughton, Macnaughton & Macnaughton." Mr Sanderson, always a little absentminded, corrected the error, and promised the boy his articles. Five years later John Blunt was a solicitor.

And now he was actually junior partner in the firm—the firm of which it was said in the City, "If a man has Macnaughton, Macnaughton, Macnaughton, Macnaughton & Macnaughton behind him, he is all right." The City is always coining pithy little epigrams like this.

There was a knock at the door of the inquiry office and a prosperous-looking gentleman came in.

"Can I see Mr Macnaughton," he said politely to the office-boy.

"There isn't no Mr Macnaughton," replied the latter. "They all died years ago."

"Well, well, can I see one of the partners?"

"You can't see Mr Sanderson, because he's having his lunch," said the boy. "Mr Thorpe hasn't come back from lunch yet, Mr Peters has just gone out to lunch, Mr Williams is expected back from lunch every minute, Mr Gourlay went out to lunch an hour ago, Mr Beamish—"

"Tut, tut, isn't anybody in?"

"Mr Blunt is in," said the boy, and took up the telephone. "If you wait a moment I'll see if he's awake."

Half an hour later Mr Masters was shown into John Blunt's room.

"I'm sorry I was engaged," said John. "A most important client. Now, what can I do for you, Mr—er—Masters?"

"I wish to make my will."

"By all means," said John cordially.

"I have only one child, to whom I intend to leave all my money."

"Ha!" said John, with a frown. "This will be a lengthy and difficult business."

"But you can do it?" asked Mr Masters anxiously. "They told me at the hairdresser's that Macnaughton, Macnaughton, Macnaughton, Macnaughton & Macnaughton was the cleverest firm in London."

"We can do it," said John simply, "but it will require all our care; and I think it would be best if I were to come and stay with you for the week-end. We could go into it properly then."

"Thank you," said Mr Masters, clasping the other's hand. "I was just going to suggest it. My motor-car is outside. Let us go at once."

"I will follow you in a moment," said John, and pausing only to snatch a handful of money from the safe for incidental expenses, and to tell the boy that he would be back on Monday, he picked up the well-filled week-end bag which he always kept ready, and hurried after the other.

Inside the car Mr Masters was confidential.

"My daughter," he said, "comes of age to-morrow."

"Oh, it's a daughter?" said John, in surprise. "Is she pretty?"

"She is considered to be the prettiest girl in the county."

"Really?" said John. He thought a moment, and added, "Can we stop at a post-office? I must send an important business telegram." He took out a form and wrote:

"Macmacmacmacmac, London. Shall not be back till Wednesday.—BLUNT."

The car stopped and then sped on again.

"Amy has never been any trouble to me," said Mr Masters, "but I am getting old now, and I would give a thousand pounds to see her happily married."

"To whom would you give it," asked John, whipping out his pocket-book.

"Tut, tut, a mere figure of speech. But I would settle a hundred thousand pounds on her on the wedding-day."

"Indeed?" said John thoughtfully. "Can we stop at another post-office?" he added, bringing out his fountain-pen again. He took out a second telegraph form and wrote:

"Macmacmacmacmac, London. Shall not be back till Friday.—BLUNT."

The car dashed on again, and an hour later arrived it a commodious mansion standing in its own well-timbered grounds of upwards of several acres. At the front-door a graceful figure was standing.

"My solicitor, dear, Mr Blunt," said Mr Masters.

"It is very good of you to come all this way on my father's business," she said shyly.

"Not at all," said John. "A week or—or a fortnight—or—" he looked at her again—"or—three weeks, and the thing is done."

"Is making a will so very difficult?"

"It's a very tricky and complicated affair indeed. However, I think we shall pull it off. Er—might I send an important business telegram?"

"Macmacmacmacmac, London," wrote John. "Very knotty case. Date of return uncertain. Please send more cash for incidental expenses.—BLUNT."

Yes, you have guessed what happened. It is an everyday experience in a solicitor's life. John Blunt and Amy Masters were married at St George's, Hanover Square, last May. The wedding was a quiet one, owing to mourning in the bride's family—the result of a too sudden perusal of Macnaughton,

Macnaughton, Macnaughton, Macnaughton & Macnaughton's bill of costs. As Mr Masters said with his expiring breath—he didn't mind paying for our Mr Blunt's skill; nor yet for our Mr Blunt's valuable time—even if most of it was spent in courting Amy; nor, again, for our Mr Blunt's tips to the servants; but he did object to being charged the first-class railway fare both ways when our Mr Blunt had come down and gone up again in the car. And perhaps I ought to add that that is the drawback to this fine profession. One is so often misunderstood.

THE PAINTER

MR PAUL SAMWAYS was in a mood of deep depression. The artistic temperament is peculiarly subject to these moods, but in Paul's case there was reason why he should take a gloomy view of things. His masterpiece, "The Shot Tower from Battersea Bridge," together with the companion picture, "Battersea Bridge from the Shot Tower," had been purchased by a dealer for seventeen and sixpence. His sepia monochrome, "Night," had brought him an I.O.U. for five shillings. These were his sole earnings for the last six weeks, and starvation stared him in the face.

"If only I had a little capital!" he cried aloud in despair. "Enough to support me until my Academy picture is finished." His Academy picture was a masterly study entitled, "Roll on, thou deep and dark blue ocean, roll," and he had been compelled to stop half-way across the Channel through sheer lack of ultramarine.

The clock struck two, reminding him that he had not lunched. He rose wearily and went to the little cupboard which served as a larder. There was but little there to make a satisfying meal—half a loaf of bread, a corner of cheese, and a small tube of Chinese-white. Mechanically he set the things out....

He had finished, and was clearing away, when there came a knock at the door. His charwoman, whose duty it was to clean his brushes every week, came in with a card.

"A lady to see you, sir," she said.

Paul read the card in astonishment.

"The Duchess of Winchester," he exclaimed. "What on earth—Show her in, please." Hastily picking up a brush and the first tube which came to hand, he placed himself in a dramatic position before his easel and set to work.

"How do you do, Mr Samways?" said the

Duchess.

"G—good-afternoon," said Paul, embarrassed both by the presence of a duchess in his studio and by his sudden discovery that he was touching up a sunset with a tube of carbolic tooth-paste.

"Our mutual friend, Lord Ernest Topwood, recommended me to come to you."

Paul, who had never met Lord Ernest, but had once seen his name in a ha'penny paper beneath a photograph of Mr Arnold Bennett, bowed silently.

"As you probably guess, I want you to paint my daughter's portrait."

Paul opened his mouth to say that he was only a landscape painter, and then closed it again. After all, it was hardly fair to bother her Grace with technicalities.

"I hope you can undertake this commission," she said pleadingly.

"I shall be delighted," said Paul. "I am rather busy just now, but I could begin at two o'clock on Monday."

"Excellent," said the Duchess. "Till Monday, then." And Paul, still clutching the tooth-paste, conducted her to her carriage.

Punctually at 3.15 on Monday Lady Hermione appeared. Paul drew a deep breath of astonishment when he saw her, for she was lovely beyond compare. All his skill as a landscape painter would be needed if he were to do justice to her beauty. As quickly as possible he placed her in position and set to work.

"May I let my face go for a moment?" said Lady Hermione after three hours of it.

"Yes, let us stop," said Paul. He had outlined her in charcoal and burnt cork, and it would be too dark to do any more that evening.

"Tell me where you first met Lord Ernest?" she asked as she came down to the fire.

"At the Savoy, in June," said Paul boldly.

Lady Hermione laughed merrily. Paul, who had not regarded his last remark as one of his best things, looked at her in surprise.

"But your portrait of him was in the Academy in May!" she smiled.

Paul made up his mind quickly.

"Lady Hermione," he said with gravity, "do not speak to me of Lord Ernest again. Nor," he added hurriedly, "to Lord Ernest of me. When your picture is finished I will tell you why. Now it is time you went." He woke the Duchess up, and made a few commonplace remarks about the weather. "Remember," he whispered to Lady Hermione as he saw them to their car. She nodded and smiled.

The sittings went on daily. Sometimes Paul would paint rapidly with great sweeps of the brush; sometimes he would spend an hour trying to get on his palette the exact shade of green bice for the famous Winchester emeralds; sometimes in despair he would take a sponge and wipe the whole picture out, and then start madly again. And sometimes he would stop work altogether and tell Lady Hermione about his home-life in Worcestershire. But always, when he woke the Duchess up at the end of the sitting, he would say, "Remember!" and Lady Hermione would nod back at him.

It was a spring-like day in March when the picture was finished, and nothing remained to do but to paint in the signature.

"It is beautiful!" said Lady Hermione, with enthusiasm.
"Beautiful! Is it at all like me?"

Paul looked from her to the picture, and back to her again.

"No," he said, "not a bit. You know, I am really a landscape painter."

"What do you mean?" she cried. "You are Peter Samways, A.R.A., the famous portrait painter!"

"No," he said sadly. "That was my secret. I am Paul Samways. A member of the Amateur Rowing Association, it is true, but only an unknown landscape painter. Peter Samways lives in the next studio, and he is not even a relation."

"Then you have deceived me! You have brought me here under false pretences!" She stamped her foot angrily. "My father will not buy that picture, and I forbid you to exhibit it as a portrait of myself."

"My dear Lady Hermione," said Paul, "you need not be alarmed. I propose to exhibit the picture as 'When the Heart is Young.' Nobody will recognize a likeness to you in it. And if the Duke does not buy it I have no doubt that some other purchaser will come along."

Lady Hermione looked at him thoughtfully. "Why did you do it?" she asked gently.

"Because I fell in love with you."

She dropped her eyes, and then raised them gaily to his. "Mother is still asleep," she whispered.

"Hermione!" he cried, dropping his palette and putting his brush behind his ear.

She held out her arms to him.

As everybody remembers, "When the Heart is Young," by Paul Samways, was the feature of the Exhibition. It was bought for 10,000 pounds by a retired bottle manufacturer, whom it reminded a little of his late mother. Paul woke to find himself famous. But the success which began for him from this day did not spoil his simple and generous nature. He never forgot his brother artists, whose feet were not yet on the top of the ladder. Indeed, one of his first acts after he was married was to give a commission to Peter Samways, A.R.A.—nothing less than the painting of his wife's portrait. And Lady Hermione was delighted with the result.

THE BARRISTER

The New Bailey was crowded with a gay and fashionable throng. It was a remarkable case of shop-lifting. Aurora Delaine, nineteen, was charged with feloniously stealing and conveying certain articles, the property of the Universal Stores, to wit thirty-five yards of bock muslin, ten pairs of gloves, a sponge, two gimlets, five jars of cold cream, a copy of the Clergy List, three hat-guards, a mariner's compass, a box of drawing-pins, an egg-breaker, six blouses, and a cabman's whistle. The theft had been proved by Albert Jobson, a shopwalker, who gave evidence to the effect that he followed her through the different departments and saw her take the things mentioned in the indictment.

"Just a moment," interrupted the Judge. "Who is defending the prisoner?"

There was an unexpected silence. Rupert Carleton, who had dropped idly into court, looked round in sudden excitement. The poor girl had no counsel! What if he—yes, he would seize the chance! He stood up boldly. "I am, my lord," he said.

Rupert Carleton was still in the twenties, but he had been a briefless barrister for some years. Yet, though briefs would not come, he had been very far from idle. He had stood for Parliament in both the Conservative and Liberal interests (not to mention his own), he had written half a dozen unproduced plays, and he was engaged to be married. But success in his own profession had been delayed. Now at last was his opportunity.

He pulled his wig down firmly over his ears, took out a pair of pince-nez and rose to cross-examine. It was the cross-examination which was to make him famous, the cross-examination which is now given as a model in every legal text-book.

"Mr Jobson," he began suavely, "you say that you saw the accused steal these various articles, and that they were afterwards found upon her?"

"Yes."

"I put it to you," said Rupert, and waited intently for the answer, "that that is a pure invention on your part?"

"No."

With a superhuman effort Rupert hid his disappointment. Unexpected as the answer was, he preserved his impassivity.

"I suggest," he tried again, "that you followed her about and concealed this collection of things in her cloak with a view to advertising your winter sale?"

"No. I saw her steal them."

Rupert frowned; the man seemed impervious to the simplest suggestion. With masterly decision he tapped his pince-nez and fell back upon his third line of defence. "You saw her steal them? What you mean is that you saw her take them from the different counters and put them in her bag?"

"Yes."

"With the intention of paying for them in the ordinary way?"

"No."

"Please be very careful. You said in your evidence that the prisoner, when told she would be charged, cried, 'To think that I should have come to this! Will no one save me?' I suggest that she went up to you with her collection of purchases, pulled out her purse, and said, 'What does all this come to? I can't get any one to serve me.'"

"No."

The obstinacy of some people! Rupert put back his pince-nez in his pocket and brought out another pair. The historic cross-examination continued.

"We will let that pass for the moment," he said. He consulted a sheet of paper and then looked sternly at Mr Jobson. "Mr Jobson, how many times have you been married?"

"Once."

"Quite so." He hesitated and then decided to risk it. "I suggest that your wife left you?"

"Yes."

It was a long shot, but once again the bold course had paid. Rupert heaved a sigh of relief.

"Will you tell the gentlemen of the jury," he said with deadly politeness, "WHY she left you?"

"She died."

A lesser man might have been embarrassed, but Rupert's iron nerve did not fail him.

"Exactly!" he said. "And was that or was that not on the night when you were turned out of the Hampstead Parliament for intoxication?"

"I never was."

"Indeed? Will you cast your mind back to the night of April 24th, 1897? What were you doing on that night?"

"I have no idea," said Jobson, after casting his mind back and waiting in vain for some result.

"In that case you cannot swear that you were not being turned out of the Hampstead Parliament—"

"But I never belonged to it."

Rupert leaped at the damaging admission.

"What? You told the Court that you lived at Hampstead, and yet you say that you never belonged to the Hampstead Parliament? Is THAT your idea of patriotism?"

"I said I lived at Hackney."

"To the Hackney Parliament, I should say. I am suggesting that you were turned out of the Hackney Parliament for—"

"I don't belong to that either."

"Exactly!" said Rupert triumphantly. "Having been turned out for intoxication?"

"And never did belong."

"Indeed? May I take it then that you prefer to spend your evenings in the public-house?"

"If you want to know," said Jobson angrily, "I belong to the Hackney Chess Circle, and that takes up most of my evenings."

Rupert gave a sigh of satisfaction and turned to the jury.

"At LAST, gentlemen, we have got it. I thought we should arrive at the truth in the end, in spite of Mr Jobson's prevarications." He turned to the witness. "Now, sir," he said sternly, "you have already told the Court that you have no idea what you were doing on the night of April 24th, 1897. I put it to you once more that this blankness of memory is due to the fact that you were in a state of intoxication on the premises of the Hackney Chess Circle. Can you swear on your oath that this is not so?"

A murmur of admiration for the relentless way in which the truth had been tracked down ran through the court. Rupert drew himself up and put on both pairs of pince-nez at once.

"Come, sir!" he said, "the jury is waiting." But it was not Albert Jobson who answered. It was the counsel for the prosecution. "My lord," he said, getting up slowly, "this has come as a complete surprise to me. In the circumstances, I must advise my clients to withdraw from the case."

"A very proper decision," said his lordship. "The prisoner is discharged without a stain on her character."

Briefs poured in upon Rupert next day, and he was engaged for all the big Chancery cases. Within a week his six plays were accepted, and within a fortnight he had entered Parliament as the miners' Member for Coalville. His marriage took place at the end of a month. The wedding presents were even more numerous and costly than usual, and included thirty-five yards of book muslin, ten pairs of gloves, a sponge, two gimlets, five jars of cold cream, a copy of the Clergy List, three hat-guards, a mariner's compass, a box of drawing-pins, an egg-breaker, six blouses, and a cabman's whistle. They were marked quite simply, "From a Grateful Friend."

THE CIVIL SERVANT

It was three o'clock, and the afternoon sun reddened the western windows of one of the busiest of Government offices. In an airy room on the third floor Richard Dale was batting. Standing in front of the coal-box with the fire-shovel in his hands, he was a model of the strenuous young Englishman; and as for the third time he turned the Government india-rubber neatly in the direction of square-leg, and so completed his fifty, the bowler could hardly repress a sigh of envious admiration. Even the reserved Matthews, who was too old for cricket, looked up a moment from his putting, and said, "Well played, Dick!"

The fourth occupant of the room was busy at his desk, as if to give the lie to the thoughtless accusation that the Civil Service cultivates the body at the expense of the mind. The eager shouts of the players seemed to annoy him, for he frowned and bit his pen, or else passed his fingers restlessly through his hair.

"How the dickens you expect any one to think in this confounded noise," he cried suddenly.

"What's the matter, Ashby?"

"You're the matter. How am I going to get these verses done for The Evening Surprise if you make such a row? Why don't you go out to tea?"

"Good idea. Come on, Dale. You coming, Matthews?" They went out, leaving the room to Ashby.

In his youth Harold Ashby had often been told by his relations that he had a literary bent. His letters home from school were generally pronounced to be good enough for Punch, and some of them, together with a certificate of character from his Vicar, were actually sent to that paper. But as he grew up he realized that his genius was better fitted for work of a more solid character. His post in the Civil Service gave him full leisure for his Adam: A Fragment, his History of the Microscope, and his Studies in Rural Campanology, and yet left him ample time in which to contribute to the journalism of the day.

The poem he was now finishing for The Evening Surprise was his first contribution to that paper, but he had little doubt that it would be accepted. It was called quite simply, "Love and Death," and it began like this:

"Love! O love! (All other things above).—Why, O why, Am I afraid to die?"

There were six more lines which I have forgotten, but I suppose they gave the reason for this absurd diffidence.

Having written the poem out neatly, Harold put it in an envelope and took it round to The Evening Surprise. The strain of composition had left him rather weak, and he decided to give his brain a rest for the next few days. So it happened that he was at the wickets on the following Wednesday afternoon when the commissionaire brought him in the historic letter. He opened it hastily, the shovel under his arm.

"DEAR SIR," wrote the editor of The Surprise, "will you come round and see me as soon as convenient?"

Harold lost no time. Explaining that he would finish his innings later, he put his coat on, took his hat and stick, and dashed out.

"How do you do?" said the editor. "I wanted to talk to you about your work. We all liked your little poem very much. It will be coming out to-morrow."

"Thursday," said Harold helpfully.

"I was wondering whether we couldn't get you to join our staff. Does the idea of doing 'Aunt Miriam's Cosy Corner' in our afternoon edition appeal to you at all?"

"No," said Harold, "not a bit."

"Ah, that's a pity." He tapped his desk thoughtfully. "Well then, how would you like to be a war correspondent?"

"Very much," said Harold. "I was considered to write rather good letters home from school."

"Splendid! There's this little war in Mexico. When can you start? All expenses and fifty pounds a week. You're not very busy at the office, I suppose, just now?"

"I could get sick leave easily enough," said Harold, "if it wasn't for more than eight or nine months."

"Do; that will be excellent. Here's a blank cheque for your outfit. Can you get off to-morrow? But I suppose you'll have one or two things to finish up at the office first?"

"Well," said Harold cautiously, "I WAS in, and I'd made ninety-six. But if I go back and finish my innings now, and then have to-morrow for buying things, I could get off on Friday."

"Good," said the editor. "Well, here's luck. Come back alive if you can, and if you do we shan't forget you."

Harold spent the next day buying a war correspondent's outfit:— the camel, the travelling bath, the putties, the pith helmet, the quinine, the sleeping-bag, and the thousand-and-one other necessities of active service. On the Friday his colleagues at the office came down in a body to Southampton to see him off. Little did they think that nearly a year would elapse before he again set foot upon England.

I shall not describe all his famous coups in Mexico. Sufficient to say that experience taught him quickly all that he had need to learn; and that whereas he was more than a week late with his cabled account of the first engagement of the war, he was frequently more than a week early afterwards. Indeed, the battle of Parson's Nose, so realistically described in his last telegram, is still waiting to be fought. It is to be hoped that it will be in time for his aptly-named book, With the Mexicans in Mexico, which is coming out next month.

On his return to England Harold found that time had wrought many changes. To begin with, the editor of The Evening Surprise had passed on to The Morning Exclamation.

"You had better take his place," said the ducal proprietor to Harold.

"Right," said Harold. "I suppose I shall have to resign my post at the office?"

"Just as you like. I don't see why you should."

"I should miss the cricket," said Harold wistfully, "and the salary. I'll go round and see what I can arrange."

But there were also changes at the office. Harold had been rising steadily in salary and seniority during his absence, and he found to his delight that he was now a Principal Clerk. He found, too, that he had acquired quite a reputation in the office for quickness and efficiency in his new work.

The first thing to arrange about was his holiday. He had had no holiday for more than a year, and there were some eight weeks owing to him.

"Hullo," said the Assistant Secretary as Harold came in, "you're looking well. I suppose you manage to get away for the week-ends?"

"I've been away on sick leave for some time," said Harold pathetically.

"Have you? You've kept it very secret. Come out and have lunch with me, and we'll do a matinee afterwards."

Harold went out with him happily. It would be pleasant to accept the editorship of The Evening Surprise without giving up the Governmental work which was so dear to him, and the Assistant Secretary's words made this possible for a year or so anyhow. Then, when his absence from the office first began to be noticed, it would be time to think of retiring on an adequate pension.

THE ACTOR

Mr Levinski, the famous actor-manager, dragged himself from beneath the car, took the snow out of his mouth, and swore heartily. Mortal men are liable to motor accidents; even kings' cars have backfired; but it seems strange that actor-managers are not specially exempt from these occurrences. Mr Levinski was not only angry; he was also a little shocked. When an actor-manager has to walk two miles to the nearest town on a winter evening one may be pardoned a doubt as to whether all is quite right with the world.

But the completest tragedy has its compensations for some one. The pitiable arrival of Mr Levinski at "The Duke's Head," unrecognized and with his fur coat slightly ruffled, might make a sceptic of the most devout optimist, and yet Eustace Merrowby can never look back upon that evening without a sigh of thankfulness; for to him it was the beginning of his career. The story has often been told since—in about a dozen weekly papers, half a dozen daily papers and three dozen provincial papers—but it will always bear telling again.

There was no train to London that night, and Mr Levinski had been compelled to put up at "The Duke's Head." However, he had dined and was feeling slightly better. He summoned the manager of the hotel.

"What does one do in this dam place?" he asked with a yawn.

The manager, instantly recognizing that he was speaking to a member of the aristocracy, made haste to reply. Othello was being played at the town theatre. His daughter, who had already been three times, told him that it was simply sweet. He was sure his lordship ...

Mr Levinski dismissed him, and considered the point. He had to amuse himself with something that evening, and the choice apparently lay between Othello and the local Directory. He picked up the Directory. By a lucky chance for Eustace Merrowby it was three years old. Mr Levinski put on his fur coat and went to see Othello.

For some time he was as bored as he had expected to be, but half-way through the Third Act he began to wake up. There was something in the playing of the principal actor which moved him strangely. He looked at his programme. "Othello—Mr EUSTACE MERROWBY." Mr Levinski frowned thoughtfully. "Merrowby?" he said to himself. "I don't know the name, but he's the man I want." He took out the gold pencil presented to him by the Emperor—(the station-master had had a tie-pin)—and wrote a note.

He was finishing breakfast next morning when Mr Merrowby was announced.

"Ah, good-morning," said Mr Levinski, "good-morning. You find me very busy," and here he began to turn the pages of the Directory backwards and forwards, "but I can give you a moment. What is it you want?"

"You asked me to call on you," said Eustace.

"Did I, did I?" He passed his hand across his brow with a noble gesture. "I am so busy, I forget. Ah, now I remember. I saw you play Othello last night. You are the man I want. I am producing 'Oom Baas,' the great South African drama, next April at my theatre. Perhaps you know?"

"I have read about it in the papers," said Eustace. In all the papers (he might have added) every day, for the last six months.

"Good. Then you may have heard that one of the scenes is an ostrich farm. I want you to play 'Tommy.'"

"One of the ostriches?" asked Eustace.

"I do not offer the part of an ostrich to a man who has played Othello. Tommy is the Kaffir boy who looks after the farm. It is a black part, like your present one, but not so long. In London you cannot expect to take the leading parts just yet."

"This is very kind of you," cried Eustace gratefully. "I have always longed to get to London. And to start in your theatre!—it's a wonderful chance."

"Good," said Mr Levinski. "Then that's settled." He waved Eustace away and took up the Directory again with a business-like air.

And so Eustace Merrowby came to London. It is a great thing for a young actor to come to London. As Mr Levinski had warned him, his new part was not so big as that of Othello; he had to say "Hofo tsetse!"—which was alleged to be Kaffir for "Down, sir!"—to the big ostrich. But to be at the

St George's Theatre at all was an honour which most men would envy him, and his association with a real ostrich was bound to bring him before the public in the pages of the illustrated papers.

Eustace, curiously enough, was not very nervous on the first night. He was fairly certain that he was word-perfect; and if only the ostrich didn't kick him in the back of the neck—as it had tried to once at rehearsal—the evening seemed likely to be a triumph for him. And so it was with a feeling of pleasurable anticipation that, on the morning after, he gathered the papers round him at breakfast, and prepared to read what the critics had to say.

He had a remarkable Press. I give a few examples of the notices he obtained from the leading papers:

"Mr Eustace Merrowby was Tommy."—Daily Telegraph.

"The cast included Mr Eustace Merrowby."—Times.

"… Mr Eustace Merrowby…"—Daily Chronicle.

"We have no space in which to mention all the other performers."—Morning Leader.

"This criticism only concerns the two actors we have mentioned, and does not apply to the rest of the cast."—Sportsman.

"Where all were so good, it would be invidious to single out anybody for special praise."—Daily Mail.

"The acting deserved a better play."—Daily News.

"… Tommy…"—Morning Post.

As Eustace read the papers, he felt that his future was secure. True, The Era, careful never to miss a single performer, had yet to say, "Mr Eustace Merrowby was capital as Tommy," and The Stage, "Tommy was capitally played by Mr Eustace Merrowby"; but even without this he had become one of the Men who Count—one whose private life was of more interest to the public than that of any scientist, general or diplomat in the country.

Into Eustace Merrowby's subsequent career I cannot go at full length. It is perhaps as a member of the Garrick Club that he has attained his fullest development. All the good things of the Garrick which were not previously said by Sydney Smith may safely be put down to Eustace; and there is no doubt that he is the ringleader in all the subtler practical jokes which have made the club famous. It was he who pinned to the back of an unpopular member of the committee a sheet of paper bearing the words

KICK ME

—and the occasion on which he drew the chair from beneath a certain eminent author as the latter was about to sit down is still referred to hilariously by the older members.

Finally, as a convincing proof of his greatness, let it be said that everybody has at least heard the name "Eustace Merrowby"—even though some may be under the impression that it is the trade-mark of a sauce; and that half the young ladies of Wandsworth Common and Winchmore Hill are in love with him. If this be not success, what is?

THE YOUNGER SON

It is a hard thing to be the younger son of an ancient but impoverished family. The fact that your brother Thomas is taking most of the dibs restricts your inheritance to a paltry two thousand a year, while pride of blood forbids you to supplement this by following any of the common professions. Impossible for a St Verax to be a doctor, a policeman or an architect. He must find some nobler means of existence.

For three years Roger St Verax had lived precariously by betting. To be a St Verax was always to be a sportsman. Roger's father had created a record in the sporting world by winning the Derby and the Waterloo Cup with the same animal—though, in each case, it narrowly escaped disqualification. Roger himself almost created another record by making betting pay. His book, showing how to do it, was actually in the press when disaster overtook him.

He began by dropping (in sporting parlance) a cool thousand on the Jack Joel Selling Plate at Newmarket. On the next race he dropped a cool five hundred, and later on in the afternoon a cool seventy- five pounds ten. The following day found him at Lingfield, where he dropped a cool monkey (to persevere with the language of the racing stable) on the Solly Joel Cup, picked it up on the next race, dropped a cool pony, dropped another cool monkey, dropped a cool wallaby, picked up a cool hippopotamus, and finally, in the last race of the day, dropped a couple of lukewarm ferrets. In short, he was (as they say at Tattersall's Corner) entirely cleaned out.

When a younger son is cleaned out there is only one thing for him to do. Roger St Verax knew instinctively what it was. He bought a new silk hat and a short black coat, and went into the City.

What a wonderful place, dear reader, is the City! You, madam, who read this in your daintily upholstered boudoir, can know but little of the great heart of the City, even though you have driven through its arteries on your way to Liverpool Street Station, and have noted the bare and smoothly brushed polls of the younger natives. You, sir, in your country vicarage, are no less innocent, even though on sultry afternoons you have covered your head with the Financial Supplement of The Times in mistake for the Literary Supplement, and have thus had thrust upon you the stirring news that

Bango-Bangos were going up. And I, dear friends, am equally ignorant of the secrets of the Stock Exchange. I know that its members frequently walk to Brighton, and still more frequently stay there; that while finding a home for all the good stories which have been going the rounds for years, they sometimes invent entirely new ones for themselves about the Chancellor of the Exchequer; and that they sing the National Anthem very sternly in unison when occasion demands it. But there must be something more in it than this, or why are Bango-Bangos still going up?

I don't know. And I am sorry to say that even Roger St Verax, a Director of the Bango-Bango Development Company, is not very clear about it all.

It was as a Director of the Bango-Bango Exploration Company that he took up his life in the City. As its name implies, the Company was originally formed to explore Bango-Bango, an impenetrable district in North Australia; but when it came to the point it was found much more profitable to explore Hampstead, Clapham Common, Blackheath, Ealing and other rich and fashionable suburbs. A number of hopeful ladies and gentlemen having been located in these parts, the Company went ahead rapidly, and in 1907 a new prospector was sent out to replace the one who was assumed to have been eaten.

In 1908, Roger first heard the magic word "reconstruction," and to his surprise found himself in possession of twenty thousand pounds and a Directorship of the new Bango-Bango Mining Company.

In 1909 a piece of real gold was identified, and the shares went up like a rocket.

In 1910 the Stock Exchange suddenly woke to the fact that rubber tyres were made of rubber, and in a moment the Great Boom was sprung upon an amazed City. The Bango-Bango Development Company was immediately formed to take over the Bango-Bango Mining Company (together with its prospector, if alive, its plant, shafts and other property, not forgetting the piece of gold) and more particularly to develop the vegetable resources of the district with the view of planting rubber trees in the immediate future. A neatly compiled prospectus put matters very clearly before the stay-at-home Englishman. It explained quite concisely that, supposing the trees were planted so many feet apart throughout the whole property of five thousand square miles, and allowing a certain period for the growth of a tree to maturity, and putting the average yield of rubber per tree at, in round figures, so much, and assuming for the sake of convenience that rubber would remain at its present price, and estimating the cost of working the plantation at say, roughly, 100,000 pounds, why, then it was obvious that the profits would be anything you liked up to two billion a year—while (this was important) more land could doubtless be acquired if the shareholders thought fit. And even if you were certain that a rubber-tree couldn't possibly grow in the Bango-Bango district (as in confidence it couldn't), still it was worth taking shares purely as an investment, seeing how rapidly rubber was going up; not to mention the fact that Roger St Verax, the well-known financier, was a Director ... and so on.

In short the Bango-Bango Development Company was, in the language of the City, a safe thing.

Let me hasten to the end of this story. At the end of 1910 Roger was a millionaire; and for quite a week afterwards he used to wonder where all the money had come from. In the old days, when he won a cool thousand by betting, he knew that somebody else had lost a cool thousand by betting, but it did not seem to be so in this case. He had met hundreds of men who had made fortunes through rubber; he had met hundreds who bitterly regretted that they had missed making a fortune; but he had never met any one who had lost a fortune. This made him think the City an even more wonderful place than before.

But before he could be happy there remained one thing for him to do; he must find somebody to share his happiness. He called on his old friend, Mary Brown, one Sunday.

"Mary," he said, with the brisk confidence of the City man, "I find I'm disengaged next Tuesday. Will you meet me at St George's Church at two? I should like to show you the curate and the vestry, and one or two things like that."

"Why, what's happened?"

"I am a millionaire," said Roger calmly. "So long as I only had my beggarly pittance, I could not ask you to marry me. There was nothing for it but to wait in patience. It has been a long weary wait, dear, but the sun has broken through the clouds at last. I am now in a position to support a wife. Tuesday at two," he went on, consulting his pocket diary; "or I could give you half an hour on Monday morning."

"But why this extraordinary hurry? Why mayn't I be married properly, with presents and things?"

"My dear," said Roger reproachfully, "you forget. I am a City man now, and it is imperative that I should be married at once. Only a married man, with everything in his wife's name, can face with confidence the give and take of the bustling City."

A FEW FRIENDS

MARGERY

I

A TWICE TOLD TALE

"Is that you, uncle?" said a voice from the nursery, as I hung my coat up in the hall. "I've only got my skin on, but you can come up."

However, she was sitting up in bed with her nightgown on when I found her.

"I was having my bath when you came," she explained. "Have you come all the way from London?"

"All the way."

"Then will you tell me a story?"

"I can't; I'm going to have my dinner. I only came up to say Good-night."

Margery leant forward and whispered coaxingly, "Will you just tell me about Beauty and 'e Beast?"

"But I've told you that such heaps of times. And it's much too long for to-night."

"Tell me HALF of it. As much as THAT." She held her hands about nine inches apart.

"That's too much."

"As much as THAT." The hands came a little nearer together.

"Oh! Well, I'll tell you up to where the Beast died."

"FOUGHT he died," she corrected eagerly.

"Yes. Well—"

"How much will that be? As much as I said?"

I nodded. The preliminary business settled, she gave a little sigh of happiness, put her arms round her knees, and waited breathlessly for the story she had heard twenty times before.

"Once upon a time there was a man who had three daughters. And one day—"

"What was the man's name?"

"Margery," I said reproachfully, annoyed at the interruption, "you know I NEVER tell you the man's name."

"Tell me now."

"Oswald," I said, after a moment's thought.

"I told Daddy it was Thomas," said Margery casually.

"Well, as a matter of fact, he had two names, Oswald AND Thomas."

"Why did he have two names?"

"In case he lost one. Well, one day this man, who was very poor, heard that a lot of money was waiting for him in a ship which had come over the sea to a town some miles off. So he—"

"Was it waiting at Weymouf?"

"Somewhere like that."

"I spex it must have been Weymouf, because there's lots of sea there."

"Yes, I'm sure it was. Well, he thought he'd go to Weymouth and get the money."

"How much monies was it?"

"Oh, lots and lots."

"As much as five pennies?"

"Yes, about that. Well, he said Good-bye to his daughters, and asked them what they'd like him to bring back for a present. And the first asked for some lovely jewels and diamonds and—"

"Like mummy's locket—is THAT jewels?"

"That sort of idea. Well, she wanted a lot of things like that. And the second wanted some beautiful clothes."

"What sort of clothes?"

"Oh, frocks and—well, frocks and all sorts of—er—frocks."

"Did she want any lovely new stockings?"

"Yes, she wanted three pairs of those."

"And did she want any lovely—"

"Yes," I said hastily, "she wanted lots of those, too. Lots of EVERYTHING."

Margery gave a little sob of happiness. "Go on telling me," she said under her breath.

"Well, the third daughter was called Beauty. And she thought to herself, 'Poor Father won't have any money left at all, if we all go on like this!' So she didn't ask for anything very expensive, like her selfish sisters, she only asked for a rose. A simple red rose."

Margery moved uneasily.

"I hope," she said wistfully, "this bit isn't going to be about—YOU know. It never did before."

"About what?"

"Good little girls and bad little girls, and fings like that."

"My darling, no, of course not. I told it wrong. Beauty asked for a rose because she loved roses so. And it was a very particular kind of red rose that she wanted—a sort that they simply COULDN'T get to grow in their own garden because of the soil."

"Go on telling me," said Margery, with a deep sigh of content.

"Well, he started off to Weymouth."

"What day did he start?"

"It was Monday. And when—"

"Oh, well, anyhow, I told daddy it was Tuesday."

"Tuesday—now let me think. Yes, I believe you're right. Because on Monday he went to a meeting of the Vegetable Gardeners, and proposed the health of the Chairman. Yes, well he started off on Tuesday, and when he got there he found that there was no money for him at all!"

"I spex somebody had taken it," said Margery breathlessly.

"Well, it had all gone SOMEHOW."

"Perhaps somebody had swallowed it," said Margery, a little carried away by the subject. "By mistake."

"Anyhow, it was gone. And he had to come home again without any money. He hadn't gone far—"

"How far?" asked Margery. "As far as THAT?" and she measured nine inches in the air.

"About forty-four miles—when he came to a beautiful garden."

"Was it a really lovely big garden? Bigger than ours?"

"Oh, much bigger."

"Bigger than yours?"

"I haven't got a garden."

Margery looked at me wonderingly. She opened her mouth to speak, and then stopped and rested her head upon her hands and thought out this new situation. At last, her face flushed with happiness, she announced her decision.

"Go on telling me about Beauty and the Beast now," she said breathlessly, "and THEN tell me why you haven't got a garden."

My average time for Beauty and the Beast is ten minutes, and, if we stop at the place when the Beast thought he was dead, six minutes twenty-five seconds. But, with the aid of seemingly innocent questions, a determined character can make even the craftiest uncle spin the story out to half an hour.

"Next time," said Margery, when we had reached the appointed place and she was being tucked up in bed, "will you tell me ALL the story?"

Was there the shadow of a smile in her eyes? I don't know. But I'm sure it will be wisest next time to promise her the whole thing. We must make that point clear at the very start, and then we shall get along.

II
THE LITERARY ART

MARGERY has a passion for writing just now. I can see nothing in it myself, but if people WILL write, I suppose you can't stop them.

"Will you just lend me your pencil?" she asked.

"Remind me to give you a hundred pencils some time," I said as I took it out, "and then you'll always have one. You simply eat pencils."

"Oo, I gave it you back last time."

"Only just. You inveigle me down here—"

"What do I do?"

"I'm not going to say that again for anybody."

"Well, may I have the pencil?"

I gave her the pencil and a sheet of paper, and settled her in a chair.

"B-a-b-y," said Margery to herself, planning out her weekly article for the Reviews. "B-a-b-y, baby." She squared her elbows and began to write....

"There!" she said, after five minutes' composition.

The manuscript was brought over to the critic, and the author stood proudly by to point out subtleties that might have been overlooked at a first reading.

"B-a-b-y," explained the author. "Baby."

"Yes, that's very good; very neatly expressed. 'Baby'—I like that."

"Shall I write some more?" said Margery eagerly.

"Yes, do write some more. This is good, but it's not long enough."

The author retired again, and in five minutes produced this:—

B A B Y

"That's 'baby,'" explained Margery.

"Yes, I like that baby better than the other one. It's more spread out. And it's bigger—it's one of the biggest babies I've seen."

"Shall I write some more?"

"Don't you write anything else ever?"

"I like writing 'baby,'" said Margery carelessly. "B-a-b-y."

"Yes, but you can't do much with just that one word. Suppose you wanted to write to a man at a shop—'Dear Sir,—You never sent me my boots. Please send them at once, as I want to go out this afternoon. I am, yours faithfully, Margery'—it would be no good simply putting 'B-a-b-y,' because he wouldn't know what you meant."

"Well, what WOULD it be good putting?"

"Ah, that's the whole art of writing—to know what it would be any good putting. You want to learn lots and lots of new words, so as to be ready. Now here's a jolly little one that you ought to meet." I took the pencil and wrote GOT. "Got. G-o-t, got."

Margery, her elbows on my knee and her chin resting on her hands, studied the position.

"Yes, that's old 'got,'" she said.

> "He's always coming in. When you want to say, 'I've got a bad pain, so I can't accept your kind invitation'; or when you want to say, 'Excuse more, as I've got to go to bed now'; or quite simply, 'You've got my pencil.'"

"G-o-t, got," said Margery. "G-o-t, got. G-o-t, got."

"With appropriate action it makes a very nice recitation."

"Is THAT a 'g'?" said Margery, busy with the pencil, which she had snatched from me.

"The gentleman with the tail. You haven't made his tail quite long enough.... That's better."

Margery retired to her study, charged with an entirely new inspiration, and wrote her second manifesto. It was this:—

G O T

"Got," she pointed out.

I inspected it carefully. Coming fresh to the idea Margery had treated it more spontaneously than the other. But it was distinctly a "got." One of the gots.

"Have you any more words?" she asked, holding tight to the pencil.

"You've about exhausted me, Margery."

"What was that one you said just now? The one you said you wouldn't say again?"

"Oh, you mean 'inveigle'?" I said, pronouncing it differently this time.

"Yes; write that for me."

"It hardly ever comes in. Only when you are writing to your solicitor."

"What's 'solicitor'?"

"He's the gentleman who takes the money. He's ALWAYS coming in."

"Then write 'solicitor.'"

I took the pencil (it was my turn for it) and wrote SOLICITOR. Then I read it out slowly to Margery, spelt it to her three times very carefully, and wrote SOLICITOR again. Then I said it thoughtfully to myself half a dozen times—"Solicitor." Then I looked at it wonderingly.

"I am not sure now," I said, "that there is such a word."

"Why?"

"I thought there was when I began, but now I don't think there can be. 'Solicitor'—it seems so silly."

"Let me write it," said Margery, eagerly taking the paper and pencil, "and see if it looks silly."

She retired, and—as well as she could for her excitement—copied the word down underneath. The combined effort then read as follows:—

SOLICITOR SOLICITOR SOLCTOR

"Yes, you've done it a lot of good," I said. "You've taken some of the creases out. I like that much better."

"Do you think there is such a word now?"

"I'm beginning to feel more easy about it. I'm not certain, but I hope."

"So do I," said Margery. With the pencil in one hand and the various scraps of paper in the other, she climbed on to the writing-desk and gave herself up to literature....

And it seems to me that she is well equipped for the task. For besides having my pencil still (of which I say nothing for the moment) she has now three separate themes upon which to ring the changes—a range wide enough for any writer. These are, "Baby got solicitor" (supposing that there is such a word), "Solicitor got baby," and "Got baby solicitor." Indeed, there are really four themes here, for the last one can have two interpretations. It might mean that you had obtained an ordinary solicitor for Baby, or it might mean that you had got a specially small one for yourself. It lacks, therefore, the lucidity of the best authors, but in a woman writer this may be forgiven.

III
MY SECRETARY

When, five years ago, I used to write long letters to Margery, for some reason or other she never wrote back. To save her face I had to answer the letters myself—a tedious business. Still, I must admit that the warmth and geniality of the replies gave me a certain standing with my friends, who had not looked for me to be so popular. After some months, however, pride stepped in. One cannot pour out letter after letter to a lady without any acknowledgment save from oneself. And when even my own acknowledgments began to lose their first warmth—when, for instance, I answered four pages about my new pianola with the curt reminder that I was learning to walk and couldn't be bothered with music, why, then at last I saw that a correspondence so one-sided would have to come to an end. I wrote a farewell letter and replied to it with tears....

But, bless you, that was nearly five years ago. Each morning now, among the usual pile of notes on my plate from duchesses, publishers, money-lenders, actor-managers and what-not, I find, likely enough, an envelope in Margery's own handwriting. Not only is my address printed upon it legibly, but there are also such extra directions to the postman as "England" and "Important," for its more speedy arrival. And inside—well, I give you the last but seven.

"MY DEAR UNCLE I thot you wher coming to see me to night but you didn't why didn't you baby has p t o hurt her knee isnt that a pity I have some new toys isnt that jolly we didn't have our five minutes so will you krite to me and tell me all about p t o your work from your loving little MARGIE."

I always think that footnotes to a letter are a mistake, but there are one or two things I should like to explain.

(A) Just as some journalists feel that without the word "economic" a leading article lacks tone, so Margery feels, and I agree with her, that a certain cachet is lent to a letter by a p.t.o. at the bottom of each page.

(B) There are lots of grown-up people who think that "write" is spelt "rite." Margery knows that this is not so. She knows that there is a silent letter in front of the "r," which doesn't do anything but likes to be there. Obviously, if nobody is going to take any notice of this extra letter, it doesn't much matter what it is. Margery happened to want to make a "k" just then; at a pinch it could be as silent as a "w." You will please, therefore, regard the "k" in "krite" as absolutely noiseless.

(C) Both Margery and Bernard Shaw prefer to leave out the apostrophe in writing such words as "isn't" and "don't."

(D) Years ago I claimed the privilege to monopolise, on the occasional evenings when I was there, Margery's last ten minutes before she goes back to some heaven of her own each night. This privilege was granted; it being felt, no doubt, that she owed me some compensation for my early secretarial work on her behalf. We used to spend the ten minutes in listening to my telling a fairy story, always the same one. One day the authorities stepped in and announced that in future the ten minutes would be reduced to five. The procedure seemed to me absolutely illegal (and I should like to bring a test action against somebody), but it certainly did put the lid on my fairy story, of which I was getting more than a little tired.

"Tell me about Beauty and the Beast," said Margery as usual that evening.

"There's not time," I said. "We've only five minutes to-night."

"Oh! Then tell me all the work you've done to-day."

(A little unkind, you'll agree, but you know what relations are.)

And so now I have to cram the record of my day's work into five breathless minutes. You will understand what bare justice I can do to it in the time.

I am sorry that these footnotes have grown so big; let us leave them and return to the letter. There are many ways of answering such a letter. One might say, "MY DEAR MARGERY,—It was jolly to get a real letter from you at last—" but the "at last" would seem rather tactless considering what had passed years before. Or one might say, "MY DEAR MARGERY,—Thank you for your jolly letter. I am so sorry about baby's knee and so glad about your toys. Perhaps if you gave one of the toys to baby, then her knee—" But I feel sure that Margery would expect me to do better than that.

In the particular case of this last letter but seven I wrote:—

"DEAREST MARGERY,—Thank you for your sweet letter. I had a very busy day at the office or I would have come to see you. P.T.O.—I hope to be down next week, and then I will tell you all about my work; but I have a lot more to do now, and so I must say Good-bye. Your loving UNCLE."

There is perhaps nothing in that which demands an immediate answer, but with business-like promptitude Margery replied:—

"MY DEAR UNCLE thank you for your letter I am glad you are coming next week baby is quite well now are you p t o coming on Thursday next week or not say yes if you are I am p t o sorry you are working so hard from your loving MARGIE."

I said "Yes," and that I was her loving uncle. It seemed to be then too late for a "P.T.O.," but I got one in and put on the back, "Love to Baby." The answer came by return of post:—

"MY DEAR UNCLE thank you for your letter come erly on p t o Thursday come at half past nothing baby sends her love and so do p t o I my roking horse has a sirrup broken isnt that a pity say yes or no good-bye from your loving MARGIE."

Of course I thanked Baby for her love and gave my decision that it WAS a pity about the rocking-horse. I did it in large capitals, which (as I ought to have said before) is the means of communication between Margery and her friends. For some reason or other I find printing capitals to be more tiring than the ordinary method of writing.

"MY DEAR UNCLE," wrote Margery—

But we need not go into that. What I want to say is this: I love to get letters, particularly these, but I hate writing them, particularly in capitals. Years ago, I used to answer Margery's letters for her. It is now her turn to answer mine for me.

CHUM

IT is Chum's birthday to-morrow, and I am going to buy him a little whip for a present, with a whistle at the end of it. When I next go into the country to see him I shall take it with me and explain it to him. Two days' firmness would make him quite a sensible dog. I have often threatened to begin the treatment on my very next visit, but somehow it has been put off; the occasion of his birthday offers a last opportunity.

It is rather absurd, though, to talk of birthdays in connection with Chum, for he has been no more than three months old since we have had him. He is a black spaniel who has never grown up. He has a beautiful astrakhan coat which gleams when the sun is on it; but he stands so low in the water that the front of it is always getting dirty, and his ears and the ends of his trousers trail in the mud. A great authority has told us that, but for three white hairs on his shirt (upon so little do class distinctions hang), he would be a Cocker of irreproachable birth. A still greater authority has sworn that he is a Sussex. The family is indifferent—it only calls him a Silly Ass. Why he was christened Chum I do not know; and as he never recognizes the name it doesn't matter.

When he first came to stay with us I took him a walk round the village. I wanted to show him the lie of the land. He had never seen the country before and was full of interest. He trotted into a cottage garden and came back with something to show me.

"You'll never guess," he said. "Look!" and he dropped at my feet a chick just out of the egg.

I smacked his head and took him into the cottage to explain.

"My dog," I said, "has eaten one of your chickens."

Chum nudged me in the ankle and grinned.

"TWO of your chickens," I corrected myself, looking at the fresh evidence which he had just brought to light.

"You don't want me any more?" said Chum, as the financial arrangements proceeded. "Then I'll just go and find somewhere for these two." And he picked them up and trotted into the sun.

When I came out I was greeted effusively.

"This is a wonderful day," he panted, as he wriggled his body. "I didn't know the country was like this. What do we do now?"

"We go home," I said, and we went.

That was Chum's last day of freedom. He keeps inside the front gate now. But he is still a happy dog; there is plenty doing in the garden. There are beds to walk over, there are blackbirds in the apple tree to bark at. The world is still full of wonderful things. "Why, only last Wednesday," he will tell you, "the fishmonger left his basket in the drive. There was a haddock in it, if you'll believe me, for master's breakfast, so of course I saved it for him. I put it on the grass just in front of his study window, where he'd be SURE to notice it. Bless you, there's always SOMETHING to do in this house. One is never idle."

And even when there is nothing doing, he is still happy; waiting cheerfully upon events until they arrange themselves for his amusement. He will sit for twenty minutes opposite the garden bank, watching for a bumble-bee to come out of its hole. "I saw him go in," he says to himself, "so he's bound to come out. Extraordinarily interesting world." But to his inferiors (such as the gardener) he pretends that it is not pleasure but duty which keeps him. "Don't talk to me, fool. Can't you see that I've got a job on here?"

Chum has found, however, that his particular mission in life is to purge his master's garden of all birds. This keeps him busy. As soon as he sees a blackbird on the lawn he is in full cry after it. When he gets to the place and finds the blackbird gone, he pretends that he was going there anyhow; he gallops round in circles, rolls over once or twice, and then trots back again. "You didn't REALLY think I was such a fool as to try to catch a BLACKBIRD?" he says to us. "No, I was just taking a little run—splendid thing for the figure."

And it is just Chum's little runs over the beds which call aloud for firmness—which, in fact, have inspired my birthday present to him. But there is this difficulty to overcome first. When he came to live with us an arrangement was entered into (so he says) by which one bed was given to him as his own. In that bed he could wander at will, burying bones and biscuits, hunting birds. This may have been so, but it is a pity that nobody but Chum knows definitely which is the bed.

"Chum, you bounder," I shout as he is about to wade through the herbaceous border.

He takes no notice; he struggles through to the other side. But a sudden thought strikes him, and he pushes his way back again.

"Did you call me?" he says.

"How DARE you walk over the flowers?"

He comes up meekly.

"I suppose I've done SOMETHING wrong," he says, "but I can't THINK what."

I smack his head for him. He waits until he is quite sure I have finished, and then jumps up with a bark, wipes his paws on my trousers and trots into the herbaceous border again.

"Chum!" I cry.

He sits down in it and looks all round him in amazement.

"My own bed!" he murmurs. "Given to me!"

I don't know what it is in him which so catches hold of you. His way of sitting, a reproachful statue, motionless outside the window of whomever he wants to come out and play with him—until you can bear it no longer, but must either go into the garden or draw down the blinds for the day; his habit, when you ARE out, of sitting up on his back legs and begging you with his front paws to come and DO something—a trick entirely of his own invention, for no one would think of teaching him anything; his funny nautical roll when he walks, which is nearly a swagger, and gives him always the air of having just come back from some rather dashing adventure; beyond all this there is still something. And whatever it is, it is something which every now and then compels you to bend down and catch hold of his long silky ears, to look into his honest eyes and say—

"You silly old ass! You DEAR old SILLY old ass!"

BETTY

THE HOTEL CHILD

I WAS in the lounge when I made her acquaintance, enjoying a pipe after tea, and perhaps—I don't know—closing my eyes now and then.

"Would you like to see my shells?" she asked suddenly.

I woke up and looked at her. She was about seven years old, pretty, dark, and very much at ease.

"I should love it," I said.

She produced a large paper bag from somewhere, and poured the contents in front of me.

"I've got two hundred and fifty-eight," she announced.

"So I see," I said. I wasn't going to count them."

"I think they're very pretty. I'll give you one if you like. Which one will you choose?"

I sat up and examined them carefully. Seeing how short a time we had known each other, I didn't feel that I could take one of the good ones. After a little thought I chose quite a plain one, which had belonged to a winkle some weeks ago.

"Thank you very much," I said.

"I don't think you choose shells at all well," she said scornfully. "That's one of the ugly ones."

"It will grow on me," I explained. "In a year or two I shall think it beautiful."

"I'll let you have this one too," said she, picking out the best. "Now, shall we play at something?"

I had been playing at something all day. A little thinking in front of the fire was my present programme.

"Let's talk instead," I suggested. "What's your name?"

"Betty."

"I knew it was Betty. You look just like Betty."

"What's yours?"

Somehow I hadn't expected that. After all, though, it was only fair.

"Orlando," I said.

"What a funny name. I don't like it."

"You should have said so before. It's too late now. What have you been doing all day?"

"Playing on the sands. What have you been doing?"

"I've been playing in the sand too. I suppose, Betty, you know nearly everybody in the hotel?"

"Oh, I play with them all sometimes."

"Yes; then tell me, Betty, do you ever get asked what time you go to bed?"

"They ALL ask me that," said Betty promptly.

"I think I should like to ask you too," I said, "just to be in the movement. When is it?"

"Half-past six." She looked at the clock. "So we've got half an hour. I'll get my ball."

Before I had time to do anything about it, the ball came bouncing in, hit me on the side of the head, and hurried off to hide itself under an old lady dozing in the corner. Betty followed more sedately.

"Where's my ball?" she asked.

"Has it come in?" I said in surprise. "Then it must have gone out again. It noticed you weren't here."

"I believe you've got it."

"I swear I haven't, Betty. I think the lady in the corner knows something about it."

Betty rushed across to her and began to crawl under her chair. I nervously rehearsed a few sentences to myself.

"It is not my child, madam. I found it here. Surely you can see that there is no likeness between us? If we keep quite still perhaps it will go away."

"I've got it," cried Betty, and the old lady woke up with a jerk.

"What are you doing, child?" she said crossly.

"Your little girl, madam," I began—but Betty's ball bit me on the head again before I could develop my theme.

"Your little girl, sir," began the old lady at the same moment.

"I said it first," I murmured. "Betty," I went on aloud, "what is your name, my child?"

"You've just said it."

"I mean," I corrected myself quickly, "where do you live?"

"Kensington."

I looked triumphantly at the old lady. Surely a father wouldn't need to ask his own child where she lived? However, the old lady was asleep again. I turned to Betty.

"We shall have to play this game more quietly," I said. "In fact, we had better make some new rules. Instead of hitting me on the head each time, you can roll the ball gently along the floor to me, and I shall roll it gently back to you. And the one who misses it first goes to bed."

I gave her an easy one to start with, wishing to work up naturally to the denouement, and she gave me a very difficult one back, not quite understanding the object of the game.

"You've got to go to bed," she cried, clapping her hands. "You've got—to go—to bed. You've got—to go—to bed. You've—"

"All right," I said coldly. "Don't make a song about it."

It was ten minutes past six. I generally go to bed at eleven-thirty. It would be the longest night I had had for years. I sighed and prepared to go.

"You needn't go till half-past," said Betty kindly.

"No, no," I said firmly. "Rules are rules." I had just remembered that there was nothing in the rules about not getting up again.

"Then I'll come with you and see your room."

"No, you mustn't do that; you'd fall out of the window. It's a very tricky window. I'm always falling out of it myself."

"Then let's go on playing here, and we won't go to bed if we miss."

"Very well," I agreed. Really there was nothing else for it.

Robbed of its chief interest, the game proved, after ten minutes or so, to be one of the duller ones. Whatever people say, I don't think it compares with cricket, for instance. It is certainly not so subtle as golf.

"I like playing this game," said Betty. "Don't you?"

"I think I shall get to love it," I said, looking at the clock. There were still five minutes, and I rolled down a very fast googly which beat her entirely and went straight for the door. Under the old rules she would have gone to bed at once. Alas, that—

"Look out," I said as she went after it, "there's somebody coming in."

Somebody came in. She smiled ruefully at us and then took Betty's hand.

"I'm afraid my little girl has been worrying you," she said prettily.

"I KNEW you'd say that," said Betty.

CINDERELLA

(BEING AN EXTRACT FROM HER DIARY—PICKED UP BEHIND THE SCENES)

TUESDAY.—Sometimes I think I am a very lucky girl having two big sisters to look after me. I expect there are lots of young girls who have nobody at all, and I think they must be so lonely. There is always plenty of fun going on in our house. Yesterday I heard Sister Fred telling Sister Bert something about her old man coming home very late one night—I didn't quite understand who the old man was, or what it was all about, but I know Sister Bert thought it was very funny, and I seemed to hear a lot of people laughing; perhaps it was the fairies. And then whenever Sister Bert sits down she always pulls her skirt right up to her knees, so as people can see her stockings. I mean there's always SOMETHING amusing happening.

Of course I have a good deal of work to do, and all the washing up, but my sisters are so big and strong that one can't expect them to bother themselves with niggling little things like that. Besides, they have so many other things to do. Only this morning, when Sister Bert was just going to sit down, Sister Fred pulled away her chair, and she sat on the floor and her legs went up in the air. She said it was a "grand slam," which some of us thought very funny. I didn't laugh myself, because I never go out anywhere, and so I don't understand topical remarks, but I do think it is nice to live in such an amusing house.

(LATER.)—A wonderful thing has happened! Two messengers came from the Prince an hour ago to invite us to the ball to-night! I'd never seen a messenger in my life, so I peeped out of the chimney corner at them and wondered if they would stay to tea. But instead of that my sisters put up what they call a "trapeze" (I never knew we had one before), and the messengers did some EXTRAORDINARY things on it, I thought they would kill themselves. After it was over, Sister Fred told them a lot of stories about the old man, and altogether it was quite different from what I expected. Ours IS a funny house.

As soon as the messengers had gone, my sisters began to get ready for the ball. I knew I shouldn't be able to go, because I haven't got a frock, and I simply COULDN'T wear anything of theirs, they are so much bigger than I am. They finished dressing DOWNSTAIRS for some reason, where anybody might have seen them—they are so funny about things like that—and we had a lot of laughter about the clothes being too tight and so on. I think anything like that is so amusing. Then they went off, and here I am all alone. It is getting dark, and so I am going to cheer myself up by singing a little.

(LATER).—I AM GOING TO THE BALL! My Fairy Godmother, whom I had often heard about, suddenly came to see us. I told her my sisters were out, and she asked where they had gone, and wouldn't I like to go too, so of course I said I should LOVE it. So I am going, and she has got a frock for me and everything. She is very kind, but not quite so FAIRY-LIKE as I expected.

WEDNESDAY.—I have had a LOVELY time, and I think I am in love. I got to the Ball just as the juggling and the ventriloquism were over—it must be a delightful Court to live in—and there was SUCH a sensation as I appeared. The Prince singled me out at once. He has the pinkest cheeks and the reddest lips of any man I know, and his voice is soft and gentle, and oh! I love him. One wants a man to be manly and a woman to be womanly, and I don't think I should love a man if he were at all like Sister Fred or Sister Bert. The Prince is QUITE different. We were alone most of the time, and we sang several songs together. My sisters never recognized me; it was most surprising. I heard Sister Fred telling a very fine-looking gentleman a story about a lodger (whatever that is) who had a bit of a head; it sounded very humorous. Wherever Sister Fred goes there is sure to be fun. I am indeed a lucky girl to have two such sisters and to be in love with a Prince. Sister Bert sat down on the floor twice—it was most amusing.

A terrible thing happened just as the clock struck twelve. All my clothes turned into rags, and I just RAN out of the room, I was so frightened. Then I remembered what my Fairy Godmother had said about leaving before twelve o'clock. I suppose she knew what would happen if I didn't. I'm afraid I left a glass slipper behind—I hope she won't mind about it.

Well, I've had a lovely time. Even if I never see the Prince again, I shall always have this to look back to. I don't mind WHAT happens now.

THURSDAY.—I AM GOING TO MARRY THE PRINCE! I can't believe it is true. Perhaps it is only a dream, and I shall wake up soon, but even if it's a dream it's just as good as if it were real. It was all because of the slipper I left behind. The Prince said that he would marry the person whom it fitted, because he had fallen in love with the lady who wore it at the ball (ME!), and so everybody tried it on. And they came to our house, and Sister Bert tried it on. She pulled her skirt up to her knees and made everybody laugh, but even then she couldn't get into it. And Sister Fred made a lot of faces, but SHE couldn't. So I said, "Let ME try," and they all laughed, but the Prince said I should, and of course it fitted at once. Then they all recognized me, and the Prince kissed me, and a whole lot of people came into the house who had never been invited, and we had the trapeze out again, and there was juggling and ventriloquism, and we all sang songs about somebody called Flanagan (whom I don't think I have ever met), and Sister Bert kept sitting down suddenly on the floor. (But the Prince didn't think this was at all funny, so I expect I must have been right all the time when I have only PRETENDED to laugh. I used to think that perhaps I hadn't a sense of humour.) And then the Prince kissed me again, and my Fairy Godmother came in and kissed us both. Of course we do owe it all to her really, and I shall tell Charming so.

I do think I am a wonderful person!

FATHER CHRISTMAS

Outside in the street the rain fell pitilessly, but inside the Children's Shop all was warmth and brightness. Happy young people of all ages pressed along, and I had no sooner opened the door than I was received into the eager stream of shoppers and hurried away to Fairyland. A slight block at one corner pitched me into an old, white-bearded gentleman who was standing next to me. Instantly my hat was in my hand.

"I beg your pardon," I said with a bow. "I was—Oh, I'm sorry, I thought you were real." I straightened him up, looked at his price, and wondered whether I should buy him.

"What do you mean by real?" he said.

I started violently and took my hat off again.

"I am very stupid this morning," I began. "The fact is I mistook you for a toy. A foolish error."

"I AM a toy."

"In that case," I said in some annoyance, "I can't stay here arguing with you. Good-morning." And I took my hat off for the third time.

"Don't go. Stop and buy me. You'll never get what you want if you don't take me with you. I've been in this place for years, and I know exactly where everything is. Besides, as I shall have to give away all your presents for you, it's only fair that—"

An attendant came up and looked at me inquiringly.

"How much is this THING?" I said, and jerked a thumb at it.

"The Father Christmas?"

"Yes. I think I'll have it. I'll take it with me—you needn't wrap it up."

I handed over some money and we pushed on together.

"You heard what I called you?" I said to him. "A thing. So don't go putting yourself forward."

He gazed up innocently from under my arm.

"What shall we get first?" he asked.

"I want the engine-room. The locomotive in the home. The boy's own railroad track."

"That's downstairs. But did you really think of an engine? I mean, isn't it rather large and heavy? Why not get a—"

I smacked his head, and we went downstairs.

It was a delightful room. I was introduced to practically the whole of the Great Western Railway's rolling stock.

"Engine, three carriages and a guard's van. That's right. Then I shall want some rails, of course…. SHUT up, will you?" I said angrily, when the attendant was out of hearing.

"It's the extra weight," he sighed. "The reindeer don't like it. And these modern chimneys—you've no idea what a squeeze it is. However—"

"Those are very jolly," I said when I had examined the rails. "I shall want about a mile of them. Threepence ha'penny a foot? Then I shan't want nearly a mile."

I got about thirty feet, and then turned to switches and signals and lamps and things. I bought a lot of those. You never know what emergency might not arise on the nursery floor, and if anything happened for want of a switch or two I should never forgive myself.

Just as we were going away I caught sight of the jolliest little clockwork torpedo boat. I stopped irresolute.

"Don't be silly," said the voice under my arm. "You'll never be asked to the house again if you give that."

"Why not?"

"Wait till the children have fallen into the bath once or twice with all their clothes on, and then ask the mother why not."

"I see," I said stiffly, and we went upstairs.

"The next thing we want is bricks."

"Bricks," said Father Christmas uneasily. "Bricks. Yes, there's bricks. Have you ever thought of one of those nice little woolly rabbits—"

"Where do we get bricks?"

"Bricks. You know, I don't think mothers are as fond as all that of BRICKS."

"I got the mother's present yesterday, thanks very much. This is for one of the children."

They showed me bricks and they showed me pictures of what the bricks would build. Palaces, simply palaces. Gone was the Balbus-wall of our youth; gone was the fort with its arrow-holes for the archers. Nothing now but temples and Moorish palaces.

"Jove, I should love that," I said." I mean HE would love that. Do you want much land for a house of that size? I know of a site on the nursery floor, but—well, of course, we could always have an iron building outside in the passage for the billiard table."

We paid and moved off again.

"What are you mumbling about now?" I asked.

"I said you'll only make the boy discontented with his present home if you teach him to build nothing but castles and ruined abbeys and things. And you WILL run to bulk. Half of those bricks would have made a very nice present for anybody."

"Yes, and when royalty comes on a visit, where would you put them? They'd have to pig it in the box-room. If we're going to have a palace, let's have a good one."

"Very well. What do your children hang up? Stockings or pillow-cases?"

We went downstairs again.

"Having provided for the engineer and the architect," I said, "we now have to consider the gentleman in the dairy business. I want a milk-cart."

"You want a milk-cart! You want a milk-cart! You want a—Why not have a brewer's dray? Why not have something really heavy? The reindeer wouldn't mind. They've been out every day this week, but they'd love it. What about a nice skating-rink? What about—"

I put him head downwards in my pocket and approached an official.

"Do you keep milk-carts?" I said diffidently.

He screwed up his face and thought.

"I could get you one," he said.

"I don't want you to build one specially for me. If they aren't made, I expect it's because mothers don't like them. It was just an idea of mine."

"Oh yes, they're made. I can show a picture of one in our catalogue."

He showed it to me. It was about the size of a perambulator, and contained every kind of can. I simply had to let Father Christmas see.

"Look at that!" I exclaimed in delight.

"Good lord!" he said, and dived into the pocket again.

I held him there tightly and finished my business with the official.

Father Christmas has never spoken since. Sometimes I wonder if he ever spoke at all, for one imagines strange things in the Children's Shop. He stands now on my writing-table, and observes me with the friendly smile which has been so fixed a feature of his since I brought him home.

MISS MIDDLETON

I
TAKING A CALL

"MAY I come in?" said Miss Middleton.

I looked up from my book and stared at her in amazement.

"Hullo," I said.

"Hullo," said Miss Middleton doubtfully.

"Are you going to have tea with me?"

"That's what I was wondering all the way up."

"It's all ready; in fact, I've nearly finished. There's a cake to-day, too."

Miss Middleton hesitated at the door and looked wistfully at me.

"I suppose—I suppose," she said timidly, "you think I ought to have brought somebody, with me?"

"In a way, I'm just as glad you didn't."

"I've heaps of chaperons outside on the stairs, you know."

"There's no place like outside for chaperons."

"And the liftman believes I'm your aunt. At least, perhaps he doesn't, but I mentioned it to him."

I looked at her, and then I smiled. And then I laughed.

"So that's all right," she said breathlessly. "And I want my tea." She came in, and began to arrange her hat in front of the glass.

"Tea," I said, going to the cupboard. "I suppose you'll want a cup to yourself. There you are—don't lose it. Milk. Sugar."

Miss Middleton took a large piece of cake. "What were you studying so earnestly when I came in?" she asked as she munched.

"A dictionary."

"But how lucky I came. Because I can spell simply everything. What is it you want to know?"

"I don't want to know how to spell anything, thank you; but I believe you can help me all the same."

Miss Middleton sat down and drank her tea. "I love helping," she said.

"Well, it's this. I've just been asked to be a godfather."

Miss Middleton stood up suddenly. "Do I salute," she asked.

"You sit down and go on eating. The difficulty is—what to call it?"

"Oh, do godfathers provide the names?"

"I think so. It is what they are there for, I fancy. That is about all there is in it, I believe."

"And can't you find anything in the dictionary?"

"Well, I don't think the dictionary is helping as much as I expected. It only muddles me. Did you know that Algernon meant 'with whiskers'? I'm not thinking of calling it Algernon, but that's the sort of thing they spring on you."

"But I hate Algernon anyhow. Why not choose quite a simple name? Had you thought of 'John,' for instance?"

"No, I hadn't thought of 'John,' somehow."

"Or 'Gerald'?"

"'Gerald' I like very much."

"What about 'Dick'?" she went on eagerly.

"Yes, 'Dick' is quite jolly. By the way, did I tell you it was a girl?"

Miss Middleton rose with dignity.

"For your slice of plum cake and your small cup of tea I thank you," she said; "and I am now going straight home to mother."

"Not yet," I pleaded.

"I'll just ask you one question before I go. Where do you keep the biscuits?"

She found the biscuits and sat down again.

"A girl's name," I said encouragingly.

"Yes. Well, is she fair or dark?"

"She's very small at present. What there is of her is dark, I believe."

"Well, there are millions of names for dark girls."

"We only want one or two."

"'Barbara' is a nice dark name. Is she going to be pretty?"

"Her mother says she is. I didn't recognize the symptoms. Very pretty and very clever and very high-spirited, her mother says. Is there a name for that?"

"*I* always call them whoppers," said Miss Middleton.

"How do you like 'Alison Mary'? That was my first idea."

"Oh, I thought it was always 'William and Mary.' Or else 'Victoria and Albert.'"

"I didn't say 'Alice AND Mary,' stoopid. I said 'Alison,' a Scotch name."

"But how perfectly sweet! Why weren't you MY godfather? Would you have given me a napkin ring?"

"Probably. I will now, if you like. Then you approve of 'Alison Mary'?"

"I love it. Thank you very much. And will you always call me 'Alison' in future?"

"I say," I began in alarm, "I'm not giving that name to you. It's for my godchild."

"Oh no! 'Alisons' are ALWAYS fair."

"You've just made that up," I said suspiciously. "How do you know?"

"Sort of instinct."

"The worst of it is, I believe you're right."

"Of course I am. That settles it. Now, what was your next idea?"

"'Angela.'"

"'Angelas,'" said Miss Middleton, "are ALWAYS fair."

"Why do you want all the names to yourself? You say everything's fair."

"Why can you only think of names beginning with 'A'? Try another letter."

"Suppose YOU try now."

Miss Middleton wrinkled her brow and nibbled a lump of sugar.

"'Dorothy,'" she said at last, "because you can call them 'Dolly.'"

"There IS only one."

"Or 'Dodo.'"

"And it isn't a bird."

"Then there's 'Violet.'"

"My good girl, you don't understand. Any of these common names the parents could have thought of for themselves. The fact that they have got me in at great expense—to myself—shows that they want something out of the ordinary. How can I go to them and say, 'After giving a vast amount of time to the question, I have decided to call your child 'Violet'? It can't be done."

Miss Middleton absently took another lump of sugar and, catching my eye, put it back again.

"I don't believe that you've ever been a godfather before," she said, "or that you know anything at all about what it is you're supposed to be going to do."

There was a knock at the door, and the liftman came in. Miss Middleton gave a little cough of recognition.

"A letter, sir," he said.

"Thanks…. And as I was saying, Aunt Alison," I went on in a loud voice, "you are talking rubbish."

"Bah!" I said angrily, and I threw the letter down.

"Would you like to be left alone?" suggested Miss Middleton kindly.

"It is from the child's so-called parents, and their wretched offspring is to be called 'Violet Daisy.'"

"'Violet Daisy,'" said Miss Middleton solemnly, trying not to smile.

"Why stop there?" I said bitterly. "Why not 'Geranium' and 'Artichoke,' and the whole blessed garden?"

"'Artichoke,'" said Miss Middleton gravely, "is a boy's name."

"Well, I wash my hands of the whole business now. No napkin ring from ME. Here have I been wasting hours and hours in thought, and then just when the worst of it is over, they calmly step in like this. I call it—"

"Yes?" said Miss Middleton eagerly.

"I call it simply—"

"Yes?"

"'Violet Daisy,'" I finished, with a great effort.

II
OUT OF THE HURLY-BURLY

"OUR dance," I said; "and it's no good pretending it isn't."

"Come on," said Miss Middleton. "It's my favourite waltz. I expect I've said that to all my partners to-night."

"It's my favourite too, but you're the first person I've told."

"The worst of having a dance in your own house," said Miss Middleton, after we had been once round the room in silence, "is that you have to dance with EVERYBODY."

"Have you said that to all your partners too?"

"I expect so. I must have said everything. Don't look so reproachfully at me. You ARE looking reproachful, aren't you?"

I let go with one hand and felt my face.

"Yes," I said. "That's how I do it."

"Well, you needn't bother, because none of them thought I meant THEM. Men never do."

"I shall have to think that over by myself," I said after a pause. "There's a lot in that which the untrained observer might miss. Anyhow, it's not at all the sort of thing that a young girl ought to say at a dance."

"I'm older than you think," said Miss Middleton. "Oh, bother, I forgot. You know how old I am."

"Perhaps you've been ageing lately. I have. This last election has added years to my life. I came here to get young again."

"I don't know anything about politics. Father does all the knowing in our family."

"He's on the right side, isn't he?"

"I think he is. He says he is."

"Oh, well, he ought to know…. Yes, the truth is I came here to be liked again. People and I have been saying awfully rude things to each other lately."

"Oh, why do you want to argue about politics?"

"But I DON'T want to. It's a funny thing, but nobody will believe me when I say that."

"I expect it's because you say it AFTER you've finished arguing, instead of BEFORE,"

"Perhaps that's it."

"I never argue with mother. I simply tell her to do something, and she tells me afterwards why she hasn't."

"Really, I think Mrs Middleton has done wonderfully well, considering. Some parents don't even tell you why they haven't."

"Oh, I'd recommend her anywhere," said Miss Middleton confidently.

We dropped into silence again. Anyhow, it was MY favourite waltz.

"You did say, didn't you, the first dance we had together," said Miss Middleton dreamily, "that you preferred not to talk when you danced?"

"Didn't I say that I should prefer to do whatever you preferred? That sounds more like me."

"I don't think it does, a bit."

"No, perhaps you're right. Besides, I remember now what I did say. I said that much as I enjoyed the pleasant give and take of friendly conversation, dearly as I loved even the irresponsible monologue or the biting repartee, yet still more was I attached to the silent worship of the valse's mazy rhythm. 'BUT,' I went on to say, 'but,' I added, with surprising originality, 'every rule has an exception. YOU are the exception. May I have two dances, and then we'll try one of each?'"

"What did I say?"

"You said, 'Sir, something tells me that we shall be great friends. I like your face, and I like the way your tie goes under your left ear. I cannot give you ALL the dances on the programme, because I have my mother with me to-night, and you know what mothers are. They NOTICE. But anything up to half a dozen, distributed at such intervals that one's guardians will think it's the same dance, you are heartily welcome to. And if you care to take me in to supper, there is—I have the information straight from the stable—a line in unbreakable meringues which would well be worth our attention.' That's what you said."

"But what a memory!"

"I can remember more than that. I can rememher the actual struggle. I got my meringue down on the mat, both shoulders touching, in one minute, forty-three seconds."

The band died slowly down until no sound could be heard above the rustle of frocks ... and suddenly everybody realized that it had stopped.

"Bother," said Miss Middleton.

"That's just like a band," I said bitterly.

"I'll tell it to go on again; it's MY band."

"It will be your devoted band if you ask it prettily enough."

Miss Middleton went away, and came back to the sound of music, looking rather pleased with herself.

"Did you give him the famous smile?" I asked. "Yes, that one."

"I said, 'WOULD you mind playing that one again, PLEASE?' And then—"

"And then you looked as if you were just going to cry, and at the last moment you smiled and said, 'Hooray.' And he said, 'Certainly, madam.' Isn't that right?"

"I believe you're cleverer than some of us think," said Miss Middleton, a trifle anxiously.

"I sometimes think so too. However, to get back to what we were saying—I came here to recover my usual calm, and I shan't be at all calm if I'm only going to get this one dance from you. As an old friend of the family, who has broken most of the windows, I beg for another."

"To get back to what I was saying—I've simply GOT to do a lot of duty dances. Can't you take me to the Zoo or the Post-Impressionists instead?"

"I'd rather do both. I mean all three. No, I mean both."

"Well, perhaps I would, too."

"You know, I think you'd be doing good. I've had a horrible week—canvassing, and standing in the streets, and shouting, and reading leaders, and arguing, and saying, 'My point is perfectly simple,' and—and—swearing, and all sorts of things. It's awfully jolly to—to feel that there's always—well, all THIS," and I looked round the room, "to come back to."

"Isn't that beautiful Miss Ellison I introduced you to just now part of 'all this'?"

"Oh yes, it's all part; but—"

Miss Middleton sighed.

"Then that nice young man with the bald head will have to go without. But I only said I'd SEE if I could give him one. And I have seen, haven't I?"

The band really stopped this time, and we found a comfortable corner.

"That's very jolly of you," I said, as I leant back lazily and happily. "Now let's talk about Christmas."

III
ANOTHER MILESTONE

"You're very thoughtful," said Miss Middleton. "What's the matter?"

"I am extremely unhappy," I confessed.

"Oh, but think of Foster and Hobbs and Woolley."

I thought of Foster; I let my mind dwell upon Hobbs. It was no good.

"I am still rather sad," I said.

"Why? Doesn't anybody love you?"

"Millions adore me fiercely. It isn't that at all. The fact is I've just had a birthday."

"Oh, I AM sorry. Many happy—"

"Thank you."

"I thought it was to-morrow," Miss Middleton went on eagerly. "And I'd bought a cricketing set for you, but I had to send it back to have the bails sawn in two. Or would you rather have had a bicycle?"

"I'd rather have had nothing. I want to forget about my birthday altogether."

"Oh, are you as old as that?"

"Yes," I said sadly, "I am as old as that. I have passed another landmark. I'm what they call getting on."

We gazed into the fire in silence for some minutes.

"If it's any comfort to you," said Miss Middleton timidly, "to know that you don't LOOK any older than you did last week—"

"I'm not sure that I feel any older."

"Then, except for birthdays, how do you know you ARE older?"

I looked at her and saw that I could trust her.

"May I confess to you?" I asked.

"But of course!" she cried eagerly. "I love confessions." She settled herself comfortably in her chair. "Make it as horrible as you can," she begged.

I picked a coal out of the fire with the tongs and lit my cigarette.

"I know that I'm getting old," I said; "I know that my innocent youth is leaving me, because of the strange and terrible things which I find myself doing."

"Oo-o-o-oh," said Miss Middleton happily to herself.

"Last Monday, about three o'clock in the afternoon, I—No, I can't tell you this. It's too awful."

"Is it very bad?" said Miss Middleton wistfully.

"Very. I don't think you—Oh, well, if you must have it, here it is. Last Monday I suddenly found myself reading carefully and with every sign of interest a little pamphlet on—LIFE INSURANCE!"

Miss Middleton looked at me quickly, smiled suddenly, and then became very grave.

"I appeared," I went on impressively, "to be thinking of insuring my life."

"Have you done it?"

"No, certainly not. I drew back in time. But it was a warning—it was the writing on the wall."

"Tell me some more," said Miss Middleton, after she had allowed this to sink in.

"Well, that was Monday afternoon. I told myself that in the afternoon one wasn't quite responsible, that sometimes one was only half awake. But on Tuesday morning I was horrified to discover myself—before breakfast—DOING DUMB-BELLS!"

"The smelling-salts—quick!" said Miss Middleton, as she closed her eyes.

"Doing dumb-bells. Ten lunges to the east, ten lunges to the west, ten lunges—"

"Were you reducing your figure?"

"I don't know what I was doing. But there I found myself on the cold oil-cloth, lunging away—lunging and lunging and—" I stopped and gazed into the fire again.

"Is that all you have to tell me?" said Miss Middleton.

"That's the worst. But there have been other little symptoms—little warning notes which all mean the same thing. Yesterday I went into the bank, to get some money. As I began to fill in the cheque Conscience whispered to me, 'That's the third five pounds you've had out this week.'"

"Well, of all the impertinence—What did you do?"

"Made it ten pounds, of course. But there you are; you see what's happening. This morning I answered a letter by return of post. And did you notice what occurred only just now at tea?"

"Of course I did," said Miss Middleton indignantly. "You ate all the muffins."

"No, I don't mean that at all. What I mean is that I only had three lumps of sugar in each cup. I actually stopped you when you were putting the fourth lump in. Oh yes," I said bitterly, "I am getting on."

Miss Middleton poked the fire vigorously.

"About the lunges," she said.

"Ten to the east, ten to the west, ten to the nor'-nor'-east, ten to-"

"Yes. Well, I should have thought that that was just the thing to keep you young."

"It is. That's the tragedy of it. I used to BE young; now I KEEP young. And I used to say, 'I'll insure my life SOME day'; but now I think about doing it to-day. When once you stop saying 'some day' you're getting old, you know."

"Some day," said Miss Middleton, "you must tell me all about the Crimea. Not now," she went on quickly, "because you're going to do something very silly in a moment, if I can think of it—something to convince yourself that you are still quite young."

"Yes, do let me. I really think it would do me good."

"Well, what can you do?"

"Can I break anything?" I asked, looking round the room.

"I really don't think you must. Mother's very silly about things like that. I'm SO sorry; father and I would love it, of course."

"Can I go into the kitchen and frighten the cook?"

Miss Middleton sighed mournfully.

"ISN'T it a shame," she said, "that mothers object to all the really nice things?"

"Mrs Middleton is a little difficult to please. I shall give up trying directly. What about blacking my face and calling on the Vicar for a subscription?"

"I should laugh in church on Sunday thinking of it. I always do."

I lit another cigarette and smoked it thoughtfully.

"I have a brilliant idea," I said at last.

"Something really silly?"

"Something preposterously foolish. It seems to me just now the most idiotic thing I could possibly do."

"Tell me!" beseeched Miss Middleton, clasping her hands.

"I shall," I said, gurgling with laughter, "insure my life."

IV
THE HERALD OF SUMMER

MISS MIDDLETON has a garden of which she is very proud. Miss Middleton's father says it belongs to him, and this idea is fostered to the extent that he is allowed to pay for the seeds and cuttings and things. He is also encouraged to order the men about. But I always think of it as Miss Middleton's garden, particularly when the afternoons are hot and I see nothing but grimy bricks out of my window. She knows all the flowers by name, which seems to me rather remarkable.

"I have come," I announced, feeling that some excuse was necessary, "to see the lobretias; don't say that they are out. I mean, of course, do say that they are out."

"But I don't think we have any," she said in surprise. "I've never heard of them. What are they like?"

"They're just the ordinary sort of flower that people point to and say, 'That's a nice lobretia.' Dash it, you've got a garden, you ought to know."

"I am afraid," smiled Miss Middleton, "that there isn't such a flower— not yet. Perhaps somebody will invent it now they've got the name."

"Then I suppose I must go back to London," I said, getting up. "Bother."

"Stay and inspect the meter," pleaded Miss Middleton. "Or ask father for a subscription for the band. Surely you can think of SOME excuse for being here."

"I will stay," I said, sitting down again, "and talk to you. Between ourselves, it is one of the reasons why I came. I thought you might like to hear all the latest news. Er—we've started strawberries in London."

Miss Middleton sighed and shook her head.

"But not here," she said.

"I was afraid not, but I thought I'd remind you in case. Well, after all, what ARE strawberries? Let's talk about something else. Do you know that this is going to be the greatest season of history? I've got a free pass to the Earl's Court Exhibition, so I shall be right in the thick of it."

"Oh, I thought last season was the great one."

"It was spoilt by the Coronation, the papers say. You remember how busy we were at the Abbey; we hadn't time for anything else."

"Whatelsedothepaperssay?Iseemtohavemissedthemlately. I've had a thousand things to do."

"Well, the Sardine Defence League has just been formed. I think of putting up for it. I suppose you have to swear to do one kind action to a sardine everyday. Let's both join, and then we shall probably get a lot of invitations."

"Do they have a tent at the Eton and Harrow match?" asked Miss Middleton anxiously.

"I will inquire. I wonder if there is a Vice-Presidency vacant. I should think a Vice-President of the Sardine Defence League could go anywhere."

"V.P.S.D.L.," said Miss Middleton thoughtfully. "It would look splendid. I must remember to send you a postcard to-morrow."

Tea came, and I put my deck-chair one rung up to meet it. It is difficult in a horizontal position to drink without spilling anything, and it looks so bad to go about covered with tea.

"This is very jolly," I said. "Do you know that my view during working hours consists of two broken windows and fifty square feet of brick? It's not enough. It's not what I call a vista. On fine days I have to go outside to see whether the sun is shining."

"You oughtn't to want to look out of the window when you're working. You'll never be a Mayor."

"Well, it all makes me appreciate the country properly. I wish I knew more about gardens. Tell me all about yours. When are the raspberries ripe?"

"Not till the end of June."

"I was afraid you'd say that. May I come down and see your garden at the end of June—one day when I'm not at Earl's Court? You can give all the gardeners a holiday that day. I hate to be watched when I'm looking at flowers and things."

"Are you as fond of raspberries as all that? Why didn't I know?"

"I'm not a bit mad about them, really, but they're a symbol of Summer. On a sloshy day in November, as I grope my way through the fog, I say to myself, 'Courage, the raspberries will soon be ripe.'"

"But that means that summer is half over. The cuckoo is what I'm listening for all through November. I heard it in April this year."

I looked round to see that nobody was within earshot.

"I haven't heard it yet," I confessed. "It wasn't really so much to see the lobretias as to hear the cuckoo that I came to have tea with you. I feel just the same about it; it's the beginning of everything. And I said to myself, 'Miss Middleton may not have a first-rate show of lobretias, because possibly it is an unfavourable soil for them, or they may not fit in with the colour scheme; but she does know what is essential to a proper garden, and she'll have a cuckoo.'"

"Yes, we do ourselves very well," said Miss Middleton confidently.

"Well, I didn't like to say anything about it before, because I thought it might make you nervous, and so I've been talking of other things. But now that the secret is out, I may say that I am quite ready." I stopped and listened intently with my head on one side.

There was an appalling silence.

"I don't seem to hear it," I said at last.

"But *I* haven't heard it here yet," Miss Middleton protested. "It was in Hampshire. The cuckoos here are always a bit late. You see, our garden takes a little finding. It isn't so well known in—in Africa, or wherever they come from—as Hampshire."

"Yes, but when I've come down specially to hear it—"

"CUCK-OO," said Miss Middleton suddenly, and looked very innocent.

"There, that was the nightingale, but it's the cuckoo I really want to hear."

"I AM sorry about it. If you like, I'll listen to you while you tell me who you think ought to play for England. I can't make it more summery for you than that. Unless roses are any good?"

"No, don't bother," I said in some disappointment; "you've done your best. We can't all have cuckoos any more than we can all have lobretias. I must come again in August, when one of the pioneers may have struggled here. Of course in Hampshire—"

"CUCK-OO," said somebody from the apple tree.

"There!" cried Miss Middleton.

"That's much better," I said. "Now make it come from the laburnum, Lieutenant."

"I'm not doing it, really!" she said. "At least only the first time."

"CUCK-OO," said somebody from the apple tree again.

There was no doubt about it. I let my deck-chair down a rung and prepared to welcome the summer.

"Now," I said, "we're off."

EPILOGUE

You may believe this or not as you like. Personally I don't know what to think. It happened on the first day of spring (do you remember it? A wonderful day), and on the first of spring all sorts of enchantments may happen.

I was writing my weekly story: one of those things with a He and a She in it. He was Reginald, a fine figure of a man. She was Dorothy, rather a dear. I was beginning in a roundabout sort of way with the weather, and the scenery, and the birds, and how Reginald was thinking of the spring, and how his young fancy was lightly turning to thoughts of love, when suddenly —

At that moment I was called out of the room to speak to the housekeeper about something. In three minutes I was back again; and I had just dipped my pen in the ink, when there came a cough from the direction of the sofa — and there, as cool as you please, were sitting two persons entirely unknown to me....

"I beg your pardon," I said. "The housekeeper never told me. Whom have I the — what did you — "

"Thanks," said the man. "I'm Reginald."

"Are you really?" I cried. "Jove, I AM glad to see you. I was just — just thinking of you. How are you?"

"I'm sick of it," said Reginald.

"Sick of what?"

"Of being accepted by Dorothy."

I turned to the girl.

"You don't mean to say — "

"Yes; I'm Dorothy. I'm sick of it too."

"Dorothy!" I cried. "By the way, let me introduce you. Reginald, this is Dorothy. She's sick of it too."

"Thanks," said Reginald coldly. "We have met before."

"Surely not. Just let me look a moment.... No, I thought not. You don't meet till the next paragraph. If you wouldn't mind taking a seat, I shan't be a moment."

Reginald stood up.

"Look here," he said. "Do you know who I am?"

"You're just Reginald," I said; "and there's no need to stand about looking so dignified, because I only thought of you ten minutes ago, and if you're not careful I shall change your name to Harold. You're Reginald, and you're going to meet Dorothy in the next paragraph, and you'll flirt with her mildly for about two columns. And at the end, I expect—no, I am almost sure, that you will propose and be accepted."

"Never," said Reginald angrily.

"That's what we've come about," said Dorothy.

I rubbed my forehead wearily.

"Would one of you explain?" I asked. "I can't think what's happened. You're at least a paragraph ahead of me."

Reginald sat down again and lit a cigarette.

"It's simply this," he said, trying to keep calm. "You may call me what you like, but I am always the same person week after week."

"Nonsense. Why, it was Richard last week."

"But the same person."

"And Gerald the week before. Gerald, yes; he was rather a good chap."

"Just the same, only the name was different. And who are we? We are you as you imagine yourself to be."

I looked inquiringly at Dorothy.

"Last week," he went on, "you called me Richard. And I proposed to Phyllis."

"And I accepted him," said Dorothy.

"You!" I said. "What were YOU doing there, I should like to know?"

"Last week I was Phyllis."

"The week before," went on Reginald, "I was Gerald, and I proposed to Millicent."

"I was Millicent, and I accepted him."

"The week before that I was—Good Heavens, think of it—I was George!"

"A beastly name, I agree," I said.

"You gave it me."

"Yes, but I wasn't feeling very well that week."

"I was Mabel," put in Dorothy, "and I accepted him."

"No, no, no—no, don't say that. I mean, one doesn't accept people called George."

"You made me."

"Did I? I'm awfully sorry. Yes, I quite see your point."

"The week before," went on Reginald remorselessly, "I was—"

"Don't go back into February, please! February is such a rotten month with me. Well now, what's your complaint?"

"Just what I said," explained Reginald. "You think you have a new hero and heroine every week, but you're mistaken. We are always the same; and, personally, I am tired of proposing week after week to the same girl."

There was just something about Reginald that I seemed to recognize. Just the very slightest something.

"Then who are you really," I asked, "if you're always the same person?"

"Yourself. Not really yourself, of course, but yourself as you fondly imagine you are."

I laughed scornfully. "You're nothing of the sort. How ridiculous! The hero of my own stories, indeed! Myself idealized—then I suppose you think you're rather a fine fellow?" I sneered.

"I suppose you think I am."

"No, I don't. I think you are a silly ass. Saying I'm my own hero. I'm nothing of the sort. And I suppose Dorothy is me, too?"

"I'm the girl you're in love with," said Dorothy. "Idealized."

"I'm not in love with any one," I denied indignantly.

"Then your ideal girl."

"Ah, you might well be that," I smiled.

I looked at her longingly. She was wonderfully beautiful. I went a little closer to her.

"And we've come," said Reginald, putting his oar in again, "to say that we're sick of getting engaged every week."

I ignored Reginald altogether.

"Are you really sick of him?" I asked Dorothy.

"Yes!"

"As sick of him as I am?"

"I—I daresay."

"Then let's cross him out," I said. And I went back to the table and took up my pen. "Say the word," I said to Dorothy.

"Steady on," began Reginald uneasily. "All I meant was—"

"Personally, as you know," I said to Dorothy, "I think he's a silly ass. And if you think so too—"

"I say, look here, old chap—"

Dorothy nodded. I dipped the pen in the ink.

"Then out he goes," I said, and I drew a line through him. When I looked up only Dorothy was there....

"Dorothy!" I said. "At last!"

"But my name isn't really Dorothy, you know," she said with a smile. "It's Dorothy this week, and last week it was Phyllis, and the week before—"

"Then what is it really? Tell me! So that I may know my ideal when I see her again."

I got ready to write the name down. I dipped my pen in the ink again, and I drew a line through Dorothy, and then I looked up questioningly at her, and...

Fool, fool! She was gone!

Il faut vivre. You'll see the story in one of the papers this week. You'll recognize it, because he is called Harold, and she is called Lucy. At the end of the second column he proposes and she accepts him. Lucy—of all names! It serves them right.